Fire and Ice

Tom felt Hilary's trembling motion, and he knew it wasn't from the cold, or the wet. He knew exactly what it was from, and he looked at her with his eyes reflecting his own degree of arousal. He moved his lips down to hers, and covered her mouth with a kiss.

His was a kiss of ice and fire, and the power of it made Hilary dizzy. Tom's hands traced fiery paths across her body, until one of them stopped, and her knees grew weak. At that moment, Tom swept her up in his powerful arms and carried her over to deposit her on the bed.

Hilary felt a sweet aching in her loins, and a heat through her body which was so intense that it was as if her very blood had turned to liquid fire.

Tom moved onto the bed with her, and he covered her with kisses on the lips, face, neck and shoulders. Then, when she thought she had experienced all the pleasure her body could stand, Tom moved over her, and Hilary knew that the wonder of it all was just beginning. . . .

Other novels by Paula Fairman from Pinnacle Books

FORBIDDEN DESTINY
FURY AND THE PASSION
IN SAVAGE SPLENDOR
JASMINE PASSION
PASSION'S PROMISE
PORTS OF PASSION
RIVER OF PASSION
SOUTHERN ROSE
STORM OF DESIRE
TENDER AND THE SAVAGE
VALLEY OF THE PASSIONS
WILDEST PASSION

PINNACLE BOOKS NEW YORK

> **ATTENTION: SCHOOLS AND CORPORATIONS**
>
> PINNACLE Books are available at quantity discounts with bulk purchases for educational, business or special promotional use. For further details, please write to: SPECIAL SALES MANAGER, Pinnacle Books, Inc., 1430 Broadway, New York, NY 10018.

This is a work of fiction. All the characters and events portrayed in this book are fictional, and any resemblance to real people or incidents is purely coincidental.

RANGE OF PASSION

Copyright © 1984 by Script Representatives, Inc.

All rights reserved, including the right to reproduce this book or portions thereof in any form.

An original Pinnacle Books edition, published for the first time anywhere.

First printing/August 1984

ISBN: 0-523-41996-1

Can. ISBN: 0-523-43287-9

Cover art by Lou Marchetti

Printed in the United States of America

PINNACLE BOOKS, INC.
1430 Broadway
New York, New York 10018

9 8 7 6 5 4 3 2 1

RANGE OF PASSION

Chapter One

A May sun, just beginning to gather heat and brilliance, rose in the east above the purple Mogollon mountain range. A dark gray haze was still hanging in the notches, though it was already beginning to dissipate, giving itself off like drifting smoke. Timbered foothills, covered with blue pine and splashed with the rainbow colors of wild spring blooms, marched down from the higher elevations. Turquoise Peak was scarred by some ancient cataclysmic event of geology to expose rocks which were blue-green in certain light. Its presence made the valley an ideal ranch site, for it towered at the north end, giving protection from the cold winds that blew from early fall to late spring.

Onto this scene rode Hilary St. John, a boyishly slim but gently rounded young girl of twenty-one. She was quite athletic, but strawberry blonde hair and golden eyes saved her from a tomboyish appearance. She rose at the crack of dawn to ride along a familiar ridgeline and look out over the sweeping grandeur of the valley that was her home. She picked her way carefully along a trail that led to a private place, a secret glen she had discovered as a little girl and to which she often came when troubled or when she wanted to be alone, just to think.

The trail climbed up the backside of a bluff, through a cathedral arch of cedar trees, across a level bench of soft spring grass and fluttering yellow, red and blue flowers, to a rocky precipice. It was the precipice which made the ride worthwhile, for from it Hilary could see the entire valley, including the main house, the foreman's house where Hilary lived with her father and the bunkhouses where the forty men who worked on the ranch slept when they weren't out on the range or in one of the line shacks. The houses: bunkhouses, barns, cookhouse, equipment shed, smokehouse and assorted other buildings, plus fifteen thousand acres of the finest rangeland in Arizona Territory, made up the spread known as the Turquoise Ranch.

But Hilary had not come here to enjoy the beautiful view. She had come here to think, for she had a decision to make.

Today she would have to give Gil Carson his answer.

It had not come as a surprise to her when, at the Cattlemen's Ball last Saturday night, Gil asked her to be his wife.

The surprise was that Hilary was even having to think twice about it. After all, with his tall, dark, brooding good looks, and his position as manager of one of the finest ranches in the Southwest, Gil was certainly the prize catch of this or any other season.

Gil had made no secret of the interest he had in the beautiful daughter of his foreman. He had been paying court to her for the past three years.

Hilary was not unaware of the effect she had on Gil, and other men as well. In fact, she rather enjoyed the attention of the men of the ranch, and she often engaged in innocent flirtation, taking a measure of pride in the fact that she could stir men so.

But Hilary's flirtations were innocent, for she was an innocent. No man had known her, though many a poor cowboy harbored just such a fantasy, and some less desirable men in Flagstaff had vowed they would pay any price for the privilege.

Many of the cowboys would have been surprised to realize that they weren't alone in their sexual fantasies. Sometimes, in the quiet moments at night in her bed alone, Hilary would be achingly aware of the fact that she was a woman, and not only a woman, but a woman with a passionate nature. During such times she often found that erotic thoughts would play their temptations upon her. Most of the time there was no form or substance to the thoughts, for she was, after all, without experience. Sometimes she thought of being a wife to Gil, with all that entailed, for after all, it was generally recognized by all that she was "Gil's girl." Hilary wasn't sure how she felt about that, though, for despite the fact that Gil was handsome, intelligent and wealthy, there was something about him that gave Hilary second thoughts.

Perhaps it was because he was exceptionally harsh with the men. Hilary had often overheard the cowboys complain about his treatment, accusing him of "not leaving a man any dignity." She had never heard anything definite, because it was not in the cowboys' nature to complain, and when they realized there was a danger of being overheard, they would immediately grow quiet.

Hilary also knew that the relationship between her father and Gil was proper but not cordial. Hilary was concerned about that, for her father was a man given to seeing good in just about anybody, and he was a friend to everyone. It was not her father's way to be so reserved in offering his friendship. And, of course, if Hilary did become Gil's wife, she would certainly want the enthusiastic blessing of her father, not only because he was a father she loved, but because he was also a man whose opinions she greatly respected.

Hilary's father, known by everyone as Big Jake, had come to Arizona from Texas back when Arizona was still considered worthless desert country. There was a shadow on his trail from Texas which a few whispered about but no one mentioned aloud, because in Arizona a man's past was considered his personal business. Big Jake had earned an honest living since coming here, and he was well paid for his work, because he was highly respected. He had married, fathered a daughter and buried a wife, all since coming to Arizona. Hilary knew nothing of her father's past, nor had she ever asked questions. All she knew was Turquoise Ranch.

Hilary had never seen the real owner of the ranch. Some said there was no owner, that the ranch was held by a banking consortium in the East. Others said the ranch was owned by English nobility, and a few even went so far as to suggest that Queen Victoria was the owner. Because the ranch was owned by an absentee landowner, the authority was entirely in the hands of the ranch manager.

When Hilary was a little girl the ranch manager was a man named Ian MacMurtry. Ian was a big, white-headed, jolly Irishman. He was like a father to the young cowboys on the ranch. To Hilary he was "Uncle Ian," though of course there was no real blood relationship between them. Ian died when Hilary was seventeen, and no one's death, except that of her own father, could have upset her as much as this one did.

After Ian came Gil Carson. Gil had been a lawyer in Flagstaff, and he vowed to bring "sound business policies" to the ranch. Ian had become a little slipshod in some things during his declining years, and Hilary had to admit, for all that she loved Ian, there were a few changes on the ranch that were immediately beneficial. Buildings were painted, vegetable gardens were put in and the place took on a younger, more vital atmosphere, in keeping with the age and personality of its new manager.

But, Hilary was soon to discover, there was a price paid for the improvements, if indeed such changes could be called improvements. There seemed to be less banter among the cowboys, fewer songs emerged spontaneously from the bunkhouse and there was less laughter. Hilary tried to reason that it was because the ranch was being run in a more businesslike way . . . but she wasn't sure she liked that. She missed the fun-loving nature of the cowboys.

It was just such disquieting thoughts as these which caused Hilary to take such time with Gil's proposal now. All logic and reason told her to say yes to his proposal, but she was nagged by the thought that there was more at stake here than logic and reason.

In the valley below, a wispy pall of wood smoke lay its diaphanous haze over the cookhouse, and Hilary knew that Sam was awake and preparing breakfast. Her father would just be waking now, and he would find her note, telling him she had gone for an early ride and asking him to eat breakfast with the cowboys this morning. It was not an unusual practice, so he wouldn't be alarmed, nor would he be angry with her for not fixing his breakfast.

Hilary sat on the ledge while the cowboys, one at a time or in small groups, moved over to the cookhouse for their morning meal. She saw her father go in to eat and knew he had read her message. She sat there until breakfast was over and the cowboys went to the barn and began throwing saddles on the horses they would be working with today.

Then and only then did she stand, brush the twigs and pine needles off her dress and mount her horse to start back down. She had come up here to make a decision as to whether she would marry Gil or not, and now that decision was made.

She would tell him *yes*.

And yet, even as she rode back down the trail she wondered if she had made the correct decision.

The men were rounding up and branding calves in a part of the ranch known as Star Canyon. Because she had not fixed breakfast for her father, and because she wanted to talk to him, Hilary decided to fry a chicken and take it to him. She knew it wasn't necessary. The chuck wagon was in the field with the men, and the stews Sam Potter cooked were very good. Jake had always made the comment that a good cook was the most valuable man on any ranch, for cowboys would stay on through just about anything if they were being fed well. Sam was a good cook. According to Jake, the best cook he had ever known. In fact, the chicken Hilary was taking to her father was cooked according to a recipe Sam had given Hilary.

Hilary put the chicken, potato salad, lemonade, and even a piece of velvet chocolate cake, in a picnic basket, hooked it on her saddle pommel and was just about to mount when Gil came out of the big house and walked over toward her.

Hilary had hoped to be able to leave before he saw her. She wanted to talk to her father before she gave him his answer.

"Well," Gil said, coming up to her and smiling broadly. "Today is the day I get my answer."

"Yes," Hilary said quietly. "Today is the day."

"Have you made a decision?"

Hilary looked at him. There was no denying it. He was an

exceptionally handsome man. He was dressed, not in the workaday clothes the cowboys wore, but in a tan suit and yellow shirt with a great, silver bolo tie. His teeth were white and perfectly formed, and not one of the black hairs on his head was out of place. He wore a small, perfectly trimmed mustache, and it was his habit to touch it often, as if combing it with the tip of his finger, though it was kept trimmed much too short for his finger to actually have any effect.

"Gil, please, I have to talk to my father," Hilary started.

"Surely not to get his permission?" Gil said quickly, almost sharply. Then, perhaps realizing how it may have sounded, he amended it. "I mean, you are twenty-one, and as such a decision will have a profound effect upon your life. I am certain he will respect whatever decision you make."

"Yes, I'm sure he will," Hilary said. "And, as you say, I will make my own decision. But he is my father, and I want to talk to him." Hilary smiled, and pointed to the picnic basket. "I've fried some chicken for a picnic lunch."

"A picnic lunch, is it? Well, then I am certain that you will put him in an excellent mood. Hilary, I want to give you time to do whatever you think is right, but please have pity on me and remember that it is agony to be held in suspense for too long a time."

"I will have an answer for you before the day is out," Hilary replied. "I promise you." She swung onto her horse and waved at him as she rode away.

Hilary was an excellent horsewoman, and she was riding a good, strong horse who could run a mile at breakneck speed or eat up ground quickly in a long, loping trot which he could maintain for hours.

The men were working about three miles away from the house, and Hilary covered that distance in just a little over fifteen minutes. She had no difficulty in finding them, for there was a cloud of dust hanging in the air where they were working. Beneath the dust cloud were several black dots, and as she grew closer the dots grew larger until they finally assumed the shape of cattle, men and horses. Because of his great size, Hilary had no difficulty whatever in picking out her father.

Jake saw Hilary approaching, and he turned his horse toward her and met her halfway to the herd.

"Well," he said, smiling at her. "My little girl left me to shift for myself this morning, did she? And what brings you around to see the old man now?"

"This," Hilary said, holding up the picnic basket. "I thought we might eat together."

"So you're trying to make up for this morning, are you?" Jake teased. "Well, it's not necessary. Sam fixed me a fine breakfast, and I'm sure the lunch will be just as good."

"Oh? Then perhaps you won't mind if I call one of the cowboys to share this fried chicken with me," Hilary said.

"Fried chicken?"

"And potato salad and lemonade and your favorite chocolate cake," Hilary went on.

"My word, girl, what a temptress you could be if you wanted to," Jake said. "With a meal like that, if you dare to call anyone else, I'll turn you over my knee and spank you. I don't want to share that with anyone."

"I thought you'd see things my way," Hilary said. She pointed to a stand of trees alongside a stream. It was the stream that made this a good place to conduct a roundup, for the cattle naturally moved their newborn calves to the protection of the canyon and the abundance of water.

Jake took the poncho and blanket from his saddle and spread it out on the ground for them, and, a moment later, Hilary and her father were enjoying their meal.

"Dad?" Hilary said as Jake reached for his third piece of chicken. "Gil has asked me to marry him."

Jake stopped with the chicken halfway to his mouth, and he looked at Hilary. For just an instant, Hilary thought she saw something in his eyes. What was it? Anger? Hurt? Resignation? Whatever it was, it had a sadness to it which Hilary found quite disturbing.

"Aren't you going to say anything?" she pleaded.

"Are you going to marry him?" Jake asked.

"I haven't given him his answer," Hilary said.

"What is your answer going to be?"

"I'm going to say yes," Hilary replied.

Jake put the piece of chicken back down.

"I see," he said.

"Dad, I want your approval."

"Girl, you are a woman, full grown now," Jake said. "You've a lifetime of making grown-up decisions before you. I sure can't make this one for you."

"I know," Hilary said. "And I have made my own decision."

"Did you think about it, Hilary? Did you think about it hard?"

"Yes," Hilary said. "That's where I was this morning."

"You went up to your ledge?"

Hilary looked a little shocked, and Jake smiled at her.

"Did you think I didn't know about it?"

"I didn't know anyone knew about it," Hilary said. "I thought it was my own, secret place."

"It is your place, girl," Jake said. "I happened by it once—oh, it must have been eight or nine years ago. It was pretty soon after your mother died, and you were having a pretty rough time of it. You left the house all upset about something and rode away quicker than the wind. I thought to go after you, to try and calm you down. When I found you, you were sitting on the ledge, looking out over the valley. You seemed so at peace with yourself then that I knew it would be best to leave you be. I've never violated your privacy there on the ledge, and I never would."

Hilary smiled through her tears, then she leaned across and hugged her father.

"I love you, Dad," she said. "I love you so much."

"And I love you, darlin'," Jake said. "But the question is, do you love Gil Carson?"

"I . . . I don't know, really," Hilary said. "I think he is a very handsome man, and I know he's smart and a good manager, and he . . ."

"Those are all very nice attributes for a man applying for a job," Jake said. "But do they qualify him to be your husband? The question I asked is, do you love him?"

Hilary sighed.

"Oh, Dad, how can I tell?" Hilary replied. "Certainly I don't love him the way I love you. But I do feel a . . . a . . ." Hilary stopped and blushed. How could she express that she felt a sexual awareness of him? She had no words to explain what she felt, and she didn't know if she would be able to say them to her father if she did know how.

But Jake understood without having to be told.

"Well, that's all a part of it, I reckon," he said, and sighed. "Girl, if you do love him, I mean truly love him, then, why of course you have my blessin'. He's a man with a good position, and if he thinks enough of you to ask you to marry him, then I have to say I admire his ambition on that score. I've no reason not to like him. Lord knows, I try to see good in every man. I have to confess, though, that if you can see enough in Gil Carson to be willin' to marry him, then you are being more successful in this case than I. When is the weddin' to be?"

"Gil wants to get married on the thirtieth of June," Hilary said.

"June? That's not too far away."

"It's about seven weeks," Hilary said.

"Seven weeks," Jake said. "Seven weeks and I lose my little girl."

"No you won't," Hilary said. She smiled broadly. "Don't you see? The best part of it is, I won't be moving away from Turquoise Ranch."

"You love the ranch, don't you, Hilary?"

"Yes," she said, looking around at the magnificent scenery which was Star Canyon. "Yes, I love it more than I can say."

"I hope you didn't confuse your love for Turquoise Ranch with love for Gil Carson. He isn't the ranch, you know. He is just the manager."

"I know," Hilary said. "And there may be something to what you say, but I don't think so. I certainly hope not. That is one of the things I was thinking about this morning, when I was on the ledge."

"Darlin', all I can say is, I hope you made the right decision."

"I do too," Hilary replied quietly.

"Yes?" Gil said later that afternoon as he stood with Hilary on the back porch of the manager's house, the house the cowboys called the big house. "The answer is yes?"

"Yes," Hilary said again.

Gil smiled broadly, then he put his arms around Hilary and swung her about once.

"Oh, darling, you have just made me the happiest man in the world!" he said. "And you'll be happy too. You'll see. Everything is going to be just great."

Gil kissed Hilary then, and though she still had too many

questions floating around in her head and in her heart to respond enthusiastically, she nevertheless allowed him to do so, because she felt that, as her fiancé, he now had that right.

"Ahem," a hesitant voice coughed.

Hilary was embarrassed by the unexpected appearance of the cowboys, and she pulled away quickly, her face flaming.

"What is it, Curly?" Gil asked angrily. "What do you want?"

"I'm about ready to go into Flagstaff and meet the train to pick up the new hired hand. I was wonderin' if there was anythin' you wanted done while I was in town."

"No!" Gil said angrily. "Just get out of here."

"Curly," Hilary said, overcoming her embarrassment to speak to him, because she had been looking for an opportunity to get into town. "Do you mind if I ride with you?"

"No'm, I don't mind a'tall," Curly said. "Onliest thang is, I wasn't a'plannin' on comin' back tonight, what with it bein' so late 'n all. I was gonna stay in town 'n get a early start 'n the mornin'."

"That's all right," Hilary said. "I'll just tell Dad not to expect me back tonight."

"Oh, I don't think you should do that," Gil said.

Hilary looked at Gil with a disapproving look on her face. Was this how he was going to be after they were married? Was he going to be so domineering that she would have no personal freedom at all?

"I really must go into town," Hilary insisted.

"If that is so, perhaps I can take you to town tomorrow and you can spend the entire day," Gil offered. "I was just going to go over some books with your dad in the morning, but we can put that off until another time."

"No," Hilary said. "Dad has been working to get the books ready, and I know he wants to go over them with you. Besides, there are some things a woman needs to do in private, and making arrangements for a dress to wear at the wedding party is one of those things." Now she was angry with herself. Why was it necessary for her to excuse her actions? Why didn't she just tell him that she wanted to go to town and that she had every right to do so without having to explain her every move to him?

Gil grinned. "A dress for your wedding. Yes, I suppose that is important, isn't it? All right, you go ahead. But, Curly, you see to it that no harm comes to her, do you understand? You be very careful with her. This is the future Mrs. Gil Carson."

"Yes, sir," Curly said, registering no expression whatever over the announcement. "I'll be careful."

Chapter Two

Gil Carson watched Hilary and Curly drive away in the buckboard, then he went back into his house to do some more work on the reports he was filing for the absentee owner, or owners of Turquoise. As he passed by a mirror, he happened to see his reflection, and he stopped and preened for a moment, adjusting his shirt collar, touching his hair to make certain that he was properly groomed.

Gil was a very handsome man, and he was very vain about it. But then, he was vain about everything. Though Turquoise Ranch didn't belong to him, he wore the mantle of authority vested in him as its manager as proudly as he would had he actually owned Turquoise.

Managership of Turquoise had come as a very lucky break to a man who was as ambitious as Gil. Of course, Gil would be quick to point out to anyone who might ask, it wasn't just a lucky break. As a lawyer he had been involved in a few dealings with Turquoise, so when Ian MacMurtry died, Gil was in an excellent position to apply to become its new manager. He had to apply through the legal firm in

Boston that handled all of Turquoise's business, though, because he had no idea who the real owner was.

Many men would have been proud to be the manager of Turquoise Ranch, for it was the biggest and most productive ranch in the Arizona Territory. They would not only have been proud, they would have been content to stay in that same position for the rest of their lives.

Gil Carson was not.

Gil Carson looked at Turquoise as a stepping-stone to bigger and better things. At the moment, however, there wasn't anything bigger or better than Turquoise Ranch. But if Gil had his way, he would stay just long enough at Turquoise to make certain that he had the wherewithal to put his plan into effect, then he would leave Turquoise for his own ranch.

Of course, he had never spoken of this aloud, not even to Hilary. First of all, she loved Turquoise so much that she would probably balk at leaving the ranch. And secondly, some of his plans depended upon taking advantage of his position at Turquoise Ranch. A few revisions on reports here and there, an occasional alteration of the numbers of cattle actually sold or lost, the omission of a few deals, and one could gradually begin to feather one's own nest.

Gil Carson was not above doing that very thing. It would not be long now before he was ready to make his move to his own ranch.

Though she didn't realize it, Hilary St. John fit into Gil's plans perfectly. She was a beautiful woman, and she would be a tremendous asset to Gil as he climbed the social ladder. Not only the social ladder but, perhaps, the political ladder as well. Surely, Arizona would one day be a state, and when that happened, who was to say that the wealthiest, most prominent lawyer in the state wouldn't be the governor? Hilary St. John would be quite an asset to a man who was seeking a high elective office. He had very carefully considered all of that before he ever asked her to marry him. In fact, when he asked her to marry him, he considered her potential practical use to him more important than love.

In his own way, he supposed that he did love her. He loved being seen with her, and he loved the idea of being the master of the woman so many men wanted. And he also loved the idea of possessing her, as he possessed Bonnie Tyre on those occasions when his need became strong. As far as Gil Carson was concerned, that was about as close to actual love as he could come. But surely that would be close enough.

He certainly didn't love Bonnie Tyre, though he had told her many times that he did. Bonnie often accommodated certain "needs" that Gil experienced. In fact, she had been doing so now for the past few years, but that shouldn't be misconstrued as love. If he had mouthed the words to her during such times, they had merely been the indiscreet murmurings of a man who was using the words and the moment to the end of his own gratification.

Bonnie Tyre was a prostitute, a "soiled dove," Gil had come to know in Flagstaff. She was young and attractive, and it was much easier to accommodate his desires with her, than it was to invest time in courting someone. Besides, Gil had made up his mind long ago that he would court no one until he found the woman who best fit his exacting requirements for a wife. She would have to be pretty, she would have to be at home on a ranch and she must be worthy enough in moral character to stand beside him as he went to the top. Hilary fit the bill perfectly, and he was pleased that she had agreed to marry him.

He wished, though, that she had let him take her into Flagstaff. He would have enjoyed the opportunity to visit Bonnie.

Gil felt a familiar twitching as he thought of Bonnie, and he rubbed himself self-consciously. Yes, he would have enjoyed celebrating the occasion tonight, in Bonnie's own bed.

Gil chuckled. That would have been a marvelous joke on both Bonnie and Hilary. It's too bad it wouldn't happen.

Gil shook his head to clear away the thoughts of sexual pleasure. No pleasure for him tonight. He would have to wait a short while. In the meantime, there was work to be done.

He went back to the reports and smiled as he looked at the numbers. They were leaning in his favor, and that was almost as satisfying as a night with Bonnie would have been.

Chapter Three

Tom Eddington stood on the deck of the *Comet*, looking out over the rolling sea and enjoying the sensation of salt sea spray in his face. It wasn't just the sensation of the sea that had brought him out on deck, though. He had come here to avoid the unpleasantness in the dining room. His recent announcement had been the cause of the unpleasantness, falling upon the others like a bombshell. Tom knew before he said anything that such would be the reaction, but he was determined to go through with his plans regardless of what anyone said. As it turned out, they had plenty to say, and he had no doubt they were still saying it.

Let them talk. His mind was made up. He was leaving home, and he was going out West.

The yacht on which Tom had come to his decision was the family yacht, the *Comet*. It was a 256-foot-long vessel, used by the Eddingtons to ferry family and friends not only from Boston to Newport or the Caribbean, but across the Atlantic to their several European residences as well. As a yacht the boat was magnificent. It could make nineteen knots and carry enough coal to travel over six thousand miles without stopping.

As impressive as its performance, however, was its interior. It looked more like a sea-going mansion than a vessel. It featured high ceilings, skylights, paneled walls and parquet floors. The dining room which Tom had so recently abandoned was exquisitely done in Louis XIV furniture, and set with the finest silver, china and crystal. It had no less than nine plushly furnished staterooms, plus a grand salon which could easily accommodate one hundred guests.

The *Comet* was operated by a crew of seventy officers and men. That was fifteen less than was required to operate J. P. Morgan's *Corsair*, but that didn't mean that the Eddington vessel was smaller, or less of a yacht. It merely meant that the *Comet* was more up to date, and possessed of all the latest labor-saving devices which enabled it to function with a smaller crew. The *Comet* was every bit as large as the *Corsair*, and certainly no less luxurious in its appointments.

The *Comet* was owned by Andrew K. Eddington, a man who had made millions of dollars in the shipping and railroad industry. The elder Eddington had made all of his money within his lifetime, for he had started life as a poor stableboy, and risen to heights of wealth and power that were the things of dreams. However, despite the fact that Andrew Eddington had fulfilled the American dream and had amassed one of the largest fortunes in America, he was never fully accepted into "society," because his money was new money, and therefore, "tainted." His money, however, was more than welcome.

It never bothered Andrew to be left out of accepted society, for he was a man at peace with himself. In his own mind, he was still the stableboy who happened to get lucky.

But Andrew married Helen Cornelius, a pretty young woman from a family that had a fine old name, though a collapse in fortunes had long ago cost them their wealth. Helen thought that the combination of her family name with Andrew's money would take care of both of them, by restoring her family to its rightful place in society, while elevating Andrew.

Despite Helen's wishes it didn't work out that way. Her family continued to be regarded as "genteel poor" and Andrew as *nouveau riche*. As a result, Helen had to put all her hopes for regaining social position in Paul, their son. After all, Paul was second-generation money, and a fourth-generation descendant of the Cornelius family, one of the finest old names in New England. Martin Cornelius had been a governor, appointed by the King of England, before the Revolution. He was written of in all the history books because he voluntarily surrendered his governorship in order to accept a commission in the Massachusetts Militia, allying himself with the American cause against the Crown. By being his direct descendant, Paul Eddington's entry into society was assured.

In order to prepare him for his station in life, Helen saw to it that Paul was educated in the best schools, met the right people and took the grand tour of Europe. Paul was groomed in every way to assume his rightful position, and Helen even saw to it that Paul married well. But Paul's reign in society was cut tragically short, for he and his wife were killed in a hotel fire in New York, leaving their young son, Tom, to be raised by Helen and Andrew Eddington.

Tom was third-generation money, and a descendant, not only of Helen's illustrious family, but possessed of quite a bit of blue blood on his mother's side as well. Because of that, he was granted automatic membership into the society to which his grandmother had so ardently aspired. But Tom, who had everything handed him, didn't want any of it. He was not only different from his grandmother in that attitude, but was different from the others in his peer group as well. Tom considered the parties, dances and endless succession of social events boring, and a waste of time. To that degree, he was much more attuned to his grandfather's no-nonsense philosophy of life.

But it wasn't just Tom's attitude which set him apart from the others. In any party or at any home, school or social gathering, Tom stood out whether he wanted to or not. That was because he was very tall, well over six feet, with broad shoulders, long arms and great, spreading hands. He had discovered the game of football in college, and though it was considered much too rough a game for those who were born to the gentry, Tom not only played it, he excelled in it. He was big and strong, and both qualities were desirable attributes for playing football, so Tom became somewhat of a sports hero, much to the chagrin of his grandmother and his social peers. The game of football broke Tom's nose and that gave his face a rugged look which tended to substantiate the impression of ruffian he gave on first meeting.

Tom was aware that his great size and rugged looks set him apart from the others, and he intensified that separation by his attitude. He avoided the parties and social events of the season as much as he could.

Despite Tom's desire to avoid what he considered the "waste of excess indulgence," it was impossible for him to avoid everything, so it was that he was more or less forced to go along on the family cruise to the Bahamas.

"We'll sweep down there for a week or two," his grandmother said. "And we'll all have a wonderful time. The Vanderbilts will be there, and so will the Mellons. Oh, and I'm sure you'll be pleased to know that the Proctor family is going with us. You won't mind that, will you, Tom? After all, Evelyn is such a lovely girl."

Evelyn Proctor *was* a lovely girl, and she and Tom were engaged to be married. Tom wasn't sure how that had come about. He could not recall asking her to marry him. He knew that his grandmother wanted them to get married, for Evelyn was the right girl from the right family, but Tom couldn't recall exactly when it became common knowledge that they were to be married. Now, he found himself trapped into an engagement that wasn't of his making and which he didn't wish to keep. Things were coming to a head, for at dinner he had informed everyone that he intended to go West as soon as they returned. At first the others thought he was teasing, then, when they realized he was serious, they tried to talk him out of it. When the atmosphere in the dining room began to get uncomfortable, Tom just got up and left the dinner table. He had been on deck ever since.

Tom was standing at the rail watching the sunset when he became aware of someone behind him. He turned and saw Evelyn Proctor. She was properly dressed in deck whites and canvas shoes, and Tom had to admit that she was devastatingly pretty. She smiled at him, making a brave effort to cover up the fact that she had been crying.

"I've been standing here for a long time," she said. "Didn't you even suspect it?"

"No," Tom replied. "I'm afraid I was thinking about something else."

"Oh, I can believe that," Evelyn said. "Knowing you, you were probably off in some totally different world, no doubt playing football or something equally as brutal."

"Something like that," Tom admitted, realizing that Evelyn just didn't want to face up to the truth.

Evelyn put her hand gently to Tom's face, and ran her

fingers down the bridge of his nose and across the lump formed by the break.

"How awful," she said, screwing her face up distastefully. "That stupid game has disfigured you for life."

Tom laughed. "I never was exactly handsome," he said.

"Perhaps not, but you certainly didn't need to go and make matters worse."

Tom laughed again. "Well, look at it this way. When I leave, you can just say 'good riddance' and go about finding someone else."

"I don't want anyone else," Evelyn pouted. "You know I care only about you."

"Really?"

"Yes, of course."

"Then come West with me." Why did he ask her that, he wondered? He didn't really want her to come with him. Or did he? Perhaps if she did, she would show him more spunk than he gave her credit for.

"Well, I'd be glad to go West for a visit. I think it might be exciting. We could put your grandfather's private car onto a train and just have a marvelous time. In fact, I think we could get several of our friends to go with us and make it a party. A wonderful, mobile party which would last from Boston to . . . wherever."

"No," Tom said. "Don't you understand? That is exactly what I don't want. I'm not going for a visit. I'm going out there to live. I am going to move to Arizona."

"Arizona? My God, that's nothing but wilderness; desert and mountain country. Arizona isn't even a state. It's full of wild Indians . . . What's that Indian's name? Jeremy?"

"Geronimo."

"Yes, Geronimo. Why, he is still scalping people, from what I understand."

"No, that has all been settled," Tom said.

"Tom, you aren't really serious, are you? You don't really mean that you are going to live out there?"

"Yes," Tom said. "My father bought a ranch out there shortly before he died. He left it to me and it has been administered by a trust ever since then. I'm going to go out there and run the ranch."

Evelyn laughed. "You are going to run a ranch? Why in heaven's name would you want to do that? Why, you don't know the first thing about ranching, do you?"

"No," Tom admitted. "But I think I can learn."

"Tom, really, you can't be serious. Please tell me you aren't serious."

"I'm very serious," Tom said, and sighed. "Evelyn, I don't fit in with all the others, and you know it. I know what they say about me . . . what they call me."

"They don't mean anything by it, Tom," Evelyn said. "You know how they are."

"Yes, I know how they are, and I don't want any part of them. They tease me because I'm bigger and stronger than most men. For some reason, they seem to find that amusing. Well, that's all right, I can handle that. But they would tease with equal vigor someone who had a club foot or some other handicap. Don't you see, Evelyn, our friends are wastrels, the lot of them. And I don't want to be like them."

"You shouldn't talk about them like that. They *are* your friends, Tom. They are people you were raised with, and they are the finest names from the wealthiest families in this country. You should be proud to be a part of them."

"Excuse me, sir, ma'am," a sailor said, walking by at that very moment. He picked up a coil of rope, then returned to the stern of the yacht, so that, once again, Tom and Evelyn were alone in their conversation.

"That was Jack Clancey," Tom said, pointing to the

sailor. "He's my age, and I have known him since he was a boy. Would you say he is my friend?"

"No, of course not," Evelyn replied. "Why, he is so far beneath your station that he couldn't possibly be your friend."

"You're right," Tom said. "But I would like for him to be my friend." Tom sighed. "The way things are, he can no more afford to be friends with me than I can to be friends with him. That's the sort of thing I want to get away from," Tom said. "And that's why I'm going out West."

"Tom," Evelyn started, then she let out a sigh. "Tom, I didn't want to say this to you. I didn't want to make it seem that I was trying to bring undue pressure on you. But, if you go West, our engagement is off."

"Yes," Tom said. "I was hoping you would see it that way."

"You were hoping . . . you mean . . . you mean you planned to break our engagement?"

"I planned to give you your freedom," Tom said. "This is something I have to do, but it isn't something I feel I can force on anyone else."

"Tom, do you know what you are saying?" Evelyn asked in a weak voice.

"Yes," Tom replied.

Evelyn began to cry softly, and Tom reached out and put his hand on her shoulder.

"Evelyn, you don't really love me and you know it. You have been in love with the idea of marrying me, but you haven't been in love with me. There are others . . . so many others . . . who are better suited to you. You'll find someone else soon. I know you will."

Abruptly Evelyn's tears of sorrow turned to tears of anger.

"When I do find another, you can bet he won't be a big, ugly ape like you!" she said angrily.

"I'm sure he won't be," Tom replied gently, and the gentleness of his reply seemed to anger Evelyn all the more.

"Oh, I hate you!" Evelyn lashed out, and she started hitting him.

Tom stood there, letting her rain blows on him until she grew tired and frustrated, and finally, with another choked sob, she turned and ran away, disappearing through a hatch that led into the grand salon of the yacht.

Tom turned back toward the sea. The sun had set, but the sky still wasn't dark. The sea looked slate gray under the dim twilight. He watched it in silence for several moments.

"I just saw Evelyn," a voice said from behind Tom. The voice was that of his grandfather, and Tom turned to see the old man, perfectly dressed in a blue blazer and white pants. The older man was wearing an ascot and smoking a pipe. He was playing the society game, and he knew it. When Tom was younger, he used to be embarrassed by his grandfather's role-playing. Then he learned that his grandfather was, in his own way, having his fun with the ultra-rich. He affected their mannerisms, not out of any desire to become one of them, but in a life-long parody of their actions. It was his way of ridiculing them, though his ridicule was so subtle that very few realized what he was doing. When Tom finally did realize it, and mentioned it to his grandfather, he and his grandfather had a wonderful laugh, and the older man seemed genuinely glad that someone else was finally able to share the joke with him. From that moment on, Tom and his grandfather had been exceptionally close.

"I imagine she told you that our engagement is off," Tom said.

"Yes," Andrew replied, sucking on his pipe. "She told me."

"Well?" Tom said.

"Well, what?"

"How do you feel about it?"

Andrew chuckled. "Makes no difference how I feel. The question is, how do you feel about it?"

"I . . ." Tom started, then he sighed and was silent for a moment.

"What is it?" Andrew asked.

"I'm ashamed to say it, Grandfather, but the only thing I can feel at the moment is a sense of relief."

"Evelyn is a lovely young woman," Andrew said.

"Yes, I know she is," Tom admitted.

"She has a lot of good qualities."

"Yes, I'm sure of that too."

"But you had no business being engaged to her in the first place."

Tom looked at his grandfather and smiled.

"Thanks," he said. "I was hoping someone could see it my way. Now, if I could just convince everyone that I am not crazy for wanting to go to Arizona."

"I don't think you are crazy," Andrew said. "If you want to go, go ahead! I think it would be good for you."

"Do you really feel that way?"

"Yes," Andrew said. "That is, if you have the courage to do it right."

"Do it right? What do you mean?"

"You are planning on going out there to take over and run your ranch, right?"

"Yes."

"What do you know about ranching?"

Tom laughed. "You sound like Evelyn. She asked me the same thing."

"Then she asked you a good question. What do you know about running a ranch?"

"I don't know anything about it. I'll admit that."

"Then I think you ought to start a little lower."

"What do you mean?"

"Go out there and go to your ranch. Work on it if you must. But don't go out there ready to take over. Tell the manager and the foreman that you want to work on the ranch as a hand for a while. That way, you'll learn it from the bottom up."

"You mean, just work as a hand?" Tom asked.

"Yes."

"That's an idea," he said. "I'll have to think about it."

"Of course you will," Andrew said. "I'm the first to admit that it doesn't have all that pleasant a sound to it. It will take courage. But you'll learn more that way than by just going out and taking over."

Tom was silent for a moment, then he smiled. "I know an even better way to learn," he said.

"What's that?"

"I'll go out there and work on the ranch, all right. But I won't tell them who I am. I'll simply take the job as a hired hand."

Andrew chuckled. "Now you're putting yourself to the real test," he said. "Are you sure you want to do that?"

"I'm absolutely positive," Tom said.

"Maybe you should tell either the manager or the foreman," Andrew suggested.

"No, I don't want to tell a soul."

Andrew said, "If you go out the way you are saying, it's going to look as if you're spying on the people you have running the ranch for you."

"Well, if they're honest, they have nothing to fear," Tom said. "If they're dishonest, then maybe a little spying wouldn't hurt."

"All right, boy," Andrew said. "It's your ranch, you have the right to run it any way you see fit." Andrew smiled broadly and ran his hand through his thin white hair. "I've only got one thing to say."

"What's that, Grandfather?"

"I wish it were forty years ago, and it was me instead of you going out there. You're going to have a fine adventure, boy. A very fine adventure. And anyone who can't see that, or the reason for your going, is a damn fool. Tom, if no one else in the whole world can understand why you're going, I can. I can, and you have my blessings."

"Thanks, Grandfather," Tom said. "It means a lot to me to know that I haven't been totally ostracized."

Chapter Four

Flagstaff was a town of some importance in the area. It was important not only because it was the largest town in the northern part of the territory, but also because of the arrival of the railroad. Flagstaff was the closest town to Turquoise Ranch, though even it was twenty-five miles away and required nearly three hours travel by buckboard.

It was quicker to go by horseback, and in truth, Hilary would much have preferred to do so. She was a very good rider, and she enjoyed the sensation of the wind in her hair and a well-muscled horse between her legs. But Curly took a buckboard because he would be bringing back a new hand and he didn't want to lead a riderless horse into town for him. Anyway, it was much more practical for Hilary, because it would be easier to carry any purchases she might make in a buckboard than it would be to tie them to the saddle of a horse.

The ride into town was passed pleasantly as far as the scenery was concerned but Curly seemed strangely reticent. Hilary had known Curly for as long as she could recall.

When Hilary was a baby, her mother was often sickly, and unable to watch after her child, so some of the hands willingly assumed the responsibility of raising the active little girl. Curly was one of those who took the job seriously, and when Hilary was barely big enough to walk, Curly would often sit her on the saddle in front of him to take her for a ride. That long association made Curly more than a casual friend, and Hilary was disturbed by his present moodiness. When she could take it no longer, she asked him what was wrong.

"Wrong?" Curly answered. "Why, I don't know as there's anythin' wrong, Miss Hilary. Why do you ask?"

Hilary laughed, though it wasn't a bubbling laugh of humor. It was a laugh of nervousness.

"Curly, come on, I've known you for a long time. Do you think I can't tell when there's something wrong? Now, what is it?"

"I was just wonderin' iffen you'd be changin' any, that's all," Curly said.

"Changing? What do you mean?"

"You've always been a sweet girl, Miss Hilary. From the time you was no higher than the knee joint on a goat's leg, you been nothin' but sweet. But they say women tend ter take on the traits of their menfolk when they get married. And so I figured that, bein' as you're gonna marry up with Mr. Carson, it would seem likely you might take on some of his traits."

"I see," Hilary said.

"Course, I hope that ain't the case," Curly went on. "But they do say that for a fac', 'n I been just sittin' here studyin' on it."

"You hope not? You mean you don't want me to assume any of Mr. Carson's traits?" Hilary asked.

"No'm, I don't."

"Do you mean to tell me, Curly, that Mr. Carson has no desirable traits?"

"Yes'm, I reckon he does at that," Curly replied. "And it would be right admirable for some folks to have them traits. He's a smart man, 'n I reckon that to a woman's way of lookin' at thangs, he's a handsome galoot too. But you are already smart, Miss Hilary, so I reckon you don't need to borrow none on that account. And I doubt as there's anyone in the whole Arizona Territory as beautiful as you are, so you won't be gainin' none there, neither."

"Why, I thank you for the compliment, Curly," Hilary teased.

"Yes'm," Curly said. "I was only speakin' the truth. But them ain't the traits I was thinkin' on. I was thinkin' that Mr. Carson has got a mean streak to him, 'n 'twas the mean streak I'm worryin' about."

"Curly, we've been friends for a long time, you and I," Hilary said.

"Yes'm, I reckon you could say that."

"And I would like for us to keep on being friends," Hilary went on. "Wouldn't you?"

"Yes'm, I certainly hope so," Curly replied.

"Then I'm going to have to ask that you not criticize Mr. Carson in front of me. After all, I am going to marry him. Can't you understand that speaking ill of Mr. Carson is the same as speaking ill of me?"

"Yes'm, I reckon that be so," Curly admitted contritely.

"Then I have your word that you won't speak so again? At least have the decency not to do it in my presence?"

"Yes'm," Curly said. "I won't say nothin' bad about Mr. Carson around you anymore."

"Thank you, Curly," Hilary said. "I appreciate that."

Except for that one meaningful exchange, the conversation for the remainder of the trip involved nothing more significant than the noting of a particularly pretty field of flowers, or a colorful bird. Finally they rolled into Flagstaff.

Flagstaff was built like a large *X*, with one track running east and west, and another running north and south. The streets of the town, and the roads running into town, accommodated themselves to the railroad tracks, for the tracks were indeed the vital center of the city.

Main Street ran east and west, and it was onto this street that the road from Turquoise Ranch ended.

The main street presented a solid row of well constructed wooden buildings: general stores, leather goods stores, a couple of laundries, and a disproportionate number of saloons and gambling halls. At a point very near the railroad there was a nice hotel, and Curly stopped there.

"You'll be wantin' to stay here, I reckon," Curly said.

"Yes," Hilary replied. "It's really quite nice, don't you think?"

"I don't know," Curly said. "I never stayed here."

"You haven't?" Hilary asked in surprise. "Why, where do you stay when you come to town?"

"Most of the time I bed down with the horses in the livery. The liveryman will let a fella do that for a dime."

"Oh, that's terrible."

"No'm, it ain't so bad," Curly said. "The straw is clean, 'n it's dry 'n warm. Fac' is, I'd rather stay there than in the hotel. Bein' upstairs in a hotel tends to make a fella feel closed up."

"Very well," Hilary said. "If you're certain that's what you want to do. But I enjoy staying in the hotel."

"Ever'body has their own preference, I guess," Curly said. "Else, there'd only be one color in the world."

Hilary laughed. "Yes, I suppose that is very true. Oh, by the way, what time will we be starting back to the ranch in the morning?"

"That all depends on you, Miss Hilary," Curly said. "We could start back before dawn 'n fix us a breakfast on the way, or we could wait 'n eat breakfast here in town 'n get started right after."

"Yes, let's do that," Hilary said. "You call for me here at the hotel right after breakfast. I promise to have everything packed and ready to go. I won't be long."

"All right," Curly agreed, and he clucked to the horses and headed the team and buckboard toward the livery stable, which was only three buildings away from the Morning Star Hotel.

Hilary had never been to a big hotel in a big city. But she had stayed at the Morning Star several times, and she had always enjoyed it. She had seen pictures of the hotels in faraway places like New York and San Francisco, and she knew they must be grand. But as it seemed unlikely she would ever see any of them, she was satisfied with the Morning Star.

Eb Deckert was the manager of the hotel, and he looked up and smiled when he saw Hilary approaching the desk. He had worked here for twenty years, so he knew Hilary and her father quite well. He welcomed her warmly.

"Your favorite room is available if you want it," Eb said. "San Francisco Peak is awfully pretty right now, with flowers at the base and snow at the top. Why, it's that pretty they was a drummer here from St. Louis last week said we ought to have an artist paint it 'n put it on one of them picture postcards. He says we could mail it aroun' the United States, 'n there would be folks come from all aroun' just to admire the beauty of it."

"Yes, I could see it on the way in," Hilary said. "Turquoise Peak is awfully pretty right now too."

"Yes'm, I reckon it is," Eb said. "There's the registration book. See? I'm puttin' you in room twenty-five. It has the best view in the house."

"Thanks, Mr. Deckert," Hilary said. "I'll take it, though I must confess that I have so much shopping to do that it'll be dark by the time I'm finished. I'm afraid it'll be too late to enjoy the view."

"Well, you'll sleep better knowin' it's there, just outside your window," Eb said, handing her the key. "And I wouldn't dream of lettin' anyone else stay in there with you in town. Will you be needin' anythin' else?"

"No, I don't think so," Hilary said. She registered, then took the key and started back out the door again, but she turned just before she went outside. "Oh, yes, there is something else. I will be purchasing several things and I am going to have them delivered to the hotel. Would you see to it that they are put in my room?"

"You just don't worry your pretty little head about a thing," Eb assured her. "I'll take care of everythin'."

"Thank you, Mr. Deckert. I really appreciate that."

"My pleasure," Eb said. "Oh, and you be sure 'n tell your daddy I said hello, when you get back out to the ranch."

"I'll do that," Hilary said.

"I'll wear my mother's wedding gown," Hilary explained to the lady in Conklin's Fine Goods store. "But I do want something special for the reception. What do you think of this one?" Hilary pointed to an illustration in a book that Mrs. Conklin had next to her cloth goods.

Mrs. Conklin was the wife of the owner of the dry goods store where Hilary went to buy the material. "Oh, yes, that is a beautiful picture," Mrs. Conklin said from her position behind the counter. "That dress is positively lovely. Does the book have a description of it?"

"Oh, yes, there is a very good description of it, right here on page one twenty-five of the *Harper's Bazaar*," Hilary said. She began to read, "This elaborate toilette is for dinners, receptions, weddings or any occasion where a high-neck dress may be worn. It is composed of white velvet, with a vest and skirt front of white satin, richly embroidered and trimmed with Chantilly lace. The front of the velvet basque opens over a narrow vest of straw-colored satin, which is almost concealed by white lace. The small collar and the ends of the long sleeves are of satin, with lace ruffles. The epaulets are double frills of lace held by richly beaded passementerie, which falls in tassels behind and before. The front breadth of the satin hangs in a drooping puff, and the side-pleatings at the foot are of plain satin, that is, without embroidery. The Chantilly lace forms butterfly bows and gathered frills that droop. The panels and the long square train are of velvet."

Hilary looked up. "Oh, Mrs. Conklin, I don't know. This all sounds so elaborate. Do you really suppose Mrs. Ivery will be able to make this for me?"

"I know she will, dear. She is a wonderful seamstress, and with that picture and description, I don't think she'll have any trouble at all. If I were you, I would go ahead and buy the material."

"Yes, you're right," Hilary said. "I've seen her work before. She is very good. I think she will make a beautiful dress."

Hilary bought all the material Mrs. Ivery would need for making the dress, plus a few other things, and asked that it be delivered to her hotel. After that, she called at a few other shops, primarily to visit, and finally she returned to the hotel for dinner. After dinner she went up to her room to go to bed. She had gotten up very early this morning, and it had been a long ride into town. Now she was tired and the thought of going to bed was very inviting to her.

Hilary didn't know how long she had been asleep when something awakened her. It may have been a noise, though as she lay in bed listening, she heard nothing. She had almost decided that it was nothing but a dream and had closed her eyes to go back to sleep when she heard a distinct sound. It was a woman's voice, and the woman had cried out. But there was something strange about the cry. It wasn't a cry of fear or pain. It was a cry unlike anything Hilary had ever heard before, and yet, though it was new to her, she realized instinctively that it was a cry of passion and pleasure.

The sound had a disquieting effect on Hilary, and she turned over, hoping to find a position that would blot out the sound. When she did turn over she made an amazing discovery. Hilary gasped as she saw, reflected in the propped-open transom glass above her door, the very thing that had caused the cry of passion. By some optical trick Hilary's transom was picking up the reflection of the transom across the hallway. As clearly as if she were looking in a mirror, Hilary could see into the room across the hallway, where the lamp was burning brightly and a scene of passion was being played out upon the bed. Hilary was, by chance, thrust into the role of unwitting witness to a secret rite of desire between a man and a woman.

Hilary could see as clearly as if she were actually in the room with them. She could hear as well, for neither of the two lovers made any effort to be quiet. The bed coverings had been cast aside, and two naked figures were clearly visible on the bed. The woman lay with her legs wantonly spread, and Hilary could see a dark tangle of hair and a pink, glistening cleft. But it was not the woman who held her attention. It was the man, for Hilary was seeing a nude and fully aroused man for the first time, and it made quite an imposing sight.

The two naked bodies came together on the bed, kissing each other with a strange mixture of tenderness and savage fury.

Hilary felt bewilderingly alive, and a strange warmth began to spread throughout her. She reached up above her and grabbed the bedpost as the kisses led to more, and the couple actually came together. She saw then, for the first time, what actually went on between a man and a woman. And yet, though she could see the couple's frenzied thrashing, some of the mystery remained. Was there some pain mixed with what was obviously pleasurable? Was making love like bringing fire and ice together? Was all lovemaking so savage, or was it just the actions of these two? As Hilary contemplated these things, her own breath began coming in gasps as short and desperate as the breathing of the man and woman on the bed in the other room.

Hilary was puzzled by the heat she felt. A moment before it had been cool enough for her to require a blanket. Now she cast the blanket aside because she was swept by such heat that she began to perspire. Her sleeping gown had worked its way up her legs, and she felt an unaccustomed breath of air on her bare legs, though the breeze did little to cool the heat which now blazed, unchecked, in her loins.

Steadily the moans of the man and woman grew louder and more urgent, while their thrashing became more frenzied. Then they seemed to reach an apex of some sort, a pinnacle of savage tenderness which brought louder and more intense little cries and grunts from both of them. Then, strangely, there was a prolonged stillness, and the two lay in each other's arms. Hilary, who was alone in her own bed, felt a devastating sense of emptiness at that moment. She wished she had not been a witness to the scene. Despite that wish, she was much too absorbed to turn away, even now, when it was finished.

After a few moments, the man rolled away from the woman, and Hilary was somewhat surprised by the difference in his appearance now from a few moments earlier. Before, he had been almost frightening with the urgent erect thrust of his manhood. Now it wasn't frightening at all, though it was just as intriguing.

The man began pulling on his pants, but the woman continued to lie on the bed with her eyes closed and a soft smile playing across her mouth. She made no effort whatever to cover her nudity. Then the man did something that nearly made Hilary gasp aloud. He put some money on her breasts.

"You're a sweet girl," the man's voice said, muffled by the walls but easily understandable.

"Thanks," the woman said. "Will you be coming into town again?"

"My sales route takes me from Denver to Phoenix," the man replied. "I'll be coming into town at least once a month from now on."

"Maybe you'll look me up again?" the woman said. "You did enjoy it, didn't you?"

The man chuckled under his breath. "Honey, you're the best lovin' whore on the line," he said. "I'll be seein' you again, you can count on that."

The woman took the money and shoved it under her pillow. "You weren't half bad yourself," she said. "Maybe I'll give you a special price, you come see me next time."

"Ha, I'm goin' to remember that," the man said. "Good night, now." The man moved out of sight of the transom, then Hilary heard the door to the room open and close, followed by the sound of his footsteps retreating down the carpeted hall.

So, Hilary thought. She had been watching a prostitute. She often wondered about them, about what they did and how they did it.

Now she knew.

Chapter Five

After Curly let Hilary off that afternoon, he put the buckboard away and had the team attended to. Then he walked back out onto the board sidewalk in front of the livery stable, rubbing his hands together in anticipation of doing a night on the town. The boardwalk ran the length of the town on both sides of the street. At the end of each block there were planks laid across the road to allow pedestrians to cross the road without having to walk in the dirt or mud. Curly waited patiently at one of them while he watched a lady cross, holding her skirt up above her ankles daintily, to keep the hem from soiling, then he stepped onto the plank himself. Just as he started to cross the street, he saw Hilary coming back out of the hotel on her way to do her shopping. Curly stepped back and walked in the opposite direction. He had been intending to cross the street and go into the Bull's Hind Quarters, one of the more popular saloons, but he didn't want Hilary to see him. He didn't have to hide his actions from her, as she probably suspected he would visit the saloons anyway. It was just that he didn't want to be quite so blatant about it.

Curly looked in the window of a leather goods shop and contemplated a pair of boots for a moment or two. When he looked back toward Hilary, he saw her stepping into a dry goods store, so he left the window and crossed the street right in the middle of the block, to go into the Bull's Hind Quarters.

It was dark enough inside the saloon so that the lamps were being lit. A great wagon wheel was lowered from the ceiling by a rope, and the bartender had a long match, lighting each of the lamps which were attached to the wheel.

Curly sidled up to the bar and leaned against it, watching the bartender as he illuminated the fixture. Then he turned back toward the bar to contemplate what he would drink, and he saw his reflection in the mirror behind the bar.

His hair was curly, thus justifying the nickname. But it was no longer jet black. Now it was laced with so much gray that one of his friends had teased him, suggesting that a more suitable nickname might be "Salt and Pepper."

Curly was a relatively short man, though the shortness came from the bowed legs, because his upper body was long. His nose had been broken in a barroom fight which would have been long forgotten had it not been for the constant reminder of it every time he looked at himself in a mirror. He was once a very good barroom fighter and often looked for fights just for entertainment. But he was into his forties now and such amusements were no longer as entertaining as they once had been.

"What'll it be, cowpoke?" the bartender asked as he came back behind the bar and pulled the rope that drew the wagon wheel lamp fixture back into position above the room.

"Whiskey," Curly replied.

The glass was set before Curly, and he took it, then turned with his back to the bar to survey the room. The evening crowd was just beginning to gather. There were several round tables which were full of drinking, laughing customers, and a few where card games were in progress. As Curly watched, one of the players left one of the games, and Curly walked over to the table.

"May I sit in?" he asked.

"Be my guest," a tall man with a handlebar mustache invited.

When Curly left the saloon a little over an hour later it was dark and he was broke. He had had very little money to start with, and any hopes of running it up into enough to have a pleasant night on the town were quickly dispelled by his run of bad luck. In truth, Curly didn't actually believe it was all bad luck. He was convinced that the man with the handlebar mustache and another man were working in cahoots to cheat him, though he had no way of proving it. Making an unsubstantiated accusation of cheating could be a dangerous move, so Curly bore his losses stoically, though he wished now that he hadn't brought Hilary into town. If it weren't for Hilary he could just pick up the new hand and head back to the ranch tonight. Now, he would have to wait until morning. All night long in town, and no money to spend.

Curly thought of the new hand he was to meet. Perhaps Curly could get the new hand to play a couple of games of two-handed poker on the come. After all, they would be working together; surely the new man would trust Curly's credit. Then Curly stopped. He realized that, if this man was like those who had come before him, he would not likely have extra money.

The new hand had answered an ad Gil Carson had placed in several newspapers. Gil Carson was a difficult man to work for, and, as a result, he had a hard time keeping enough hands on to do the work. By now his reputation had spread so that local cowboys didn't want to work for him, so he had to come by his new hands by advertising.

Curly had stayed on, and so had half a dozen or more of the other, older hands. But they had stayed on out of loyalty to Big Jake. Of all the cowboys on the ranch, only Sam, the cook, had been with Big Jake longer than Curly. Sam had come from Texas with Jake. Curly hadn't been with Jake in Texas, but he had known him a long time, and he had no interest in leaving now, despite the difficult personality of Gil Carson.

The younger hands had no such loyalty, though, so there was a rather rapid turnover, and Curly had seen many new hands come and go. Often they were green young men, frequently from the East, coming West out of a spirit of adventure. Others were discharged soldiers, interested in trying their hand at cowboying. Some were people who had been in trouble with the law, looking for a new start, and some, Curly suspected, were on the dodge from the law and looking for a place to hide out. But they almost always had one thing in common. They were almost always broke, having spent their last cent just to get here. That meant there would be no sense in trying to interest the newcomer in a game of cards. He would, no doubt, be just as broke as Curly was.

Curly wandered down to the depot to wait for the night train. The depot was one of the most substantial structures in town. It was fairly large, with a waiting room, warehouse, dining room, freight and dispatch offices all inside one building. It was painted green, with a red-painted shake roof and a proud white sign announcing "Flagstaff."

The arrival of the train was always an important event in a small Western town, and Flagstaff was no exception. There was a carnival atmosphere to the crowd. There was a great deal of laughing and joking going on, and a constant cry of salesmen who were trying to take advantage of the crowd to move their wares.

Curly leaned back against the depot wall and watched the crowd mill about on the platform. He rolled a cigarette, lit it, then smoked quietly as he waited for the train.

"Here it comes!" someone shouted, and with the shout, the laughing and joking ceased as everyone grew quiet to await the train's arrival.

Curly watched as the people on the platform moved closer to the track to stare in the direction from which the train would come. Those who looked could see the headlamp first, a huge, wavering yellow disc—actually a gas flame and mirror reflector—shining brightly in the distance. They could hear it now as well, the hollow sounds of the puffing steam came not only from the train, but rolled back in echo from the surrounding mountainsides. As the train grew even closer one could see glowing sparks spewing out from the smokestack, whipped up by the billowing clouds of smoke.

The train pounded into the station with sparks flying from the drive wheels and glowing hot embers dripping from its firebox. Following the engine and tender were the golden patches of light that were the windows of the passenger cars. Inside, Curly could see that those people who would be getting off here were already moving toward the exits at the end of the cars.

Curly was in no hurry to meet the new hand, so he just stood quietly until everyone was off the train. Many of the passengers were being met, but there were several who weren't. Most of those who weren't being met were drummers, calling on Flagstaff as part of their circuit. They were easy to pick out, for they were all dressed in business suits, vests and ties, proud emblems of their profession.

The passengers who would be leaving with the train got on then, and with the conductor's shout of "All aboard!" a gush of steam and a quick, impatient whistle, the train started up. Curly watched until it was gone, then, on the nearly deserted platform he saw a single figure standing alone, looking around as if trying to decide what he was about to do. Curly knew, without having to be told, that this was the man he was to meet.

The man was big. He was even taller than Big Jake. Curly guessed that he must stand at least six feet three, and he probably weighed around two hundred pounds. He had big shoulders and long, powerful-looking arms. If he couldn't do anything else, he should certainly be good for any job around the ranch that required brute strength, for Curly could tell by looking that here was a man who was exceptionally strong.

As Curly moved closer to him, he couldn't help but feel an affinity with him, because the man had a nose just like Curly's. It had obviously been broken, and Curly smiled as he wondered how big the other fella had been to be able to do this.

The man wasn't handsome by any stretch of the word, but there was something about him that made Curly think he would probably like him. There seemed to be a sense of humor in his eyes and the suggestion of a laugh around his mouth. Curly walked over to him.

"Hello," the big man said, sticking a large mitt out for a friendly handshake. "Are you from the Turquoise Ranch?"

"Yes," Curly said. "Folks call me Curly."

"I'm Tom," the big man said. "Thomas Eddington."

Curly laughed.

"What is it? What's wrong?"

"Nothing, really," Curly said. "It's just that out here, we don't often hear a man's full handle."

"Should I not give it?" Tom asked innocently.

"You ain't wanted by the law, are you?" Curly asked.

"No, no, of course not," Tom said easily. "Why would you ask that?"

"If you ain't wanted by the law, there ain't no reason why you can't tell a feller your whole handle iffen you want to," Curly said. "Fac' is—" Curly looked around, then in a quieter voice, he continued sheepishly, "My real name is Joshua. Joshua Michaels. Only, they don't many people know that. I prefer to go by Curly."

Tom laughed. "All right, Curly it shall be," he said. Tom walked over to the baggage cart then, and he picked up a trunk which two men were struggling with and lifted it easily to his shoulder.

"Did you bring a wagon or something into town?" Tom asked. "I can put away my trunk. Then, if you don't mind, we could go get something to eat. I'm starved."

"I, uh, brought a buckboard," Curly said. "It's over in the livery, about a block from here. That's pretty far to have to carry that. If you want, you can leave it here and I'll go hook up the buckboard."

"No, there's no need," Tom said easily. "Just show me where it is."

Curly led the way down the street toward the livery, and Tom kept up an easy conversation for the entire distance, showing absolutely no strain from carrying the trunk. When they reached the livery, Curly showed Tom the buckboard, and Tom set his load down easily. The buckboard sagged under the weight.

"Now," Tom said, brushing his hands together. "What do you say we get something to eat?"

"I have some jerky here in the buckboard," Curly offered.

"Jerky? Jerky is all right when you have to eat it," Tom said. "But I was thinking more along the lines of a big steak, with a healthy side of potatoes. A half-dozen biscuits would go well with it too."

"A meal like that would cost nearly a dollar," Curly said. "I don't have any money."

Tom smiled. "Well, I have a little," he said. "In fact, I have enough for both of us. Have you eaten?"

"No," Curly said. He smiled sheepishly. "Truth is, I lost all my money playin' poker to a couple of slick-dealin' galoots afore I come down to meet you."

"You don't say? Well, you'll have to show me the fellows you were playing with. I'll want to be sure and avoid them if I get into any poker games."

"Yeah," Curly said grimly. "Yeah, I'd say that would be a pretty good idea."

A short while later, Curly pushed his plate away. He was so stuffed that he could scarcely breathe.

"How about passing the rest of the biscuits this way if you aren't going to eat any more of them?" Tom asked, and Curly, amazed at Tom's appetite, handed the plate of biscuits across to Tom. Tom had already finished his steak and potatoes, and now he set to work finishing the rest of the biscuits. He had just finished the last one when a couple of men came in through the front door. Curly glanced over toward them and saw that they were the two men in the game he had suspected of cheating. The fact that they were together now, talking and joking, proved that they weren't casual acquaintances who happened to meet in the game. That tended to substantiate Curly's suspicions.

"Well," Curly said, "there they are."

Tom looked over toward them. One was tall and wore a handlebar mustache. The other was shorter and clean-shaven. Both wore city-style clothes.

They sat at a table next to Curly and Tom.

They were laughing, and one of them said something that was so quiet no one else could hear. Both of them laughed again. Their laughter was low and evil, and Curly intuitively knew that it was not the light banter of the kind he was used to with cowboys.

"What did that fella say her name was again?" the tall one asked.

"Hilary," the other answered.

"That's purty, ain't it? Hilary."

"Sure it is," the short one replied. "But then, all them whores got purty names." He rubbed his crotch and laughed. "Wouldn't I like to crawl in a sleepin' roll with her, though?" he said, and he laughed again, more raucously than before.

Curly tensed, and Tom noticed it.

"What is it?" Tom asked.

"Hilary," Curly said. "They are talkin' about Hilary."

"Who is Hilary?"

"She's the sweetest girl you'd ever want to meet," Curly said. "She's the daughter of Big Jake, our foreman. I brung her into town with me today, and she'll be goin' back with us tomorrow."

"If you are goin' to get in that girl's sleepin' roll, you probably got to wait 'n line. A whore that's a looker like that has probably got a lot of customers."

"Mister, you mind your tongue!" Curly said. "I'll not listen to that kind of language about Miss St. John."

"Miss St. John, is it?" the tall one with the handlebar mustache said. He chuckled. "And who are you, her flunkie?"

"I happen to work at the Turquoise Ranch," Curly said. "And you are spreading filthy lies about a fine young girl."

The shorter of the two men said, "Hey, Luke, you know who this is? This here is the sucker cowboy we took in the poker game. Only he was such shortchange, he wasn't hardly worth the effort."

"Looks like we ain't the only one to take him," Luke replied. "Seems to me like he's been took by the girl as well. What's an old geezer like you doin' sniffin' aroun' a young girl, anyway? Why, she could throw you offen her like a . . ."

The gambler didn't get a chance to finish his remark, because Curly was over to his table in a flash, and he brought the back of his hand across the gambler's face so hard that it sounded like someone clapping hands.

"Why you dried-up old prairie dog, you hit me!" the gambler said in surprise, running his fingers across his cheek, which was now showing a red welt.

"You're damned right I hit you, and I'm about to do it again if you don't apologize for those remarks about Miss St. John." Curly drew his hand back again, but he just let it hang there when he saw a small derringer suddenly appear in the gambler's hand.

"No, I don't think you will," the tall gambler said menacingly. "Because I'm going to put a ball right between your eyes." The gambler raised his pistol to fire, but before he could Tom reached up and clamped his big hand around the gambler's wrist. Tom squeezed the wrist so hard that the gambler let out a yelp of pain, and the gun clattered to the floor.

"Let go of his wrist, mister, or I'll put a bullet in your brain!" the smaller gambler said, and now he was also armed. But he was too preoccupied with keeping a wary eye on Tom to notice Curly, and Curly took advantage of that preoccupation to pick up a chair. He brought it crashing down on the second gambler, who fell like a sack of potatoes. Tom increased the pressure on his man's wrist until the tall man sank to his knees, crying out in pain. Finally Tom released him.

"You damn fool . . . I think you broke my arm!" the gambler said.

"No," Tom said. "But if I had wanted to do it, I could have done so quite easily."

The gambler was still whimpering in pain and he took off his jacket to look at his arm. When he did, the action revealed a clamp and an accordion-like device on his arm.

"What the? What is that?" Curly asked.

"It's called a sleeve holdout," Tom said.

"A what?"

Tom reached down and took the device from the gambler's arm.

"It would appear that your suspicions were well-founded," Tom said. "This man was cheating, and this is the proof. It's a small machine, arranged to allow him to slip a card into the palm of his hand anytime he needs it. I once saw a demonstration of just such a device."

"Mister, you owe me two dollars and fifty cents," Curly said.

Slowly, painfully, the gambler reached into his vest pocket and pulled out a handful of money. He dropped it on the floor in front of him.

"Here," he said. "Take it. Take it all. Just, for God's sake, get this giant away from me!"

"I only want what's mine," Curly said, picking up his share of the money. He put it in his pocket, and looked at the other gambler, who was just beginning to come around. "I suggest that you and your friend stay out of our sight for the rest of the time we're in town."

"Don't you worry none about that," the gambler said as he helped the other man to his feet. "If I ever see either one of you again, it will be too soon for me."

Both gamblers hurried out of the restaurant while Tom gallantly set the chair back up and carefully moved the tables back to the way they were. He looked at the proprietor of the restaurant, who, when the trouble began, had moved with the other customers to the far side of the room.

"I'm sorry for the disturbance," Tom said. "I hope you will forgive us."

"Mister, those two hyenas have been nothing but trouble ever since they came into town," the restaurant owner said. "Believe me, it does my heart good to see them run off. You don't have my forgiveness. You have my thanks."

"Come on," Curly said, now grinning broadly. "Seein' as how I've got my poke back, I can show you how to have a little fun in this town."

Chapter Six

When Tom opened his eyes the next morning, he was so cold that he found himself groping for cover. But there was no cover because he wasn't sleeping in a bed; he was sleeping in a stall in the livery stable. For just a moment he wondered where he was and how he got here, then he looked over and saw Curly, who was skillfully burrowed down in the straw, sleeping comfortably. When he saw that, he smiled, and he remembered.

Tom made the offer to put them both up in a hotel last night, but Curly wouldn't hear of it. Curly had insisted that Tom save his money. Besides, Curly explained, sleeping in a livery stable was better anyway, because a fella wouldn't feel "cooped up" that way.

That was all well and good for Curly, Tom thought. He had experience in sleeping this way, and he was able to make himself quite comfortable. But Tom had not passed as good a night. It took him a long time to get to sleep, and when he did get to sleep his body was still cold. Now, in the gray light of early morning, he felt exceptionally cold, so he looked around to try and find some way to get warm.

Tom blew on his hands and wrapped his arms around himself, then he saw a saddle blanket hanging across a partition. He smiled as he thought of his grandmother and her insistence that the bed linen be changed every day. What would she think about wrapping up in a saddle blanket, just to get warm? The truth is, Tom didn't relish using it, but it would be better than nothing. In fact, at the moment, Tom was grateful for it. He took the blanket from the partition and wrapped it around his shoulders. The blanket was covered with frost, stiff and cold, but he knew that his body heat would warm it, then it would be better, so he braved the initial discomfort.

There was a window open at the back of the stable, and Tom, holding the blanket securely around his shoulders, went to the window to look outside. From here he could look up to the top of San Francisco Peak, and he could see snow there. Being able to see the snow made him feel all the colder, and he saw that it was cool enough to see his breath when he breathed. That surprised him a little. He had not expected it to be this cool in the mornings this late in the spring. Especially as he had always regarded Arizona as being in a warm climate.

"Well, Grandfather, I am here," Tom said under his breath. "You've spoken of the days when you used to be a stableboy. Was it a stable just like this, I wonder? Well, I just spent the night in this one, so we have come full circle." Tom shivered and wrapped the frosty blanket more tightly around him. "Why didn't you ever tell me it would be so cold, though?"

"O-oh," Curly moaned from the straw in the corner, and Tom was embarrassed that he might have been overheard talking to himself, so he turned and looked in Curly's direction. Curly was just now sitting up. He rubbed his head gingerly. Straw hung from his hair and clung to his shirt. Tom laughed.

"Good morning," Tom said. "Did you pass a pleasant night?"

Curly looked toward him. His eyelids drooped heavily, and he blinked several times, as if gingerly testing the world he had so reluctantly abandoned the night before.

"Say," Curly said, "by chance, did a horse happen to step on my head during the night?" He rubbed his head again.

"No, my friend," Tom said. "Any pounding in your head comes from within, I'm afraid. You put away a prodigious amount of whiskey last night."

"What did I do?" Curly asked, not understanding the comment.

"You drank a lot," Tom said simply.

Curly smiled. "Did I have a good time?"

"You appeared to have a wonderful time," Tom said.

Curly stood up, then walked over to a watering trough. He bent over and stuck his head down in it, then jerked it out again, shaking the cold water from his face and hair and making a *brrr*ing sound with his lips. Tom winced because he couldn't bear to think of immersing his head in cold water on a morning as cold as this.

"I *hope* I had a good time," Curly said. He began combing out his hair with his fingers. "I hope it was worth all this."

"Well, what do you say?" Tom asked. "Are you about ready for breakfast?"

"Breakfast?" Curly moaned. He shook his head. "No, thank you. I don't think I could look food in the face this morning."

"Come on," Tom said. "A half-dozen eggs or so, a few

pieces of ham and a handful of biscuits would fix you right up."

Curly looked pale. "If you mention food again, tenderfoot, I'll shoot you where you stand," he said menacingly.

"How are you going to shoot me? You don't have a gun," Tom teased.

"Damned if I don't," Curly agreed. "Then I'll strangle you with my bare hands, and . . ." Curly started, then, looking at Tom and his size, he stopped in mid-sentence and groaned.

"Oh, please, can't you just have mercy on me?"

"All right." Tom laughed. "I won't insist that you eat breakfast. But I hope you don't mind if I do."

"No, I don't mind," Curly said. "Only be back here right after, 'cause as soon as Miss Hilary is ready, we're headin' back to the ranch."

"I'll be here," Tom promised.

Tom stripped off his shirt and washed himself at the water trough, braving the cold water in the name of cleanliness. After he washed he opened his suitcase, then he pulled out a clean, light-blue shirt and put it on. Curly watched him.

"What'd you do?" Curly asked. "Roll over inter somethin' while you was asleep? The stable keep said this was a clean stall."

"No, I didn't roll into anything," Tom said as he buttoned the shirt.

"Then what are you puttin' on another shirt for?" he asked.

"I just felt the need for one," Tom answered without elaboration. "Don't you ever feel like just changing shirts?"

"I only got me three," Curly said. "An' one of them is my Sunday go-to-meetin' shirt, only since I don't go to

Sunday meetin's, I don't hardly ever wear it none. The other two shirts I wear one week at a time, then I change."

"This is my week," Tom said.

"Oh," Curly replied, and that seemed to satisfy him. "Don't forget now, you come back here right after breakfast. I don't want to keep Miss Hilary waitin' on account o' some tenderfoot that can eat more'n any three men I ever knowed."

"All right," Tom answered.

Tom left the livery stable and walked along the boardwalk. He looked around the town, seeing it in daylight for the first time. In the bright light of day, the town didn't seem quite as intimidating. It wasn't nearly as large as he had imagined it to be last night. And it wasn't nearly as boisterous either.

Last night Tom had seen Flagstaff only by the golden glow of the many lamps and lanterns which splashed patches of light onto the streets. With Curly, he had started on one side of the street, gone into every saloon they encountered, then they crossed the street and went into every one on the other side as they worked their way back.

Tom had enjoyed it, even though he did no more than nurse a beer in each of the saloons. He enjoyed it because it was all new and strange to him, and he was absorbing new experiences. He watched the bargirls and the gamblers and the cowboys with an intense, though guarded interest. Guarded, because he did not want to make anyone uneasy by this observation.

Curly drank straight whiskey as if that were his mission in life. The bargirls fluttered to them like moths to a light as soon as the men stepped through the swinging doors of a new saloon. They were drawn to Tom by his size, and to Curly by the hope that he would be generous enough to spread some of his money around. When they discovered that Tom wasn't interested in anything they had for sale and that Curly was doing a maximum amount of drinking on a minimum investment, the girls left them alone, and Curly, after finishing a drink in one bar, would leave abruptly and head for another. By the time they left the final saloon, Curly was staggering drunk, and Tom had to help him back to the livery stable.

Tom planned to take his breakfast at the restaurant where he and Curly had eaten dinner last night, but as he passed the hotel, he saw that it also had a restaurant. Since it was close to the livery stable, and since he had promised Curly he would return immediately, he thought it would be more convenient to eat his breakfast here. He stepped inside and went to the dining room.

Hilary was in the hotel dining room, looking at the menu, trying to decide what to order for breakfast. A shadow fell across her table, and it was so large that it seemed as if the very sun had been blotted out. She looked up to see a tall man standing in the door looking around the dining room. He wasn't just tall, he was very big, with wide shoulders and long, powerful-looking arms. The man looked over the dining room for a moment, saw an empty table, then walked over to it. Hilary watched him as he moved. Despite his great size he moved with a fluid gracefulness which was pleasant to watch. Hilary was reminded of a powerful stallion with a sleek black coat and muscles which rippled just under the skin.

Hilary's father was a big man, and as a little girl she had always thought that she would grow up to marry a big man. How different things were about to turn out, for Gil, though not small, was not as large as her father. This man was even bigger than her father.

Hilary continued to stare at him as he took his seat. She

covered her curiosity by holding the menu in front of her face. The man's eyes, she couldn't help noticing, were light blue. In fact, their color very nearly matched his shirt. He looked up as the waiter brought him a menu, and he smiled, an easy, comfortable smile. The smile did something to his face. It softened the rough features and minimized the effect of the misshapen nose. Hilary thought that it became a very appealing face then.

Inexplicably, Hilary felt a quickening of her pulse and a spreading warmth in her body, not unlike that which she felt last night when she had been witness to the scene of passion in the room across the hall. She suddenly got an image of that same scene, only instead of the strange man and the prostitute, she saw herself in that bed with this man. What was this? No man had ever made her feel this way before. Besides, she was engaged to be married. If anyone made her feel this way it should be Gil. And yet, despite all her musings, she had never imagined Gil in this way. Then, to Hilary's great embarrassment, the man must have sensed her looking at him, because he looked over toward her. At first there was a question in his eyes, as if he wondered who was looking at him. Then, when he saw who it was, he smiled broadly and acknowledged her unabashed interest with the slightest nod of his head.

Hilary looked away quickly and felt her face flaming red in embarrassment. She had been caught staring. She was angry with herself, and unreasonably angry with the man for catching her. She moved the menu pointedly so that she couldn't see him and he couldn't see her. She was glad that the waiter came to take her order, because it had the effect of breaking the uncomfortable contact that had been established between them.

Hilary ate a light breakfast, not because she wasn't hungry, but because she wanted to leave the dining room as quickly as she could. When she did leave a few moments later, she managed to steal one more glance at the tall man. She was relieved to see that he was now occupied with his own breakfast. Because of that, she was able to get away without another awkward exchange.

"Oh, Miss St. John," Eb Decker called out as Hilary walked through the lobby. "What do you want me to do with these things you bought yesterday?"

"Curly will be by for me shortly," Hilary said. "Just have them stacked up out front, and Curly will pick them up in the buckboard."

"Yes, ma'am, I will," Eb said. "Oh, and Miss St. John, you won't be too hard on Curly, will you? After all, it was you he was fighting over."

Hilary had just started up the stairs to her room, but when she heard that, she stopped and looked over toward the front desk in confusion.

"What?" she asked. "What are you talking about? Who fought over me?"

"Why, Curly did," Eb said. "That is, Curly and the new hand he picked up. They took on those two tinhorn gamblers that have been robbin' ever'one in town. The robbers both had guns, and Curly and your new man were unarmed, but that didn't stop them." Eb chuckled. "No, sir, that didn't slow 'em down one whit. And after they was through, why them two no-'count gamblers lit out. Truth to tell, I think they even left town."

"What do you mean they were fighting over me?" Hilary asked.

Eb blinked a couple of times, then cleared his throat, realizing that he may have spoken out of turn.

"Uh, well, nothin' much," he said.

"Mr. Deckert, if Curly fought over me, there must have been something."

"I . . . I think the two tinhorns passed some uncomplimentary remark about you, that's all," Eb said.

"But, how can that be? I don't even know the two men you are talking about."

"The thing is, I think they seen you yesterday when you was shoppin'," Eb said. "You know how men like that are sometimes. They can be awful insultin' just from meanness."

"I see," Hilary said. "And over some stupid remark they may have made, Curly felt it was necessary to defend my honor, is that it?" Hilary said icily.

"Yes, Miss Hilary, I reckon it was," Eb said. " 'Course, it wa'nt only Curly. It was the new hand too. They was together."

"Thank you for the information," Hilary said.

"Yes," Eb said. "Well, uh, I only tole you this 'cause you might of heard it somewhere else, 'n they might not have got all the fac's straight. It wa'nt Curly's fault, Miss Hilary."

"Oh, I'm sure it wasn't," Hilary said coolly. "And you are right, Mr. Deckert, I am glad I heard it from you first."

A few moments later Hilary was standing on the front porch of the hotel, patting her foot impatiently as she waited for Curly to show up with the buckboard. Her purchases were in boxes, stacked neatly beside her. She had bought material, ribbons and lace for a dress to wear at her wedding party. Mrs. Ivery, the seamstress, had come to the valley with her husband about a year ago. Mr. Ivery was a lumberjack, and he had a contract to cut lumber from the Turquoise Ranch. For the year or so it would require to take the lumber out, the Iverys were living in one of the range cabins on the ranch, so it would be very convenient for her to make the dress.

The buckboard arrived shortly after Hilary came out onto the porch, and Curly pulled it up to the porch and stopped it, then hopped down to start loading the packages. He helped Hilary onto the seat.

"I thought you picked up a new hand last night," Hilary said.

"I did," Curly said. "He's back at the stable, takin' care of the bill. We'll go back and pick him up."

Hilary was tempted to take Curly to task now for his unauthorized defense of her honor on the night before, but if the new hand had been involved, she decided she might as well wait and include him. After all, if she let them know right now how she felt about such things, perhaps it would prevent it from ever happening again.

Curly swung the team in a wide, U-turn in the street in front of the hotel and drove back over to the livery stable. He stopped out front and gave a loud whistle.

"Ah, there he is," Curly said and chuckled under his breath. "Oh, I forgot to tell you. He's a big 'un."

Tom came out of the barn and started to get onto the buckboard.

"*You!*" Hilary said, mouthing the word with such expressiveness that both Tom and Curly looked at her in surprise.

"Miss Hilary, do you . . . do you know Tom?" Curly asked.

"No," Hilary said, flustered now by what she had done. She had been angry with herself for the way she reacted to the sight of Tom when he was in the restaurant earlier in the morning. Now she was giving voice to that anger, and yet, to do so would certainly let him know that he had affected her. She had a moment of panic, wondering how she would cover up her blurted remark. Then she thought of the fight the men had last night. That would provide the excuse for her anger.

"No, I don't know him," Hilary went on. "But I'm angry with him. And you too! Curly, just what makes you think I could possibly appreciate your fighting, for whatever reason?" she asked. "And to bring me into it . . ."

"Now, hold on, Miss Hilary. I didn't bring you into it, those two galoots did," Curly said. "Miss Hilary, you don't know what all they were sayin'."

"You should have just let them babble on," Hilary said. "What did it matter what they were saying? It is obviously untrue."

"But Miss Hilary, it was a matter of honor," Curly protested.

"Is it honorable to bring me into a . . . a common saloon fight?"

"It wasn't a saloon, it was a restaurant," Curly said.

"Then all the more reason you should have done nothing. If you were offended by what they were saying, there were other things you could have done, other ways you could have fought."

"Like what?" Curly asked.

"Well, you could have ignored them," Hilary suggested.

"What? And do nothing?" Curly asked.

"Yes."

"But . . . what good would that have done?" Curly asked.

"I think what Miss St. John is suggesting, is that discretion is the better part of valor," Tom said.

Hilary looked around in quick surprise.

"Something like that, yes," she said. "Though I wouldn't have expected to hear such a remark from you."

"Why not?" Tom asked. "Don't you think anyone my

size has ever read a book? It might interest you to know that I have read several books."

"You went to school?"

"Yes."

"I wouldn't have thought . . ." Hilary let the sentence die.

"You wouldn't think a big, dumb-looking brute like me would go to school, is that it?"

"I didn't say that," Hilary replied quickly.

"You didn't have to," Tom said. "I know what people think about men my size. They all think we are all dumb."

"Your size has nothing to do with it at all," Hilary said. "I was thinking more along the lines of the profession you've chosen for yourself. You are obviously an educated man. Why would an educated man want to be a cowboy?"

"A spirit of adventure?" Tom replied.

"Well, I beg of you, Tom, don't get your adventure by defending my honor. My honor doesn't need defending."

Hilary called him Tom, because she called all the hands by their first names. And yet, for some reason, she felt self-conscious about doing it with him. Self-conscious and, though she wouldn't admit it to herself, a little thrilled as well.

What was she doing? Why was she reacting so to him? He wasn't nearly as handsome as Gil, he was only a hired hand and she had just met him. And yet, she felt herself tremble a little, just being this close to him. What was wrong with her?

Chapter Seven

"It's good to see you back," Gil said, kissing Hilary lightly on the cheek. "Did you have any problem finding everything you wanted in town?"

"No," Hilary said. "Everything went just fine."

"Who is the big, dumb lummox you and Curly brought back with you?"

Hilary looked toward Tom. He was busy unhitching the team from the buckboard, and without even realizing it, she reflected in her facial expression some of the reactions she had already had to him.

"Don't let his size fool you," Hilary said. "He isn't dumb," she added with conviction.

"Oh?" Gil replied, raising an eyebrow as he spoke. Gil had seen her strange reaction to Tom, and he was disturbed by it. "How did you find out so quickly? What did he do, recite poetry for you or something?"

"No," Hilary answered, blushing under Gil's taunt. She suddenly realized that she might be telegraphing her feelings. "It's just the way he talks, that's all. I get the feeling he isn't dumb."

"Then what's he doing working for twelve dollars a month and found?" Gil challenged.

"I don't know," Hilary admitted. "He told me he's looking for adventure."

"He must talk a great deal. Either that, or perhaps you just have a little more than the usual interest in this cowboy. I don't think I like that, and I don't think I'm going to like him very much!"

"Don't be silly, Gil," Hilary said quickly. "I don't have any more or any less interest in him than in anyone else. He's just another cowboy, that's all."

"That's right," Gil said. "He's just another cowboy."

Gil took a special interest in Tom, whether Hilary had one or not. He wanted to make certain that, in Hilary's eyes, he just stayed another cowboy. Gil pointed out the bunkhouse to Tom, and told him which remuda he could select his horse from, and gave him the rules of the ranch.

"The most important rule of all," Gil said as the two men stood at the fence, looking out over the horses, "is that you remember your place around Miss St. John."

"Remember my place?" Tom replied. "And just what would that place be?"

"You know what that place is," Gil said. "You are nothing but a hired hand. In fact, you are the lowest and least important hand on this ranch. I am going to marry Miss St. John. I don't want you near her, do you understand?"

Tom looked at Gil. "Do you give such instructions to every hand on the ranch?" he asked.

"No," Gil replied. "That isn't necessary."

"Then why do you consider it necessary with me?"

"Because I don't like the way Miss St. John . . ." Gil started, then he stopped. "Uh . . . there is no reason, really. It's just a word to the wise, that's all. Now, get your tack put away while I go find Big Jake. I'll see to it that he finds some work for you to do."

Tom returned to the buckboard for his trunk, while Gil went over to the foreman's house to speak with Jake.

"I've hired a new hand for you," Gil told Jake.

"So I see," Jake said. "He's a big, strong-looking man. Is he a good hand?"

"I don't know," Gil said. "I don't know anything about him. I guess it's just going to be up to you to find out. But keep me posted, will you? I'm going to take a special interest in this man."

"Yes, sir," Jake said. "I'll keep you posted."

As with all new cowboys, the jobs Tom received were the worst of the lot. For the next several days he dug fence-post holes, stretched barbed wire, pitched hay and greased wagon axles. All were jobs that had to be done, but they were a far cry from the spirit of adventure Tom had hoped for when he came West.

Near the end of the first week Tom drew the assignment of stringing fence again for the third day in a row. He took a wagonload of wire out to the outer fence line, and there he began to work.

As he worked Tom stripped off his shirt, seeking some relief from the heat. It was a little cooler without his shirt, but he had to be careful, lest he get sunburned.

The wood of the wagon was bleached white by the sun, and it gave off a pungent aroma as it baked in the afternoon heat. Tom picked up a big roll of barbed wire and carried it over to one of the posts he had just put in. He nailed one end of the wire to the post and started stringing the wire out toward the next post. Then he heard someone approaching.

When he looked up he saw Hilary St. John. He smiled at her.

Hilary had ridden out to Mrs. Ivery's cabin to bring her the material the seamstress would be using for Hilary's dress. It was such a lovely day for a ride that she decided to take the long way back. At least, that was what she told herself. In fact, she had discovered that even while riding, she was actually looking for something, and when she saw Tom Eddington stringing the wire, she knew what she had been looking for.

Hilary saw him before he saw her, and she stopped her horse and stared down at him for a moment. He was working without a shirt, and she could see his smooth muscles flexing under the sun. He reminded her of some animal, a mountain lion, sleek and beautiful and powerful, and she got the unbidden image of a lion leaping upon its prey. She shuddered, for instinctively she knew that she could easily be his prey. All logic and reason told her to ride away now, but there was something in her that was more powerful than logic and reason, and it drove her on. A moment later she found herself approaching him, and he looked up at her and smiled.

"Good morning, Miss St. John," he said. His voice was deep, well-modulated and cultured, and it never ceased to surprise Hilary to hear such a voice come from such a powerful-looking man. Perhaps that was the secret of his mysterious power over her.

"Don't you know better than to work out in this sun without some protection?" Hilary asked. "You will burn very badly."

Hilary swung down from her horse and walked over to him. His shoulders were already red, and she put her fingers on his skin there. When she moved her fingers away, they left little white marks on his skin. Tom winced in pain.

"Do you see what I mean?" she asked.

"Yes," Tom said. He started for his shirt and gave a little self-conscious laugh. "I guess I'm not used to the Arizona sun." He started to put the shirt on, then he winced even more as the rough texture of the shirt material came into contact with his skin.

"Here," she said. "You'd better let me help. I'll hold the shirt and you try and put your arms into the sleeves."

Hilary held the shirt and Tom moved toward her. Now she was so close to his naked torso that she could see the smallest hairs on his skin, and she could feel the heat of the sun on his body.

Hilary caught her breath, and instead of holding his shirt up for him, she just stood there for a moment as if mesmerized by the situation. Tom had his back to her, reaching for the sleeve. When he couldn't find it with his arm he turned to look, and when he did, he saw the expression on her face. For an instant, but only for an instant, he was puzzled, then he felt a thrill pass through him, for he knew exactly what was going through her mind.

"Hilary," he said softly, and turned toward her and reached for her.

Hilary had not expected such reaction from him, and his move caught her completely by surprise. She tried to react against it, but she was too late, for he managed to grab her by the shoulders. He pulled her to him, crushing her lips against his. His arms wound around her tightly, pulling her body against his. She could feel the heat of his skin, or was it the heat of her own body? Now she could no longer be sure.

At first, Hilary tried to struggle against the kiss, but the harder she struggled, the more determined Tom became to hold her. And with Tom's great strength she knew he could do whatever he determined to do. Finally, she allowed herself to go limp in his arms.

From the moment she surrendered, things began to happen. She abandoned all pretense of resistance to allow herself to float with the pleasure of the moment. And never had any moment been more pleasurable. Tom's lips opened on hers and his tongue pushed into her mouth. It was shocking and thrilling at the same time, and involuntarily a moan of passion began in her throat. Now her blood was as hot as his skin, and she never felt a heat such as the heat which coursed through her body. The kiss went on, longer than she had ever imagined such a thing could last, and her head grew so light that she abandoned all thought except the quest for this forbidden pleasure. Finally, Tom broke off the kiss, and Hilary had to lean against him for support, for now she was weak as a milk-fed kitten.

"I'm . . . I'm weak," Hilary admitted, holding onto him for support. She breathed deeply. "That took my breath away."

"Has Gil Carson ever made you feel this way?" Tom asked.

At the sound of Gil's name, Hilary suddenly realized what she had done, and she gasped and covered her mouth with her hand.

"Oh, no," she said, looking at him in fear. "Oh, please, he must never find out that I let you kiss me. He . . ." She took a couple of steps back from him.

"Tell him," Tom said.

"What?" Hilary asked weakly.

"Tell him that you don't love him," Tom said. "Break your engagement. It isn't too late."

"No!" Hilary said. "No, I won't do that. Besides

. . . where do you get off saying I don't love him? What makes you think that? I never told you such a thing."

"Well, maybe not in so many words," Tom admitted. "But you can tell a lot by a kiss. You can't kiss one man the way you kissed me, and claim to love another. You don't love him, not if you can kiss me the way you just did."

"May I remind you *Mister* Eddington," she said, setting the word *Mister* apart from the rest of the sentence. "It was you who kissed me, not the other way around."

"But you were willing," Tom replied.

"Willing? It cannot have escaped your attention, sir, that you are much larger that I. I had no choice but to succumb to your force. But I assure you, it will not happen again."

With that, Hilary got back on her horse, then, slapping her heels against the side of the horse, she rode away at a gallop.

Tom spent the next few hours thinking about Hilary's strange visit. He had lots of time to think, for stringing wire was a solitary job, and there was no one there to disturb his thoughts. The work was not only lonely, it was hard. It was backbreaking and often painful, and he had several cuts and punctures from the barbs on the wire. Then, later in the day Curly happened by. Tom straightened up and wiped his face with his bandana, happy to see the one cowboy who did not treat him like the tenderfoot he was.

"Hi, Curly," Tom called.

"They got you stringin' wire again?" Curly replied. He swung down from his horse and took a long drink of water from his canteen.

"Yep," Tom answered. "By the time I get finished with this wire, I'm going to have the entire territory of Arizona fenced in. No one will be able to come or go," he teased.

Curly put the cap back on his canteen, and wiped his mouth with the back of his hand. A dark stain of perspiration spread from beneath his arms, and Tom wondered in passing when Curly would deem it necessary to put on a new shirt. This was still the same shirt Curly had worn to pick him up, and that was nearly a week ago.

"What I want to know is, which one of the bosses did you go 'n get mad at you?" Curly asked. "Was it the foreman or the manager?"

"Mad at me? Why would one of them be mad at me?"

"That's what I don't know," Curly said. "But you must have done somethin'. Elsewise, they wouldn't keep you on this detail for a whole week. This is punishment kind of work. They don't make nobody, not even a tenderfoot like you, do more'n his share of this kind of work. You must'a made somebody mad."

Curly swung back onto his horse, gave Tom a slight tip of his hat and went back to whatever duties he was attending to that day.

Tom, on the other hand, had to return to his own duties. He worked hard for the remainder of the day, stringing as much wire as any three men could do on an ordinary day. Then, after supper that night he made a special effort to get cleaned up. He intended to go to Big Jake and find out just what was going on. Why was he singled out for such disagreeable duty?

It wasn't dark yet, though the sun had disappeared, leaving in its wake a brilliant sky splashed with reds and purples. Tom was admiring the view from the front porch of the foreman's house when the door opened. It was Hilary who had answered his knock.

"You," she gasped. "What are you doing here? What do you want? I don't want to see you."

"Don't worry, Miss St. John," Tom said. "I didn't come to see you."

"You didn't? Then why are you here?"

"I came to call on your father, if he's in and receiving."

"Tom, you aren't going to talk about . . . that is, you aren't going to mention," Hilary started, then she stopped, at a loss for words.

"Don't worry," Tom said. "My visit has nothing to do with us."

Hilary let out a sigh of relief. "Thank you," she said. "Please, come on in. I'll go get Dad."

Tom walked inside, then stood in the living room with his hat in his hand while Hilary went to get her father. Tom looked around at the room. There was nothing remarkable about the furnishings; an overstuffed sofa and chair, a cane-bottom rocking chair, and a lamp table. The kerosene lamp on the table had not yet been lit, but the many glass facets which hung from the mantel shroud shone with the last reflected light of the setting sun. On the wall was a large, oval-framed picture of an attractive woman, and Tom noticed some resemblance between the woman and Hilary. He guessed it must have been Hilary's mother. Tom had learned during the week that Hilary's mother had died of a high fever years ago.

"Yes, Tom, did you want to see me?" Jake asked, coming into the room with Hilary at that moment.

"If you don't mind," Tom said politely.

"Dad, I'm going to step over to the big house for a few minutes," Hilary said. It was obvious to Tom that she didn't want to be around while they were talking.

"What on earth for?" Jake answered. "You were with him most of the afternoon."

Tom looked at Hilary and she looked away, as if guilty. Tom smiled. If he could make her feel guilty about spending the afternoon with her fiancé, then he must be making some headway with her.

"Gil wanted my help in planning the guest list," Hilary explained.

"All right, but don't stay over there too long, darlin'," Jake advised. "It'll soon be dark, and that won't look too good to the cowboys."

"Dad, Gil and I *are* engaged," Hilary said with a pointed look at Tom as if by that statement showing him exactly where things stood. "I'll be moving into the big house soon."

"You may be engaged, but you aren't married," Jake said. "Don't stay there too long."

"I won't," Hilary promised, kissing her father on the cheek.

Jake watched his daughter leave before he turned back to Tom.

"I wish—" he started. Then, realizing that he was about to think aloud, he cut his remark short. "Never mind. What is it you wanted to see me about?"

"It's about the work you're having me do," Tom said. "Curly says that it isn't routine to assign such tasks to the new men on a permanent basis."

"I see," Jake said. "Is the work too hard for you?"

"No," Tom said. "It isn't that, it's just . . ."

"It's just not what you had in mind when you came West," Jake finished for him.

"No, this isn't what I had in mind at all."

Jake walked over to the lamp table and picked up a pipe which lay there. He filled the pipe with tobacco from a pouch in his pocket, then he lit the pipe and blew out a long cloud of blue smoke before he spoke again.

"Tell me," Jake said. "Exactly what did you have in mind when you came out here?"

"I'm not certain," Tom admitted. "But I didn't think I'd spend all my time stringing fence."

"Have you been reading the dime novels? Did Ned Buntline's action stories get you to thinking that there would be an Indian or a cattle rustler behind every rock?"

"No," Tom said. "Not exactly."

"But you have read the stories?" Jake said.

"Who hasn't?" Tom defended himself.

"I'd say most of the cowboys I've known haven't read them, and for a very good reason. They can't read."

"Oh, I'm sure there must be a few who can't read," Tom said. "But would you go so far as to say most of them can't read?"

"That's right," Jake said. He studied Tom through narrowed eyes. "You take Sam, now. He's the best cook I've ever known, but he's had to teach himself everything. Sam has never read a recipe, nor is he likely to, because he can't read. Neither can your friend, Curly."

"I knew Curly was an uneducated man, but . . ."

"Hold on there," Jake interrupted. "I didn't say Curly was uneducated. I said he couldn't read. There's a difference between not being able to read and being uneducated. A big difference. In the things Curly does, he has as good an education as any man you might ever run across. He can read trail sign, he can doctor cattle, he can ride a horse like he was a part of the animal. No sir, Curly isn't uneducated."

"I really didn't mean that the way it sounded," Tom apologized. "I suppose it did sound pretentious, didn't it? I apologize."

"Pretentious," Jake scoffed. He took a deep breath. "All right, Tom, your apology is accepted."

"Thanks," Tom answered.

"Tell me, Tom, are you sorry you came out West?"

"No, not at all," Tom replied quickly.

"Even though it isn't what you expected?"

"I'm not sure what I expected," Tom admitted sheepishly.

"Well, I can tell you this," Jake said. "Despite what you may have read in Mr. Buntline's stories, cowboying isn't adventurous. It is hard work. And don't think ridin' the crooked trail is any more glamorous, because it isn't. You've no idea what it's like to sleep out in the rain or the cold because you're afraid to show your face in town. You don't know what it's like to have paper on you all over the country so that no matter where you go you see your picture staring back at you from a wanted poster. The rewards get bigger and bigger until soon you're afraid to sleep, even around your friends."

Tom looked at Jake in some surprise, and for a moment he thought he saw a distant, haunted expression in his eyes. Then Jake cleared his throat and the expression left his face. He smiled.

"I knew a desperado once, and he used to tell me stories," Jake explained. "But, back to the business at hand. Cowboyin' is honest work, but it's hard work."

"Yes, sir, I know," Tom said.

"Digging holes, stringing wire, pitching hay and the like is part of that work," Jake went on.

"I realize that too," Tom answered.

"What if I told you that I was going to keep you doing that kind of work from now on? Would you quit?"

"No, sir," Tom replied.

"Why not?"

"Because, as you say, it is important. Someone has to do it, and you are the boss. If you think I am better utilized doing that kind of work, then that is the kind of work I'll do."

"Without complaint?"

"None, other than the complaint I've just registered, and

as far as I am concerned, you've just explained it to my satisfaction. I will make no further protests."

Big Jake puffed on his pipe for a moment longer and just stared at Tom. "What is your relationship to Gil Carson?" Jake finally asked.

"I beg your pardon?"

"Do you know Gil Carson from somewhere?"

"No, I never met him before I came here," Tom replied. "Why do you ask?"

"No reason, I guess," Jake said. "But he took such a special interest in you when you arrived that it makes me wonder a bit. I been thinkin' on the possibility that you might be workin' for him."

Tom laughed. "Of course I'm working for him," he said. "We all are, aren't we?"

"I didn't mean workin' for the ranch, I meant workin' for Gil personally," Jake said.

Tom was puzzled by the strange comment, and his expression reflected his bewilderment.

"What do you mean, working for him personally?" Tom asked.

Jake paused for a moment, as if measuring Tom. "You are an intelligent and educated man, Tom, and I must confess that I like what I have seen of you. I should learn to trust my instincts more 'n my suspicions less. Still, there's somethin' queer goin' on around here, and in the long run, I think it pays a fella to be cautious."

"Queer? In what way? Mr. St. John, what on earth are you talking about?"

"Well, I'll tell you now that it's nothin' you are goin' to have to worry about," Jake said. "But if my suspicions are correct, well, I reckon there is goin' to be some trouble around here. A few heads are goin' to roll when the ranch owners find out what's goin' on. I'm innocent of it 'n that's the God's truth. But like most men, I've got a background that won't stand too much lookin' into. When things start happenin' around here, I'm likely to be the first one to get the blame. And it's probably only right, since I am the foreman and it won't seem likely that anythin' can go on around here without my knowin' of it." Jake took several more long, thoughtful puffs on his pipe. "Maybe I'm a foolish old man, and I'm suspicious for no good reason."

"Mr. St. John, are you saying the owner of this ranch is being cheated?" Tom asked. Tom obviously had more than a casual interest in the question, though he thought it best to keep the degree of his interest quiet for the time being.

Big Jake dumped the contents of his pipe in a nearby ashtray, then he took out a pocket knife and started cleaning out the bowl. He worked diligently for a long moment before he looked back at Tom.

"All I know is that we are moving more cattle to market than we ever have, but the profit keeps going down. Now how can that be, unless something underhanded is going on?"

"Have you investigated it?"

Jake let out an explosive laugh which had no humor.

"Now why the blazes should I do that? If I'm right, who would I report it to? Carson? Chances are he's the one doin' it, 'n if he's not, then that lays the blame squarely onto me. And if he is doin' it, how would I report it to the owners? I don't even know who they are. The truth is, whoever they are, they've probably already forgotten Turquoise Ranch. They're probably so rich that they don't even care what happens out here. I tell you what I should be doin'."

"What's that?"

"I should be gettin' in on this thing, grabbin' off as much for myself as I can. Instead, it's all goin' to break someday, and I'm the one gonna be left suckin' hind teat."

"Maybe not," Tom said. "Maybe the situation is not quite as hopeless as you believe."

"Yeah, it could be you're right," Big Jake said. "And it could be there's nothin' at all goin' on. Still . . ." Jake let the word hang for a moment. "Well," he finally said, "for Hilary's sake, I sure do hope I'm wrong."

Tom was silent, for it was obvious that a reply wasn't expected. Finally, Jake looked at Tom and smiled.

"Well, but that's neither here nor there for you, is it, young man? You got a itch to be more of a cowboy 'n less of a handyman. I can't say that I blame you any. I apologize for my suspicions, and you have my word that things will be different for you from now on. Now, get on back about your business, 'n let me be to mine. Oh, and Tom?"

"Yes?" Tom answered.

"I'd take it kindly iffen you didn't go speakin' about the things I was talkin' about. I was just thinkin' out loud anyway, 'n like as not there ain't nothin' to it. You will keep quiet?"

"Yes," Tom said.

"You're a good man," Jake replied. He chuckled. "I happen to know that Hilary's taken a shine to you, regardless of the fact that she's engaged to Gil Carson. You may be nothin' but a cowboy now, but I got my suspicions that you been more in the past, 'n you'll be more in the future. Truth is, she could do worse than you. And I'd rather see her take up with you than with Gil Carson."

Tom didn't reply to that remark because he was too shocked by it. Could it be true? Could it be that he actually did have a chance with Hilary?

Tom left Big Jake's house and walked across the yard to the corral. Inside the corral were several horses, and two of them were nibbling playfully on each other's neck. Beyond the corral was the barn, and beyond that the wide open spaces which led to Turquoise Peak. Tom was just beginning to realize how beautiful Turquoise Ranch was.

And, he thought with a thrill which sent a small chill shivering through him, he owned it!

How wrong Big Jake was when he said that the owner of the ranch was unaware of it. Tom was so aware of it that he could let out a shout for joy, right here and now.

And in fact, he did just that!

Chapter Eight

Hilary stood at the fireplace in the big house, watching the flames consume a log. The fire popped and snapped, and the flame that licked hungrily at the wood was blue at the base, then it passed through various shades of red, orange and yellow until, at the tip, it curled away into smoke. Hilary had come to the big house, not to discuss plans with Gil as she had told her father, but to escape Tom Eddington.

Hilary poked at the burning log and thought of the big tenderfoot. For reasons she couldn't explain, she felt hot and shaky every time he came near her. It was not right that she experience such feelings. She was engaged to Gil Carson. If she had to have such feelings, then she should have them around Gil Carson, not Tom Eddington. But, of course, as she was unmarried such feelings were wrong anyway, no matter who inspired them.

Whether they were right or wrong, she couldn't deny her feelings. Since she couldn't deny them, she could only fight them. Right now, the best way she could do that, it seemed, was to leave the house when Tom came to speak with her father. Thus it was that when Tom arrived, Hilary made an excuse to an evening call on Gil. Gil was pleasantly surprised by his unexpected good luck. He walked up behind her.

"On a night like this when there is just a bit of a nip outside and a warm fire inside, there is nothing better than a glass of good wine," Gil said. Hilary heard the tinkle of glasses, then the splashing sound of wine being poured. Gil handed her a glass. The deep red liquid glowed brightly in the reflection of the fire, as if it had trapped some inner flame of its own.

"Thank you," Hilary said.

"To us, my dear, and to a future of many evenings as pleasant as this." Gil held his glass up and Hilary touched the rim of hers to his. There was a pleasant ring as the glasses touched.

"Drink up, my dear," Gil said.

Hilary drank the wine and tasted the controlled fire of its fruit on her tongue. When she finished, she held her glass out for a second, and then a third. As the wine began to take effect, she felt a relaxing warmth course through her, and, or so it seemed, that relaxation stilled some of the confusion and turmoil which raged within.

Why did she react so every time she was around Tom Eddington? It couldn't be because of his handsome features, for, compared to Gil, Tom wasn't handsome at all. Hilary looked at Gil. She had to admit that Gil Carson was an exceptionally handsome man. His features were well-formed, almost aristocratic, and his eyes were penetrating and his lips were full and sensual.

Gil sensed that Hilary was staring at him, and he smiled.

"Is something wrong?" he asked.

"No," Hilary said. "Nothing is wrong. I was just thinking what a handsome man you are, that's all."

"Careful, Hilary," Gil said. "It can be dangerous for a woman to tell a man she thinks he is handsome."

"Why?" Hilary asked innocently.

"I think you know why," Gil said. "Such talk can easily inflame the senses. In my case, this is particularly so. But then, I am certain that I'm telling you no secrets. You have long been aware of my ardor. I think you know not only what I feel about you, but also what I want . . . what I *must* have."

As Gil looked at Hilary the expression on his face reflected his words. He wanted her very much, and that naked want showed in the set of his lips and in his eyes. It particularly showed in his eyes, because they were reflecting the flames from the fireplace, glowing deep red as if from the fires of his own wanton desire.

To know that she was the cause of such feeling pleased Hilary, but it frightened her too. Involuntarily, she drew a short, audible breath.

"My God, you are a beautiful woman," Gil said. He put his hand on the bare skin of her neck, then let the fingers trail down until they rested on her breast. Hilary felt a sudden surge of heat through his fingers, and her breast burned as if he had laid a hot coal there. Her fear intensified. It grew so that it was a fear, not only of him, but of the moment . . . and of her own feelings.

"Gil, please!" she said. "I must be going now."

"No," Gil said simply. "Not this time, Hilary. It's not that easy. We are engaged. Soon you will be my wife. I will not be put off again."

Gil raised his hand to her chin and lifted her head so that her lips were close to his.

Hilary started to back away, but she couldn't. Then, with a sudden flash of reason born from desperation, she decided that she didn't want to back away. She had been confused by her strange reaction to Tom Eddington, and maybe this was the answer. Maybe it wasn't Tom Eddington who made her blood run hot. Maybe it was just the fact that she was a young woman of strong passions. Tom Eddington was a young man who had showed some interest in her, that's all. Perhaps the desires she had so long held down were so strong that she could no longer keep them in check. Maybe they were so strong now that they could be awakened by anyone. If that was true, wouldn't it be better to have those desires tested by the man she was to marry than to let someone else break through her resolve?

Gil moved his lips to hers, and when he did, Hilary returned his kiss with all the intensity and ardor she had learned was at her command.

Gil was surprised by Hilary's response, and he acted quickly to press the advantage. His hands moved about her, and Hilary could feel them as they traced paths of fire on her body. One hand stopped on her breast, and it began to burn, and her nipple ached as it strained upward. His other hand moved across her hip. Then slowly but deliberately, Gil began to undress her. A moment later, she felt herself being lowered, nude, to the soft bearskin rug which lay on the floor in front of the fireplace.

For an instant Hilary felt a quick surge of fear. What if her father came in?

But even as Hilary considered the possibility, she knew that it was unlikely. There was nothing to prevent this from going any farther now, but her own resistance, and she knew that she couldn't or, she admitted to herself, wouldn't do anything now to stop it.

The wavering orange fire cast a soft golden glow across her nude body. Then she realized that it wasn't just her body that was glowing nakedly, but his as well, for he had quickly divested himself of his own clothes and was now lying down beside her.

Hilary felt another spasm of fear run through her. This had gone much farther than she ever dreamed it would, and now, for the first time in her life, she was feeling the body of a nude man next to her. He was not only nude, he was aroused, and Hilary recalled the sight of the aroused man in the hotel room when she had been in town. There she had been a safe witness, for she had viewed that passionate event through the reflection in the transom. Now she wasn't just a witness, she was a participant.

As Gil pulled her body against his, she could feel the hardness of him in contrast to her own softness.

The heat she felt now had built to a roaring inferno, and Hilary knew that it was not from the blazing logs but from the raging fires within her own body. Her mind made one last desperate, though unheeded, scream that this was wrong. But her body urged her ahead.

Gil's kisses became more demanding now, and Hilary felt the tip of his tongue darting across her lips. She opened her mouth instinctively and Gil's tongue stabbed inside. The white heat she was feeling changed to an urgent craving, and she knew that tonight, for the first time in her life, she was going to have the mysterious hungers in her body answered. For the moment at least, Hilary was willing to put aside all questions as to whether this was right or wrong, or whether she loved Gil Carson enough to marry him. Here, with this handsome young man, she was willing to accept the fact that everything was right, and nothing was wrong. His skilled, tender supplications explored her body with easy confidence, and soon those bubbling passions which always lay just beneath the surface in Hilary spilled over until she was hungrily, boldly returning his caresses.

Then, when Gil moved his hard and demanding body over her soft, yielding thighs, Hilary was ready to receive him.

She let out a low whimper of pain as he found her, and then a sharper exclamation as she felt him thrust into her. It was painful only in the beginning, however, for the pain was soon mixed with pleasure. Thus the cry of pain turned to a whimper of pleasure not unlike the sounds she had heard in the hotel room on that night, and she blushed as she rose to meet him. Then, inexplicably, through the blazing flames of this union, she found that at the supreme moment the face she wanted to see over her was not the handsome countenance of Gil Carson, but the strong, rugged features of Tom Eddington.

After Tom left the foreman's house, but before Hilary returned, Jake went over to the fireplace and sat down to watch the flames lick at the wood. He had told Tom he knew a desperado once. What he didn't tell Tom was that he was that desperado. The wanted posters he spoke of were his own posters. He had seen them plastered all over Kansas, Arkansas and Texas—during and after the war. He had been a soldier, or so he thought. He had conducted raider operations behind the enemy lines. He had been good at his job, so good that the Yankees weren't willing to forgive and forget when the war ended.

Jake poked at the fire and remembered one mission in particular . . .

Jake St. John and a handful of riders were waiting under a cluster of trees near the Lawrence turnpike. It was snowing, and he and the other men wore sheepskin coats, and hats which were brimful of snow. They were waiting for a Yankee ambulance to come by, because they had learned from Quantrill that the ambulance would be carrying a shipment of gold.

"Iffen ya'll want my opinion, they ain't no Yankees gonna come out in weather like this," one of the men said. He squirted out a stream of tobacco juice, and it landed in a snowbank where it was brown for just a moment before it was buried by the falling snow.

"It'll be here," one young man said.

"What makes you think so?" the first man asked.

"If Quantrill says it will be here, it will be here."

"Yeah? How come you always willin' ter take as gospel ever'thin' Quantrill says? What's the ole man got for you, boy? A pocket full o' sugar titties?"

The young soldier who had defended Quantrill unbuttoned his coat and faced his challenger. That action exposed his pistol, and his hand moved over it.

"Pull your gun, you son of a bitch," the boy said menacingly.

"Jesse, let it be," Jake said. "He didn't mean anything by it."

"I want the son of a bitch to pull his gun," Jesse said again. He smiled, but it was a smile without mirth. "I'm goin' to shoot him, and watch him die."

"Dingus, he's one of our'n. Iffen you got such an all-fired itch to kill, save it for the Yankees," one of the other riders said.

"Nobody talks to Jesse James like that 'n gets away with it," Jesse said.

"Frank, you're his brother, can't you calm him down?" Jake asked. "He listens to you."

Frank rode over to Jesse and put his hand on Jesse's shoulder.

"Dingus, close your coat, will you? You're gonna get a chill."

There was a moment of tension, then Jesse smiled easily. He buttoned his coat.

"Sure, Frank, if you say so," Jesse said.

"Ha, I thought you might . . ." the challenger started to say, but he never finished his statement, because Jake backhanded him so hard that the man nearly fell from his saddle. He kept his mount only by grabbing onto the saddlehorn.

"What the hell?" the man shouted, rubbing his chin and looking at Jake in angry surprise. "What the hell did you do that for?"

"I thought I could shut you up in time to save your life," Jake said. "But if you keep this up, there won't be anything I can do for you."

Jake moved away from the others to the side of the road to wait for the ambulance. He was a Texan, sworn to support Texas, and when the war came, there was no question in his mind which side he would fight for. But this was not the kind of fighting he had planned on. He had thought to be in a cavalry unit, charging pell-mell across the field of battle, clashing sabers with enemy soldiers. Instead, he had been selected by his general to lead raiding parties such as this one. They were deep behind enemy lines. Here, there were no armies to fight, just cattle to rustle and money shipments to rob. Occasionally they would cut telegraph wires or destroy railroad track, but they were never in a classic battle. For the last two months, on orders from his commander, he had joined forces with Quantrill. He didn't particularly like Quantrill, nor the type of men Quantrill attracted. Jesse and Frank James, and their cousins, Jim, Bob and Cole Younger, were typical of the men who rode with Quantrill and they were little more than cold-blooded killers and thieves. Jake had the idea that Quantrill was just using the war as an excuse, and it didn't really make any difference which side he fought for. Jake would be glad when this particular mission was over, so he could return to his own men. Only Sam Potter had come with him on this mission. Everyone else was a rider for Quantrill.

Through the muffling of the snowfall, Jake heard the whistle and shout of the ambulance driver, urging his team on.

"All right," Jake said to the others. "I hear 'em comin'."

"How far away are they, Jake?" Sam asked.

Sam, like Jake, was from Texas. They had known each other for a long time. Sam had volunteered to come with him on this mission, and for that Jake was thankful.

"Not too far," Jake said. "Sam, I'm going to ride out there and stop 'em."

"How you gonna do that?"

"Well, they're in an ambulance, aren't they? I'm goin' to tell them I got an injured man."

"Yeah, but they aren't really an ambulance."

"We aren't supposed to know that, though," Jake said. "My hope is he will stop, at least to yell at me to get out of the road. When he does that, we can hit them. If we're lucky, we'll be able to take the gold without firing a shot."

"If we're lucky," Sam said.

Jake put the rest of the men back in the trees, then he rode out into the road and stood there.

The ambulance driver saw Jake while he was still quite a ways off. He shouted at Jake, "Get out of the way! Get out of the way before I run you down!"

"Stop!" Jake called, and he held his hand up.

For a moment, it looked like it was going to work. The driver was going to stop. But one of Quantrill's men grew anxious, or careless, and he moved out of the woods too soon. The driver saw him and realized that something was wrong. He raised his rifle and shot Jake.

Jake felt himself knocked from his horse and slammed into the snow. He was surprised by it, because he never did feel the bullet hit him. He was in the saddle one moment, and in the snow the next, and he wasn't sure why.

From the moment Jake was down, the others began shooting. Jake saw the driver pitch off the seat of the ambulance and land in the snow with his blood staining the pristine white. There were two men riding with the ambulance, and they turned and tried to run, but they, too, were cut down by a hail of gunfire.

The riders reined up alongside the ambulance with their horses prancing about in excitement and breathing clouds of steam into the cold air.

Sam rode over to where Jake lay in the snow, and he hopped off his horse and looked down at him.

"Jake, are you bad hurt?" Sam asked.

"I've got a bullet in my shoulder," Jake said. "Help me onto my horse."

Sam, very carefully, helped Jake onto his horse, while Jesse, Frank and the others anxiously tore the canvas away from the ambulance.

"Yahoo!" one of them called, holding up a sack of gold. "We're rich, boys! We're rich!"

"That money belongs to the South," Jake said through teeth which were clinched tight against the pain of the bullet.

"Let the South get their own money," Jesse said. "This here money belongs to Quantrill's Raiders!"

Jake, who could barely hold himself erect in the saddle, watched as Jesse and Frank James, the Youngers and the others of Quantrill's Raiders, rode away with the moneybags thrown across their saddles.

"Damn!" Jake swore. "This wasn't a military operation. We just helped them commit robbery."

"Never mind that," said Sam Potter. "We've got to get some doctorin' done on you."

Jake tried to follow Sam, but he could scarcely ride. Finally Sam came back and took the reins of Jake's horse.

"You just hold onto the saddlehorn, Jake," he said. "Just hang on."

Jake did what Sam said, and hung on for dear life while Sam led his horse. The pain finally stopped, and a warming numbness set in, and it was that numbness which allowed him to keep up with Sam as they rode away. Somewhere during the ride Jake must have passed out, because he could remember nothing of it. He could recall only stretches of cold and spinning dizziness and then, at last, he woke up in a safe house with his shoulder bandaged and Sam smiling down at him while feeding him soup.

"Where am I?" Jake asked.

"You're safe," Sam replied. "We're back with our own people. Don't worry none about it."

"Tell 'im," someone said.

Jake looked around to see Corley McQuade, one of his Texas men.

"Tell me? Tell me what?"

"Ah, nothin' much," Sam said. "Here, eat some more soup."

"Nothin' much, you say? When this war's over, I'd like to go back to livin' like normal folks. We can't do that now. Not with paper on us."

"Paper? What paper are you talking about?" Jake asked.

"Wanted posters, Jake," Sam said. "They sayin' we ain't soldiers. They're callin' us criminals, 'n they got posters out on us all over the place."

"Well, that's just because of the war," Jake said. "They'll call 'em in after the war."

"You think so?" Sam asked.

"Sure I think so," Jake replied. But he was lying, even to himself.

Chapter Nine

The next morning Tom was shaken awake while it was still dark.

"Hey, Tom Tenderfoot, roll out of that sack," Curly said. "You been wantin' some real cowboyin', well, it starts now. Get up 'n see how you like it."

Curly was cheerful enough, but at this early hour and this stage of sleepiness, Tom could have done with a little less cheer and a little more sensitivity.

Tom sat up. He had not yet gotten over his surprise as to how cold it could be in the mornings in this strange Arizona Territory. It seemed especially strange now that it was nearly summer and the days were so hot.

"Where are we going?" Tom asked. He was barely able to keep his teeth from chattering as he talked. He pulled on his boots, and the shock of the cold leather against feet which had been warmed from the bed covers almost made his toes draw up.

"Big Jake thinks there may be some beeves up in

Candlestick Draw, 'n he wants us to ride up there 'n take a look aroun'."

"Do we have to find them in the middle of the night?" Tom asked. "Won't they still be there in the daytime?"

"Ha," Curly said. "That's a pretty good joke. It'll be daytime before we get there," he said. "Maybe you just don' know how far away this here Candlestick Draw is."

"How far is it?"

"It's near twenty miles, 'n that's all cross-country," Curly said. "Now shake a leg, Sam's got us some biscuit 'n bacon and hot coffee, iffen I can drag your tenderfoot hide over there 'fore he throws it out."

"You mean Sam got up early just for us?" Tom asked. "He must be something special."

"Yeah," Curly said. "I'm glad you noticed it as somethin' special. Most tenderfeet don't, you know. They figger they got it comin', 'n they ain't grateful when they get it, 'n they raise Cain when they don't. But the fac' is, you won't hardly get a belly robber on any other spread to do that. No sir, we are lucky that Big Jake has a friend like Sam Potter, 'cause he is somethin' special indeed."

Outside the bunkhouse the dark sky stretched over their heads like the vaulted ceiling of a great cathedral. Except for the blazing of thousands of stars, the sky was forebodingly silent and empty.

Tom looked up at the sky. The stars ranged from the very brightest, which were white and blinking almost like beacons, to the dimmest, which were no more than a suggestion of stardust shimmering mysteriously in the trackless distance.

The big house, the foreman's house and the bunkhouse were all dark. Only the cookhouse showed a light, and it was just a small, square patch of yellow which splashed out from the kitchen window as if keeping some lonely vigil.

Tom looked toward the foreman's house. He knew which window was Hilary's bedroom, and he looked toward it with a secret sense of longing in his heart. Her room was dark, but Tom knew that just on the other side of that window, burrowed down snug and warm in her bed was the most beautiful, most intriguing girl he had ever met. At that precise moment, he wanted more than anything in the world to be in that bed with her. Perhaps that was a disrespectful thought, but it was a thought that filled his mind with desire.

"I know exactly what you're thinkin', pard," Curly said.

"What?" Tom asked, shocked by the intrusion. Did Curly really know what he was thinking? Had he thought aloud? "You know what I'm thinking?"

"I sure do. Would you like me to tell you?"

"If you think you can," Tom said. He didn't really want Curly telling him what he was thinking. Not if Curly was right. He considered his wanton desire for Hilary to be his own personal and very private business. Still, he must play the game if he didn't wish to make matters worse. So he had to pretend that he wanted Curly to guess.

"I seen you lookin' toward Miss Hilary's room," Curly said. "You was lookin' over there, 'n all the time you was thinkin' what a shame it is she's gonna marry a galoot like Gil Carson. You was thinkin' how you wish she would marry you."

"Yeah," Tom said, breathing easier now that he realized Curly was just guessing. At that, Curly wasn't too far wrong. "Yeah, you're right. I am thinking what a shame it is she's planning on marrying Gil Carson. What do you suppose she sees in an hombre like that, anyway?" Tom asked.

"He's got money," Curly said.

"Is that all?"

"That's important to a girl."

"There are some things that should be more important," Tom said.

"What could be more important?"

"Whether or not she loves him, for one," Tom suggested. "It would seem to me like that would be the most important thing of all."

"Well," Curly chuckled, "you couldn't hardly expect someone like Miss Hilary to love a no-'count cowpuncher, could you? Let alone marry one."

"I . . . I guess not," Tom said. "Still, a man could have some hope."

"Tom, don't tell me that you . . ." Curly started, then he stopped. "Damn me if I don't think you haven't gone and done it."

"Gone and done what?" Tom asked.

"Fallen in love with Miss Hilary," Curly said. He chuckled again. "I don't know why I expected you to be any different from any other cowpoke, though. I guess all of us have been in love with her at one time or another. Even me, 'n I've knowed her since she was just a little girl. Onliest thang is, me 'n all the rest knowed just how unlikely it was, so we looked at her like some sort of princess or somethin'. We could fall in love as long as we didn't expect nothin' to come of it."

"Except for Gil Carson," Tom suggested.

"Beg pardon?"

"Gil Carson expected something to come of it, and it did," Tom suggested.

"Yeah," Curly said bitterly. "Except for Gil Carson. But then, they ain't nobody ever accused Gil Carson o' playin' by anybody's rules 'ceptin' his own."

They were talking as they walked, and had crossed to the cookhouse by now. Curly pushed the door open, then they walked inside. A warm, cheery glow came from the kitchen, not only from the lantern Sam had lit, but also from the wood-burning stove, which was roaring and popping and filling the little cookhouse with its inviting heat. The rich aroma of coffee and frying bacon permeated the room.

"Sam, damn me if you don't make gettin' outa bed worth it in the mornin'," Curly said as the two men walked back to the kitchen and warmed their hands over the roaring stove.

Sam laughed. "Well, biscuits 'n coffee will work pretty good iffen you ain't leavin' anythin' pretty in bed behind you," he said.

"What's a poor cowboy like us ever gonna leave in bed, 'ceptin' a little trail dirt?" Curly asked, pouring himself a cup of coffee. "I was just tryin' to explain that to my educated pard here as we was walkin' over to the cook shack."

"Friend, don't tell me you took on a cowboy's life without understandin' all there was to know about it," Sam said as he took the strips of bacon up from the pan. Into the bacon drippings he sprinkled a handful of flour and some milk, and a moment later produced a bowl of gravy for Curly and Tom to put over their biscuits. Both men helped themselves to generous amounts.

"I figure it's never too late to learn," Tom said.

"No, that's a fact," Sam agreed. "A fella can always learn, if he is of a mind to. But it 'pears to me you could'a picked somethin' else to learn. There sure as hell ain't no future in cowboyin'."

"Sure'n someone told me that self-same thing when I was young," Curly said, cheerfully slurping some coffee. "I didn' pay no never-mind to it, 'n I don' reckon Tom is either. I reckon on that point, he's about as bull-headed as I was."

"Well," Sam chuckled. "Iffen he's bull-headed, then he's already halfway to bein' a cowboy. I ain't ever met a one what had good sense."

" 'Ceptin' maybe Big Jake," Curly put in.

"Now that's a fact," Sam agreed. "Big Jake is one of the finest men I've ever knowed. But then, they just ain't many men like him, cowboy or no."

"Sam rode with Big Jake back in Texas, didn't you, Sam? They was in the war together."

"You and Sam fought in the Civil War?" Tom asked.

"Up North they called it a Civil War," Sam said. "We called it the War Between the States. It was a noble cause we rode for. But that cause is dead now, like lots of good men who fought it."

"That was a long time ago," Tom said.

"Yeah, I reckon it was," Sam said. "It's been twenty-five years since I last heard the sound of battle."

"Do you miss it?"

Sam chuckled. "Now that's a fool question to ask of a man. Who would miss battle? But I tell you what. I miss the men we was with then. War brings out the best in men." Sam was quiet for a moment. "And the worst too, I reckon, for I seen both kinds."

Tom shivered. "I hope I never have to experience that. If I have my way I'll never go to any war."

Sam looked at Tom, then gave him another helping of bacon.

"You're all right, son," Sam said. "Lots of young guys are all full of spit 'n vinegar, spoutin' off how they wisht they'd been aroun' to fight. You got a little more sense than that, I see."

Sam's acceptance of him pleased Tom very much, and he was secretly glad that he had such a man working for him.

He wished he could tell him that now, only this wasn't the opportune time. But that time would come. Until then, Tom would just watch, learn and wait.

They had been riding for the better part of an hour, and it was still dark. In fact it was even darker, because a cover of clouds had moved down from the mountains, and the clouds blotted out the moon and the stars. Objects that had been clearly discernible in the moonlight now became nothing but mysterious shapes and shadows.

"It's gonna rain soon," Curly said. "Did you bring your slicker?"

"Yes," Tom said. He had learned the hard way how quickly a rainstorm could build up in the mountains, so that a perfectly clear day could turn into a downpour in a matter of minutes. He had been caught out without his slicker once, and he vowed never to be caught short again.

"Look over there," Curly said, pointing to a shadow which became a small cabin. "Do you see that buildin'?"

"Yes, I see it," Tom said, barely able to make it out in the darkness. "What is it, someone's house?"

"Yeah, maybe your house," Curly said.

"My house?" Tom answered with a surprised gasp. Had Curly discovered Tom's secret?

Curly chuckled. "It'll be your house if you are ever caught out and need one. Actually, it's a line shack. In the wintertime, when the snow is deep 'n we're out ridin' the herd, we spend a lot of time in line shacks. It's easier than tryin' to get back into the bunkhouse ever' night."

"Are there many of them?"

" 'Bout twenty or so, I would say," Curly answered. "Some of 'em is kept up better'n others. We try 'n keep 'em all stocked with a little food, but ever' now 'n then a drifter, or an Injun comes through 'n cleans it out." Curly rubbed his chin. "Gil complains that it's costin' the ranch a lot of money, 'n he said we should shoot anybody we ever catch lootin' one of the places. But the truth is, I've been an uninvited guest in line shacks myself a few times in my day. It's sort of an unwritten law that a man who is hungry 'n desperate can take shelter for a while iffen he don't abuse it."

"Are they abusing these line shacks?" Tom asked.

"No," Curly answered. "Carson can't pull that ole' dodge. That ain't where the money is goin'."

"What money?" Tom asked.

"Ah, don't worry about it, pard," Curly said. "It ain't no bother of ours. We're just the small fish in this kettle of stew. Let the owners worry about it. If they don't care that Carson is stealin' 'em blind, why should I?"

Tom was suddenly very attentive. Big Jake had alluded to this same thing. Now he realized more than ever how fortunate it was that neither of them realized he was the owner. Tom understood that if they knew, their strange sense of honor would prevent them from talking about it to him. Whatever was going on, Tom was going to have to find out on his own hook.

"Are you saying Carson is a crook?" Tom asked, being careful not to appear too interested.

"Well, I guess there's degrees of being crooked," Curly said. "Truth is, I reckon near 'bout ever' rancher in the West has thrown a long rope at one time or another, prob'ly even includin' Big Jake. The story is, that's why he left Texas."

"A long rope?"

Curly looked at Tom and laughed. "Say, you really don't know much, do you? A long rope is when a cattle rancher sort of accidental like runs another man's cows in with his own. 'Course, it's only accidental if he gets caught. Otherwise, it's just plain smart ranchin'."

"Is that what Carson and Big Jake are doing? Throwing a long rope?"

"I don't really think Big Jake is in on it," Curly said. "I don't see him as teamin' up with Carson on somethin' like that."

"Just Carson then?"

"Yeah," Curly replied. "And the thing is, Carson ain't too particular where his rope lands. You see, he ain't stealin' from his neighbors, he's stealin' from the hand that's feedin' him. He's takin' Turquoise cows for his own."

"How can he do that?" Tom asked.

"They's lots of ways of doin' it," Curly said. "One way is to sell five hunnert head 'n only report four hunnert. Another way is to report losin' ten to twenty more cows than was actual in a winter blizzard. Fac' is, I got me a hunch these here cows we're goin' after today might be somethin' like that."

"What do you mean?"

"Well, they ain't no legit reason for these cows to be in Candlestick Draw, 'lessen they was put there to wait out the winter. I 'spect they already been counted dead. Yes, sir, whatever we find up here, we will sell; 'n you can make book that all the money is goin' to wind up in Gil Carson's pockets."

"Didn't you say Big Jake sent us after these cows?" Tom said.

"Yes, he did."

"Then that means he must be in on it, doesn't it? I mean, if he knows where the cows are."

"I don't know, pard," Curly said. "I don't want to think that, but I just don't know."

Tom recalled the conversation he and Jake had when he

asked to be relieved of the handyman jobs. Jake had protested his innocence then, protesting even before an accusation was made. Did he, perhaps, protest too much?

"What do you think, Curly? Are we helping Big Jake and Gil Carson rustle these cows right now?"

Curly pulled his hat off and rubbed his hair for a moment.

"Now, pard, I just don't have the answer to that," he said. "On the one hand, I don' see how Big Jake could be foreman here 'n not know what's goin' on. Particular bein' a man with a past like he has."

"What sort of past, exactly, does Big Jake have? I've heard it alluded to a couple of times, but no one has ever been specific."

"No, 'n you ain't likely to get anyone to be specific," Curly said. "But I hear tell that ole Jake went bad durin' the war."

"What do you mean, went bad?"

"He took some things, some money, cattle, things like that, for the South. Only the South never got any of it. Then, after the war, he got into some more trouble in Texas, 'n it had somethin' to do with cows 'n gunplay. But that was a long time ago, 'n ever' one is entitled to keep a door closed on his past iffen he's of a mind to. Besides, near as I know ole Big Jake has rode a straight path for some number of years now. I know I ain't never met no man who was straighter with me. 'N I'll be honest with you, Tom, it would sore disappoint me iffen I was to find that he was in some sort of trouble now. The truth is, I'd have to be on his side, no matter what!"

"Even if the owner had proof that Big Jake was stealing from him?" Tom asked. "You'd still side with Big Jake?"

"When I got throwed from a horse a few years back and was busted up somethin' awful, it wa'nt the owner who patched me up," Curly said. "It was Big Jake. Yes, sir. If push ever come to shove, you'd find me in Big Jake's corner."

Tom was quiet for several minutes after that. This was something he would have to think about.

Chapter Ten

The slanting bars of the brightly shining moon fell through the window onto Hilary's bed. Had someone looked in then they would have seen a picture of loveliness, for Hilary's strawberry blonde hair was fanned out upon the pillow in such a way as to frame her face with beauty. Her eyes were closed in sleep, and no artist could have painted a more tranquil scene.

The scene may have been tranquil, but the sleep was not, for unknown to the fanciful casual observer, Hilary's sleep was fitful. She was bothered by her dream. There was an uneasiness, a sense of displacement that disquieted her. She turned in her bed to will the dream away, and it had the desired effect of waking her. She lay in bed for a moment, trapped on the line between waking and sleep, wondering why she was discomforted. Then she remembered. But when she tried to recall the dream, it slipped away into the shadowed recesses of the night.

Now she was fully awake, and she turned and fluffed her pillow and looked at the wall where the brightly shining moon created a magic lantern show by projecting lace shadows formed by the trees and curtains. She heard a horse blow, then, onto her private viewing screen came the shadowed figures of two men on horseback. Even from the shadow images she could tell that one of them was Tom Eddington. She could tell that by the great size of the rider, and by the width of his shoulders and the proud, erect way he held his head.

Hilary got out of bed and crossed over to the window. She saw that it was Tom and Curly, and she wondered where they were going so early in the morning. Then, even as she thought that, she found herself wishing that she could change places with Curly so that she, and not Curly, would be riding off with Tom.

Hilary felt a strange heat over the forbidden thought. The heat may have started in her face as a blush, but it spread rapidly through her body. She recalled the night before, when she had given herself to Gil Carson, and suddenly she realized that the sensations she was feeling were no longer mysterious. She knew them now for just what they were. They were the stirrings of sexual desire. At that moment she was wanting Tom. She wanted him as she had had Gil on the night before. Last night she had taken the irrevocable step that took her, forever, across the line from girlhood to womanhood. And now, from her new perspective, she was able to examine her feelings critically. She had glimpsed the stars last night when she and Gil made love. She had stood just on the outside of total ecstasy. Now, with the awareness that had come with her first experience, she knew that though Gil Carson opened the door for her, there were vast areas of her sensuality yet to be explored. And then, unbidden, a quick hot thought surfaced. If it had been Tom instead of Gil, would the door have just been opened, or would those depths have already been explored?

Hilary turned away from the window and moved back to her bed. But as she started to turn the covers back, a sudden thought hit her. It was a wild, unreasonable thought which she ought to have dismissed immediately. And yet she knew that all the second thoughts in the world wouldn't change her mind. She was gripped by an irresistible impulse, and she was going to carry it through. With a heady sense of dizziness over what she was about to do, she reached for her clothes.

The moon and stars which had shined so brightly overhead when Tom and Curly left and which had splashed into Hilary's room, were gone now, to be replaced by the clouds that had moved down from the mountains.

The wind freshened, bringing on its breath the rain Curly had warned of a few moments earlier. Off in the distance, there was a long, low rumble. Curly reached into his saddle roll and pulled out his poncho, and Tom followed suit.

"I told you so, pard. We are about to get wet," Curly called. "You're gonna find yourself wishin' you were back doin' chores. At least you wouldn't have to be out in weather like this."

A long, jagged streak of lightning split the night sky, and for just an instant the rugged terrain around them was brightly illuminated. It reminded Tom of a photograph, a split second of time lifted out of the continuum and frozen for an eternity.

The rain began then. At first it was no more than a few, fat heavy drops. Then there was more, and more still, until finally the rain was cascading down in sheets.

The rain gushed down as they rode. It slashed into them in stinging sheets, and ran in cold rivulets off the folds and creases of their ponchos. It blew in gusts across the trail in front of them and drummed wickedly into the rocks and the trees around them.

Curly held his hand up, giving a signal for Tom to stop. He said something, but Tom couldn't hear him.

"What?" Tom shouted.

Curly had to cup his hand around his mouth and shout in order to be heard above the storm. He pointed to a draw in front of him.

"You go on up to the end of this draw," he shouted. "You'll find a line shack there. Go on in and get out of the rain. When it gets light, ride down the draw and see if there are any cows. If you find any, push 'em on through." Curly was shouting, but his voice was thin against the wind and the rain.

"What are you going to do?" Tom shouted back.

"This draw wanders around for a bit, then it comes out about another mile down the trail. When you push 'em through, that's where they'll come out. I'll be waitin' there for 'em."

"Do you have a place to get out of the rain?" Tom shouted.

"Better'n you," Curly replied, smiling broadly. "Why do you think I sent you in here?"

Tom returned Curly's smile. "I don't know," he said. "Maybe I just thought you were being friendly."

"I'm only friendly when it don't cost me nothin'," Curly replied with a laugh. He slapped his chap-covered legs against the side of his horse and rode on.

Tom watched Curly for just a moment, then he started up his end of the draw. It was a long, narrow, twisting canyon, filled with rocks which had tumbled down from the steep walls, and cut with cross ravines and gullies which made its transit difficult. The fact that it was dark and storming made it even more difficult, so when Tom finally emerged at the other end and saw the dark shadow of the line shack, he was more than a little relieved.

There was a small lean-to horse shelter to one side of the shack, and Tom led his horse into the shelter and tied it off.

"Sorry you can't come in with me," he said. "But you'll be just fine here."

Tom went inside, found a kerosene lamp on a wooden table and lit it. A soft golden bubble of light filled the room, and he looked around to examine his temporary quarters. There was a small wood-burning stove in the middle of the room and a coffeepot on the stove. Tom wished he had some coffee, but short of putting the pot outside to catch the rain, he had no idea of how he would get water. Finally, he gave up that idea, but he did decide to build a fire. He figured it would be an hour or so before he started after the cows, so he might as well try to warm himself.

Within moments the fire was roaring, and already the room was beginning to warm. Then Tom got an idea. Why not take off his clothes and hang them over a chair near the stove? They would dry, or nearly dry, and even if it was still raining when he started after the cows, he would at least have had the advantage of being out of the wet things for a short time.

Tom undressed and a moment later he stood before the stove, totally naked, enjoying the radiant heat on his body.

What a fool idea this had turned out to be, Hilary thought. It was dumb to leave her warm bed to follow Tom and Curly. She wished she hadn't done it, but she had, and there was nothing she could do about it now.

What would she tell Tom and Curly when she saw them? Or perhaps, she should say, *if* she saw them, for shortly after the rain began she lost them. Now she had no idea where they were, and that made her situation even more ridiculous.

At least she wouldn't have to face Tom with an explanation as to why she had come out. She wouldn't have to face Tom, but she would have to face her father and Gil. What would she tell them?

For the time being, at least, what she would tell her father and Gil was the least of her problems. She was cold and wet, and she wanted to get out of the weather. When she came to Candlestick Draw, she decided to abandon her chase of Tom and Curly and go to the line shack she knew was just a little ways from the mouth of the narrow canyon. She may have lost Curly and Tom, but she wasn't lost. She knew every square inch of Turquoise Ranch, and if necessary, she believed she could find her way back home blindfolded. Hilary turned her horse into the canyon and started toward the line shack.

She rode on through the rain, but it was now much more than a downpour. It was an electrical storm of such magnitude that the sky seemed to be a constant flash of lightning bolts. Thunder boomed in a steady roar.

Hilary squinted her eyes against the slashing rain and the blinding flashes of lightning and saw the shack in the distance. She hurried her horse on toward it.

The rain fell in cold rivulets and blew in sheets across the narrow gauge of the canyon. For a moment, Hilary thought of the creeks and streams that snaked their way through Turquoise Ranch, and she tried to remember if there was one in this valley. If so, there might be a danger of flash flooding.

But no, if that were the case, the cabin would have never been built right here. And, here the cabin was.

Thank goodness she had made it.

Chapter Eleven

When Hilary reached the line shack a few moments later, she saw a glow of light shining through the windows. For just a moment she was frightened. Drifters were known to use the shacks frequently, and if this was the case, the present occupant might be dangerous. But if it was a drifter, he wouldn't be so foolish as to show a lamp. It had to be Tom and Curly.

Hilary sighed. Perhaps she was in no physical danger from Tom and Curly, but she wasn't prepared to meet them either, for she had no idea what she would say to them. They would surely ask her why she was here. And what could she say? She certainly couldn't tell them she was here because she had been driven by some irresistible urge to follow them this morning.

As Hilary led her horse into the lean-to, she saw only one other horse. Was it Tom's or Curly's? And why only one?

Hilary tied her animal next to the horse already there, then she walked around front, opened the door, and stepped through to the welcome warmth inside.

"Oh, Tom, my God!" Hilary said, gasping as she saw him standing by the stove, warming himself.

Tom was facing her, totally nude, and the skin of his body was glowing in the soft light. His stomach was flat, and his shoulders broad, with droplets of water clinging like tiny diamonds in the mat of hair on his chest. Hilary spoke out so because she had felt a sudden and overwhelming charge of sexual excitation over the scene displayed before her.

"Hilary! What are you doing here?" Tom asked. Then, Tom suddenly realized that he was naked, and he reached quickly for his pants. He tried to step into them, but he was so surprised by Hilary's unexpected appearance that he tripped and stumbled forward. Involuntarily, he reached out for support, and he grabbed Hilary.

"No!" Hilary called out, and though her mind told her she should retreat, her body refused to accept the command. Instead, she stayed where she was, trembling with excitement over his touch.

"Please," Hilary said, more quietly now. "Please, don't do this."

Tom felt Hilary's trembling motion, and he knew it wasn't from the cold or the wet. He knew exactly what it was from, and he looked at her with his eyes reflecting his own degree of arousal. He moved his lips down to hers and covered her mouth with a kiss.

This kiss, like the kiss he had given her when he was stringing fence, took her breath away. It was a kiss of ice and fire, and the power of it made her dizzy.

Once before Hilary had tested herself with him by allowing the kiss to go to its limits just to see where it would go. She needed no such test this time, for this kiss started beyond where the first kiss had left off. She found that she had no control whatever, and she totally abandoned herself to it, feeling her head spin faster and faster in dizzying excitement until, finally, she feared she would pass out from the intense pleasure of it.

By now Hilary was so overcome by the pleasurable sensations of the moment that she lost track of time and space. She felt Tom's hands at her dress, and her only thought was about how right it was. She twisted and turned, not to avoid his hands but to facilitate them, and when he opened her dress and gently slipped it down across her shoulders, waist and hips, it was she who made the final move so that she stood nude and damp before him.

Tom's hands traced fiery paths across her body until one of them stopped at that sensitive place between her legs which was now the center of all her feelings.

Hilary's knees grew so weak that she didn't think she could support herself any longer, but that support wasn't necessary, for Tom swept her up in powerful arms and carried her over to deposit her on the bed.

Hilary lay on the bed and looked up at him, not yet able to grasp the reality of it. She was still floating in the sensations of pleasure, and she wasn't sure she could discern whether this was really happening, or whether it was merely a dream. If it was reality, then never had reality had such a dizzying, overpowering quality to it. And if it was a dream, then surely no dream of pleasure could ever seem so real.

Hilary felt a sweet aching in her loins and a heat through her body which was so intense that it was as if her very blood had turned to liquid fire.

Somewhere, in some inner chamber of her mind, a distant voice whispered that this was wrong. She was engaged to Gil Carson and to give herself like this to another man was a sin. And yet, if her mind told her it was wrong, there was an inner recess of her heart that was even more powerful, and it screamed with all the persuasiveness it could muster that this was right! Never had anything been more right!

Tom moved onto the bed with her, and he covered her with kisses on the lips, face, neck and shoulders. Then, to her amazement, but oh so sweet joy, his eager lips and tongue went to her breasts where each straining nipple was kissed and attended to until Hilary wanted to shout with the joy of it. Then, when she thought she had experienced all the pleasure her body could stand, Tom moved over her, and Hilary knew that the wonder of it all was just beginning.

Hilary gasped as Tom made the intimate connection. It was a gasp of delight, for not even in her most intimate fantasy had Hilary ever dreamed of pleasure this exquisite. She put her hands on his back, then clawed at his skin with her fingernails, and she gave him as much as she took, for hers wasn't to be the passive role. She thrust her tongue into his mouth and gave herself up to him to take him deeply into her, rushing toward the golden promise which waited just ahead.

Somewhere during the next few moments she overtook the peak she had attained with Gil on the night before, and she sped far beyond that until she reached the sounding chord of her innermost being. Then, from deep, deep inside, the waves of pleasure began coming back on themselves, intensifying, growing with every second, building up until they burst over her in a golden wonder of ecstasy that made her cry and whimper with the joy of it. Her skin tingled from her feet to her head, and she felt an overpowering dizziness which nearly swept her into unconsciousness. Lights seemed to flash, and her body jerked in uncontrollable convulsions as she was swept away by the orgasmic shudders.

This was so far beyond what she had experienced with Gil Carson that there was no comparison. And with Gil, even that relatively modest plateau was the culmination, for there was nothing beyond that. Not so now, for no sooner was Hilary adjusting to the first explosive pleasure wave, when another, totally different event swept over her, then another still. Then, when she heard Tom gasp and felt his muscles tighten and knew that he was joining her, she was swept away by a fourth which was as great as the first. During that moment of sweet sharing she had the seemingly implausible but totally real experience of feeling that she and Tom were sharing everything. It was as if their nervous systems had meshed, their bloodstreams joined, their souls united, and she felt as he felt, thought as he thought, and the rapture of his climax was also her own.

After the stormcrest of sensation, Hilary began to coast back down, but even in this she returned as she had risen, exploring all the valleys and peaks of pleasure a second time, and finding them just as sweet as they had been at first.

They lay together after that, but they didn't speak for a long time. Tom put his hand on Hilary's hip. He put it there easily, possessively, and Hilary could feel it on the sharpness of her pelvic bone, across the tender, yielding flesh, and into the soft cushion of hair. In its own easy, understated way, this was more an act of intimacy than that which had just occurred.

Outside the rain had stopped, and darkness had given way to the gray of early morning. Hilary gloried in those moments, for in her mind she could almost believe this was as it should be. She wished hard that it had to be true, that she and Tom had every right to be here, and that this was just one of the thousands of dawns they would welcome together.

"Hilary? You don't love Gil Carson," Tom said. "You can't love him."

The spell was broken. Tom's voice had not only brought Hilary back to reality, it had brought her back sharply, by reminding her of a basic and unshakable truth. She was engaged to Gil Carson. She had no right to be here. Now Tom's hand, which had felt so wonderful, so right before, was a flaming brand, and she reached down and pushed it aside.

"Please, Tom," she said. "Please don't talk now."

"But we have to talk," Tom said. "Don't you understand that?"

Hilary sat up. Why was he asking her to talk? Couldn't he understand the mood she had established? Didn't he realize that for a moment she had managed to escape into a pleasurable fantasy which could never be more than a fantasy, but which, for the moment, was real enough to hide behind?

"You don't love Gil," Tom said again.

"I'm sorry," Hilary said. "I have to go."

Hilary walked over to her clothes and was about to put them back on, keeping her mouth tightly shut lest she give in to the tears that waited for release.

"Yeah," Tom said, now reaching for his own clothes. "I guess you do. And I've got some cows to find."

"Tom?" Hilary asked.

"Yes?"

Hilary looked at him, at the expression of hope which was in his eyes and on his face, and she wished more than anything that she could answer that hope. But she knew that she couldn't.

"Please try to understand," she said, asking him to do something that she herself could not do.

"I can only understand one thing," Tom said.

"What's that?"

"I love you," Tom said.

"Tom, no, you can't," Hilary replied. "You mustn't."

"Perhaps not. But then, we don't always do what we're supposed to do, do we?"

Hilary got up and walked over to the window, padding naked across the floor. She peeked outside.

"The rain has stopped," she said. "I've got to get back home. Dad will be worried."

Tom walked over and stood behind her. He put his hands on her shoulders, and she quivered under his touch. When he put just a little pressure on her shoulders, she leaned back against him and she felt his nude body against her naked skin. A moment later she realized the reawakening of desire wasn't hers alone, for he soon gave physical evidence of his renewed interest.

"Tom," she said, turning toward him. "Tom, we can't . . ." but her protest was smothered by his kiss, and as she felt the iron-hard bands of his arms wind around her, and pull her against him, all internal resistance and resolve melted away. She was his once again, to do with as he wished.

Gently, Tom carried her back to the bed where he stretched her out and lay beside her. He moved his now familiar hands across her body, kneading the flesh of her breasts until they were literally throbbing with pleasure, dipping adroitly into that area that he had so recently awakened.

Tom positioned himself over her. Then, more gently than before, because this time the terrible urgency had been replaced with a more leisurely pleasure, he thrust into her. Hilary raised herself to meet him, pushing against him to share with him this thing that was now so much a part of both their bodies.

Hilary gasped with the pleasure of it, and cried with the joy of it, freeing herself from all thought save this building quest for fulfillment. Her senses were like a restless willow in a windstorm, moving, tightening, latent with the promise of more. At the peak, a crest of pleasure broke over her like a thunderclap. It was a pleasure equal in intensity to those she had enjoyed earlier. It did not seem possible that this quickly after she had been to the summit of sensation she could so soon return, and yet, here she was again.

Hilary was unable to control her reactions to the orgasm. Though she tried to hold back her screams of joy, moans of pleasure escaped her lips and she threw her arms around Tom and pulled him to her, trying to accept all of him into her womb until the last shudders of ecstasy died away full moments later.

"Now, Hilary," Tom said, when all was finished. "Deny that you found that pleasurable."

"Tom, please . . ." Hilary said, and tears suddenly pooled in her eyes. She sat up, pulling away from his reaching hand, and moved quickly to the clothes which still lay in a heap on the floor. This time, she would not make the mistake of remaining nude. She began dressing, even as he watched her.

"Can you deny it?" Tom asked again.

"No," Hilary said quietly. "I can't deny it. I did find it pleasurable. It was more thrilling than anything I have ever experienced in my life, but . . ."

"But what?"

"But I am engaged to Gil Carson. I must marry him."

"Why must you marry him?" Tom asked in exasperation.

"Because," Hilary said, without explanation. "Because I must."

"I won't let you. I won't allow it," Tom said. "Tonight

I'll come to your house. I'll talk to your father, I'll tell him . . ."

"Tom, please, no!" Hilary said, literally screaming the plea. "You mustn't speak to my father, you mustn't. In fact . . . I . . . I don't even want you to speak to me again. I don't want to see you."

"You can't mean that."

"Yes, I do. I mean it more than I have ever meant anything."

"Very well," Tom said coldly. "If it's avoidance you want, it's avoidance you shall have."

Now it was Tom's time to get up from the bed, and he walked over to get his clothes from the chair by the stove where he had hung them to dry. Hilary turned her eyes away from him, though she ached to look at his muscular body, to burn into her memory the sight of this man who had propelled her to the stars with his lovemaking.

"I have to go," she said.

"Go," Tom said coolly. "Go to Gil Carson. After all, he is the one with the money, isn't he?"

"Tom!" Hilary said. "You can't mean what you just said!"

"Don't I? What other reason would you have?"

"It isn't the money," Hilary said. "It isn't."

Tom was finished dressing now, and he reached for his hat and put it on. A few drops of water dripped down from the brim and fell on his cheek. One of the drops of water caught the early morning sun, which now peaked through the clouds, and the drop of water exploded into a rainbow spectrum of color. Hilary had an almost uncontrollable urge to kiss it, but she knew better. She looked away.

"I have some cows to round up," Tom said, starting for the door.

* * *

Tom rode away from the shack without looking back. He was afraid to look back, because if he did, he was afraid he would ride back to her and beg her on bended knee to give up her crazy notion to marry Gil and marry him instead. He would do anything he could to win her over. If necessary, he would even tell her that he was the real owner of the ranch. If it was money that drove her to Gil, then he would offer her more money. More money than she had ever dreamed about.

But no, he couldn't do that! He would lose, no matter how it turned out. If she said yes, then he would never know if it was him or his money. If she said no, then he would have lost her forever, because her pride would never let her come to him under such circumstances.

Tom had never faced such a situation before. But then, Tom had never known a woman like Hilary before. She was the most beautiful woman he had ever known. And though he had not led a celibate life, he had never known pleasure like the pleasure of their lovemaking this morning.

What could he do? How could he win her love? Tom pondered the situation as he rode toward the end of the canyon, and he finally decided that the best thing he could do for the time being was just what she wanted him to do. He would just have to stay away from her, to give her the opportunity to make up her own mind. Surely what they experienced this morning would mean something to her. Maybe his best bet would be to just let the memory of their lovemaking work on her, and hope that she would change her mind.

"Tom?" Curly called then. "Tom, is that you?"

"Yes."

"Where you been, boy? I thought you were going to push the cows out to me."

"I'm sorry," Tom said. "I guess it just took me a little longer to get up here than I thought."

"Ah, that's all right," Curly said. "This is your first time. I should'a taken this part and let you wait at the other end. Come on, I spotted them. Let's move 'em out."

"Where are they?"

"They're back in the blind draw there," Curly said. "Damnedest thing."

"What?"

"It looks like they was put in there of a purpose. Tom, them are rustled cattle sure as God created you and me. Onliest thing is, who rustled them, and who was they rustled from?"

Chapter Twelve

The sun was up more than full disk as Hilary rode back to the house. She could feel a heaviness in her loins, and even as she sat in the saddle a small tingling of pleasure remained with her, a residue of the rapture she had shared with Tom.

Hilary blushed despite the fact that there was no one to see her. What an amazing night this had been! She had lost her virginity to Gil Carson on the evening before and had made love with Tom on the morning after, not once, but twice! But her experience with Gil last night had merely been a peek at what was to come with Tom this morning. Hilary contrasted the two events. Gil had taken something from her. Tom had given her something. Gil had taken her virginity while Tom had given her an awareness of what it was like to be a woman.

Hilary knew she should feel some degree of shame for her actions, but she didn't. She felt only the slowly dying tinglings of pleasure.

Then, even as she thought of it, those warm tides of pleasure began to ebb. They began to fade under the reality of the situation. This morning Tom told her he loved her. It was a reasonable enough remark. They had just made love and it had been wonderful, and Tom told her he loved her. All he asked of her was that she should love him. But Hilary couldn't do that. Surely Tom could see that she couldn't love him. Surely he could understand that she must honor her commitment to Gil Carson.

And yet, had she honored it? Hadn't she betrayed her honor and broken her commitment this morning when she surrendered to the primitive passion that swept over her?

No, she thought. What took place between her and Tom this morning was just passion, and nothing else. And one cannot be ruled by passion. One must be ruled by reason.

Hilary's reason told her that Gil Carson was the right man for her. And as she was being coldly dispassionate, she realized that Tom was close to the truth when he said she was interested in Gil's money and position. What he didn't understand was that it wasn't Gil's money, it was the fact that he managed the ranch. If she married Gil Carson, then her own position on the ranch would be secure. It wasn't the money; it was the ranch itself, and the love she felt for it. If she married Gil, she would always be a part of it. What could she possibly hope for by falling in love with Tom Eddington?

Hilary looked out over the ranch, which was now rain washed and sparkling bright under the morning sun. Though she saw it every day, she never had a day in which she didn't find some new aspect of its beauty to appreciate. The ranch was so big that it was like a kaleidoscope. One never got the same perspective twice, even if looking at the same view. This morning, for example, she was struck by the sight of the droplets of water clinging to the bushes and lying on the petals of the wild flowers. At this precise moment the sun was at just the right angle to catch the droplets so that there were millions of diamondlike prisms spread out before her, breaking the morning sunbeams into a rainbow spectrum of brilliant color. The sight was positively breathtaking.

Hilary stopped and stared at the scene, enraptured by its beauty. Unfortunately it only lasted for a few moments, because the continued rise of the sun gradually bent the angle of the falling light until the diamonds disappeared.

How could she even consider leaving this place? She was right not to tell Tom what her heart pleaded with her to say. She was absolutely correct not to tell him that she returned his love. Hilary suddenly recalled the drop of water on Tom's cheek this morning, and how it, too, had captured all the colors of a sunbeam. In that one event, Tom and Turquoise Ranch seemed, somehow, linked. Oh, if only that were true. If only she could somehow have Tom and Turquoise Ranch too.

Tom had not been to this part of the ranch before, and he looked around as he and Curly pushed the cattle back to the main herd. How magnificent it was! And to think it all belonged to him. Oh, perhaps he should tell Hilary. How could he blame her for loving this place so?

The sun was well up now, shedding a vast, clear, golden light over the entire range. This part of the ranch looked like a beautiful park, covered with sun-bleached grass and dotted with clumps of trees in mottled shades of green. Mountains rose in majestic grandeur all around.

"Curly," Tom said. He took in the surrounding countryside with a sweep of his hand. "Curly, don't you just love it?"

Curly laughed. "I reckon I do, pard," he said. "I reckon I do."

Curly watched Tom. He had never seen any tenderfoot

take hold so fast, nor had he ever met a tenderfoot he liked as quickly. Most tenderfoot cowpokes lost interest in adventure as soon as hard work started. Not Tom. He was willing to pull his share and then some.

There was a moment this morning when Curly was a little concerned, however. He had waited in the shack until the rain stopped, then he went to the head of the draw to wait for Tom to push the cattle down to him. When the cattle didn't come, he rode up the draw to see what was wrong. Curly reached the cattle, but still saw no sight of Tom. He was concerned that Tom had gotten lost or, worse, had fallen asleep in the cabin. He was just about to ride back and see what was keeping him when he saw him arrive. Curly breathed a sigh of relief then, not because the work would have been too much for him to handle by himself, but because he had not wanted to be disappointed in the man he had come to like. Let the others tease him about being a tenderfoot all they wanted. Curly had ridden with a lot of men, but seldom had he encountered a man he thought more of than Tom Eddington.

"Where have you been?" Gil asked when Hilary returned to the ranch. There was a proprietary degree of sharpness to his voice which first surprised, and then angered Hilary.

"I wasn't aware that I had to report my every movement to you," she replied indignantly.

Hilary's anger was genuine, for she really didn't believe Gil had any right to demand an accounting of her whereabouts. But she used the anger as a convenient cover for the guilt she was feeling after her encounter with Tom this morning.

Then Gil saw that she was angry and he suddenly realized that he might have overstepped his bounds, so he quickly recanted.

"I'm sorry, Hilary," he apologized. "I didn't mean to be so harsh. It's just that I was worried about you. Your father said you weren't there when he got up this morning, and I had no idea where you could have gone." Gil grinned, a knowing, intimate grin. "Besides, you have to admit that after last night I do have some justification in being concerned about you."

"I don't see what the one thing has to do with the other." She blushed over his reference to the night before. "I am my own person, and I will not answer to you for my every move, either now or after we are married."

"Hilary, I know you are a headstrong person. I think one of the things I like about you is your spirit. And perhaps I am being a bit overly concerned. But I think you should understand that once we are married, I have every intention of being aware of your whereabouts at all times. After all, you will be my wife, and as my wife, you will occupy a position of some responsibility. Don't forget, I am a man of importance. You won't be the daughter of a mere foreman anymore, you will be the wife of a cattleman. A cattleman's wife has an obligation not only to her husband, but to her social position. I shall certainly expect you to conduct yourself accordingly."

"A mere foreman? You call my father a mere foreman? What are you but a glorified foreman?" Hilary asked angrily. She surprised herself by the sharpness of her response, but she was stung by what she considered to be a derisive reference to her father.

"I would hardly call my position that of a foreman, my dear," Gil said.

"What would you call it?" Hilary asked. "After all, you don't own Turquoise Ranch, you just run it."

"Perhaps I don't own it," Gil said. "But I do control it, and that is practically the same thing. The fate of this ranch, its owners, and everyone on it, depends upon me and the decisions I make. Your father's position, as well as the position of all the cowboys, is subject to my approval, or," he added ominously, "my disapproval."

"Are you threatening my father's position here?" Hilary asked.

"Hilary, have I made such a threat? You know that as long as we are married, your father's position as foreman of this ranch is safe."

As long as we are married? Hilary thought. There it is again, an implied threat. Does that mean she has to marry him to insure her father's job? No, surely not. Perhaps it was just her own sense of guilt that was causing her to think this way. After all, as they were engaged, Gil did have the right to be concerned about her. And she had left before dawn, and in a driving rainstorm . . . though it wasn't raining when she first left. That would cause someone to wonder. And of course if Gil had known what she really did during her absence this morning, then he would have legitimate cause for anger. She would rather not lie to him, but his prying left her no choice. She couldn't tell him the truth. That left a lie as her only alternative.

"I'm sorry," she said. "I have a secret place I go to sometimes. I've been going to it for years. Dad knows about it. I went there this morning, then the rain came up suddenly. I was forced to take shelter under a ledge of rocks. That is what caused me to be late. I didn't realize anyone would be worrying about me."

Gil softened before Hilary's new strategy, and he smiled at her. "That's all right," he said. "It's just that I wanted to find you because I'm expecting some important people for lunch. This will give you your first opportunity to perform some of the social functions which will be expected of you after we are married. I want you to come to lunch with us. Will you?"

"Of course I will," Hilary said, smiling sweetly. She was glad that the subject had been changed, and though she really didn't want to join him for lunch, she felt as if she didn't have any choice. She felt that she owed him that.

Hilary didn't care for Gil's guests. They were identified to her as "important cattle buyers from the East," and they wore their titles as badges of authority.

"Yes, thank you," one of them answered in response to a question. "We have enjoyed a great deal of success over the past year. You might say we have had a banner year."

"Another year this good, and we can get out of the business," the other one said.

"Why would you want to leave a business that is obviously so successful?" Gil asked.

"Why? You work and live around these smelly animals, you deal with the type of man who becomes a cowboy, and you ask why? The cattle business is a good business to make money, especially if you are as . . . shall we say, lucky . . . as we have been. But I certainly don't like the people who are associated with the business. For the most part I find them to be among the lowest specimens of life. They are unwashed, uneducated, and uncouth."

That was not the only derogatory comment made about ranching in general and cowboys in particular. Several other times during the course of the conversation, they said things that implied their disdain for the cowboys and others who honestly toiled for a living. Hilary heard about as much as she could take, and she was tempted to ask them if they thought they could have the success they were enjoying if it weren't for the cowboys who made everything go. They were obviously enjoying their success. They were both dressed in expensive suits and tooled-leather boots.

One of the men was very large, and rolls of fat spilled across his tight collar. His suit, though expensive, was too small, and he was sweating, though Hilary did not believe it was actually that warm. He kept sticking his finger between his collar and his neck, pulling it out, as if trying to get room to breathe. He had close-set, beady eyes, and Hilary could feel them burning into her as he watched her hungrily all through the meal. Hilary knew that the hunger in his eyes wasn't for food, and the thought of being with him the way she had been with Gil and Tom made her flesh crawl.

The fat man's name was Ponder. The other man was cadaverously thin with sunken cheeks and deep, dark brown eyes. He had only looked at Hilary once, and that was when they were introduced. Where Ponder's eyes were clouded with undisguised lust, the thin man, whose name was Stallings, had eyes that were as expressionless as those of a dead fish.

He seemed to have an interest in only one thing, and that was cattle.

"What a beautiful creature your fiancée is," Ponder wheezed over a glass of wine. "Don't you think so, Mr. Stallings?"

"What?" Stallings asked. He looked up from some papers which had occupied a prominent position by his plate all during lunch. "Oh, yes, she is lovely." Stallings moved his facial muscles in what may have been a smile, but he returned immediately to his work. He was a cold fish, but in fact Hilary much preferred his indifference to her over Ponder's long, lustful glances. She also didn't particularly care for the way they were speaking of her in the third person, as if she weren't even there.

"My dear, have you ever been to the city?" Ponder asked.

"I've been to Flagstaff several times," Hilary answered.

"Flagstaff? Oh, no, my dear. I mean a real city. Denver, perhaps. Or San Francisco."

"No," Hilary said. "I've never been there."

"Too bad. A lovely creature like you would have a wonderful time there. There are so many things to do. You could go to the ballet, the opera, the theater . . . or you could just visit the fine restaurants. I am a connoisseur of fine restaurants. Do you know what that means?"

"You eat a lot?" Hilary said innocently.

Gil laughed, and so did Ponder. Only Stallings remained expressionless.

"Oh, you sweet thing," Ponder said. "As a matter of fact, you can, no doubt, tell from my appearance that I do eat a lot as you so adroitly put it. But in truth a connoisseur is a person with exquisite taste, possessed of an acute discrimination when it comes to making selections. If you were to visit a restaurant with me, you may be assured it would be a wonderful experience for you."

"Oh, well, I think Gil would have something to say about that," Hilary said.

"Mr. Ponder is a business associate, my dear. If he chose to take you to a restaurant, I would hope you would be honored to accept the invitation."

Hilary looked at Gil in surprise. Did he know what he was saying? Didn't he realize that Mr. Ponder had more than visiting a restaurant on his mind? Couldn't Gil see the lust in Ponder's eyes? Or, worse, did he realize it but disregard it because Ponder was a business associate, and he didn't want to offend him? Was this what Gil meant when he said that as a cattleman's wife she would have certain responsibilities?

"Mr. Carson, may we get back to business?" Stallings asked.

"Yes, of course," Gil replied.

Stallings went on, "I have here the invoices from the last shipment. As you can see, everything is all accounted for, including the loss in transit, etcetera."

"Are the invoices for the Colorado Cattle Company included?" Gil asked.

Stallings looked up sharply, then he glanced over toward Hilary. In that one glance she saw more expression in his face than she had seen at anytime since he arrived.

"I would prefer not to talk about that in front of . . ."

"Don't worry about her," Gil interrupted easily.

"I don't know," Stallings said. "I'm not sure it is a good thing to discuss the business of the company at all. It is especially dangerous to discuss it around outsiders."

"I told you, don't worry about her," Gil said again, more sharply than before. "She is not exactly an outsider. She is Jake St. John's daughter. Obviously she has her father's best interests at heart. That means she won't do anything to jeopardize our business."

"You are certain she understands the consequences of any indiscretion?"

"What consequences?" Hilary asked, confused now by the direction of the conversation.

"I will see that she understands," Gil said. "Now that that is settled, what about new business? Have you any new business for me?"

"Yes, as a matter of fact I do," Stallings answered. "We have a requirement of fifty-five hundred head on your next shipment."

"Fifty-five hundred?" Gil said. He whistled. "I don't know, that may be a little larger than I can handle. You've never taken more than twenty-five hundred head before . . ."

"Yes," Stallings said. "But now we have a government contract to sell cattle to the San Carlos Apache Indian

Reservation, down near Phoenix. We must meet that quota or we will lose the contract. You can see that it is imperative that we get all the beef. It is preferable to get it all from one source. We were hoping you would be that source."

Gil pulled out a long, thin cheroot, bit off the tip and put it in his mouth. Hilary lit a match and held it to the end of the cigar.

"Uhmm, thanks," Gil said, puffing on the cigar until it was lit. He pulled the cigar from his mouth, and with his head ringed in a cloud of aromatic blue smoke, he looked at Stallings and Ponder.

"That's quite an order. I'm not certain I can come up with fifty-five hundred head," he said. "The losses we have been reporting back East have been exceptionally large as it is. Something like this would just be too much."

"I think you will find that this deal is worth it," Stallings said. "We are willing to pay top price."

"Oh?" Gil said with interest. "What would that be?"

"Twenty-five dollars a head," Ponder said.

"That would be over one hundred thousand dollars," Stallings added.

Gil smiled. "One hundred thousand dollars, you say?"

"All in cash," Ponder put in. "Untraceable."

"Provided, of course, that the cattle you provide us are the same. That is to say, untraceable."

Gil put the cigar back in his mouth and cocked it up at a jaunty angle.

"Gentlemen, I think you have just found your untraceable cattle," he said, smiling broadly. "Shall we drink a toast to it?"

Chapter Thirteen

It was late in the evening of that same day before Tom and Curly returned from their job. Big Jake invited both of them in for coffee and Curly accepted gratefully, but Tom mumbled some excuse as to why he couldn't come and he left Curly to make the report.

"What's the matter with Tom?" Big Jake asked as he poured coffee for the two of them. "He acted like he didn't want to come in."

"Beats me, boss. Here I thought this was what he wanted to do, but damned iffen he ain't been actin' strange this livelong day."

Hilary was in her bedroom, and when she heard the voices she came in to see who was there. When she saw Curly she was afraid that Tom might be with him. She couldn't face Tom. Not now, not after this morning. She stopped and started to go back to her room, but her father called out to her.

"Hilary, girl, come join us," Jake said. "Curly and Tom just got back from a long hard day."

"Is . . . is Tom here?" Hilary asked.

"No, he wouldn't come in," Big Jake said.

When she heard that he wasn't there, she breathed a quiet sigh of relief, and went on into the room to join Curly and her father.

"Well, I suppose I can sit with you two for a while," she said.

"Oh ho, listen to that now, will you?" Curly said. "Time was when you was a little girl, I couldn't keep you away from me."

"You were my hero then," Hilary smiled.

"Uh huh, 'n I ain't no more. Well, that I can understand. Little girls grow up to be big girls 'n then they put away childish things. I reckon heroes is one of 'em." Curly took a drink of coffee from his cup and eyed her over the rim. "They is one thing I can't understand, though, girl, 'n that's why you got it in for Tom. Iffen you ask me, he is as fine a cowboy as ever forked a horse, though truth be told, he ain't really no cowboy. He's somethin' much finer'n any cowboy I've ever known, which makes it hard to understand what you got ag'in him."

Hilary looked shocked. "Why Curly, I don't have anything against Tom. Why would you think such a thing?"

"It's just somethin' I've noticed," Curly said. "I see it in the way he acts. He don't want to talk none about you, 'n all the while we was comin' back here, he was actin' real strange, liken as if he was afraid he was gonna run into you when we come to talk to Big Jake. Why, I bet he asked me a hunnert times iffen I didn't think I could make the report without him, 'cause he didn't want to upset you, by bein' around you. Now what I want to know is, why would it upset you for him to be around?"

"Daughter, have you taken a dislike to Tom for some

reason? Does it upset you for him to be around?" Jake asked.

Hilary looked down at the floor, and she felt her cheeks flaming. She hoped her father didn't realize she was blushing, but she didn't know how he could miss it.

"No, Dad," Hilary said. "Not exactly."

"Not exactly? What do you mean by not exactly? That's no answer."

"It's just that Tom has ideas that perhaps, that is, we might . . ." Hilary paused in midexplanation.

"You might what?"

"Dad, Tom seems to harbor some hope that a . . . romance . . . could exist between the two of us. Of course, such an idea is ridiculous, but he seems to harbor it, nonetheless."

"Why is it so ridiculous?" Jake asked. "For my way of thinkin', Tom Eddington is a good man. Curly has vouched for him, and you can't get a higher recommendation in my book."

"Why thank you, boss," Curly said, genuinely moved by Jake's endorsement of his judgment.

"Dad, you know why it is ridiculous," Hilary said. "I'm engaged to Gil Carson. Or have you forgotten?"

"No," Jake said. "I'm not likely to forget that. Have you?"

"Have I? What do you mean?"

"I mean how can you account for Tom's strange belief that there might be somethin' between the two of you, unless you have led him on a bit?"

"I don't know," Hilary said quietly. Now her cheeks burned so that she knew they must be beet red. "I can't explain that."

"Well now, boss, truth to be told, Miss Hilary may have nothin' to do with it anyway. For all that I like the man, I got to say that sometimes there don't seem to be no accountin' for how Tom acts," Curly said. "He's about the most different person I ever laid eyes on."

"What do you mean?" Big Jake asked. "In what way is he different?"

"Different from all the other cowboys I know," Curly said. "Now you take his education. He's a educated man, I know that," Curly said. "He don't look educated—I mean he's so big—but he's educated all right. He's always talkin' 'bout things he's read in books, 'n you know it takes a educated man to be able to talk about things in books. And strong? Boss, I always thought you was the strongest man I'd ever seen, but Tom can go you one better. Have you heard about what he did with the tie-bar offen the grain wagon?"

"No," Big Jake said. "What about it?"

"The other day, we was usin' the grain wagon to haul some barbed wire. Well sir, we was up at Tooley Creek where all them boulders has been washed down from the mountains, don't you know, and the wagon hit a rock. The driver had just whipped the team up to make the upgrade, so when it hit the rock, well, the tie-bar got bent up somethin' awful. You know how downright hard it is to straighten one of them things out. You got to heat it up in a fire, then you got to pound it out over a forge. Well, Tom didn't know that, 'n when one of the boys, just jokin' mind you, told Tom to straighten the tie-bar out, well, Tom commenced to do just that!"

"Are you telling me that Tom Eddington straightened a bent tie-bar?" Jake asked, impressed by the feat of strength.

"He did just that," Curly said. "Ole Tom just pulled that tie-bar offen the wagon, stuck one end of it down in a rock crevice, then he pulled on the other end with both hands until it straightened out pretty as you please, just liken it was in the first place. You should'a seen him, boss. He took off his shirt and he had muscles poppin' out on top of muscles."

Hilary felt an involuntary shudder pass over her. She had seen those muscles just this morning. Indeed, she had felt them, and she realized a little thrill now over Curly's description of Tom's strength. She wished she had been there to witness it. No, on second thought, she was glad she had not been. She was having enough difficulty with her emotions now.

Big Jake let out a soft sigh of surprise. "He must be one strong son of a bitch," he said.

"Ain't that the truth, though?" Curly answered, and Hilary noted some pride in Curly's voice, as if he was sharing in Tom's accomplishments because he was Tom's best friend. "But, now here's the kicker. He's always doin' things like that without givin' it a second thought. It's as if his strength comes so natural to him that it don't seem nothin' unusual."

"I must confess to a degree of curiosity over Mr. Eddington's background myself," Big Jake said. "He comes here from the East, he is educated and, though I don't know for sure, I get the idea that he is from a fine family. Most young men like that fold when the going gets tough. Mr. Eddington has stayed on. There's a mystery there all right, but I sure don't know what it is. I would be very interested to find out."

"Please," Hilary finally said in exasperation. "Must we always talk about Tom Eddington? It seems like ever since he arrived, I've been seeing him or hearing about him. I'd like to just get him out of my mind for a while!"

It was hard enough carrying around her memory of this morning. To have his name constantly bandied about just made her job of forgetting him all the more difficult.

Big Jake and Curly looked at Hilary with some surprise over her sudden outburst. When Hilary realized what a thing she had made over it, she glanced quickly down to the floor, and once more her cheeks flamed. She had better be careful. She was going to give herself away if she didn't watch out.

"I mean, you can talk about him if you want to, but I thought a man's personal life was his own. If Tom Eddington wanted people to know more about him, he would tell them."

"You know, Curly, the girl is right," Big Jake said. "I got things in my own past I don't particularly like to talk about, so I reckon we got no business speculatin' about Tom's past."

"No, I guess not," Curly said.

"Tell me about your job," Big Jake said, changing the subject. "Did everything go all right?"

"Yeah," Curly said. "Boss, you know they was near on to a hunnert head of cattle we caught up there in Candlestick Draw."

"One hundred head you say?" Big Jake whistled. "We're lucky they didn't die in there. That would've been three thousand dollars lost, right there."

Hilary looked at her father in surprise.

"Yeah, well, here is the funny thing, boss. Them cows was as good off in there as the ones we was runnin' out on the range. Fac' is, someone had took the trouble to damn up a creek 'n send some water into the draw. Why, them cows had ever'thin' they needed in there. It was almost like they was put in there of a purpose."

Big Jake looked at Curly for a long, musing moment.

"What are you trying to say, Curly?"

"It looked to me like some rustlers might have took the notion to cut out about a hunnert head. For some reason they couldn't get 'em off the ranch, so they run 'em into Candlestick Draw, aimin' to come back later 'n pick 'em up. Leastwise, that's my way of thinkin' on the subject."

"That's a possibility," Big Jake agreed. "That's certainly a possibility."

Curly set his coffee cup down on a nearby table and stood up, then stretched.

"Boss, it ain't that I don't enjoy jawin' with you, you unnerstan', but I gotta tell you, I'm one tired cowpoke."

"Yes Curly, well, you go ahead and turn in," Big Jake said. "You put in a good day of work today. And tell Tom that goes for him, too."

"Right, boss. Good night," Curly said. "And good night to you too, Miss Hilary."

Hilary watched her father walk to the door with Curly, then after Curly was gone, she spoke to him.

"Dad, what did you mean when you said that those one hundred head of cattle were worth three thousand dollars?"

Big Jake chuckled. "Now you're beginning to see why Turquoise Ranch is worth so much money, are you? Well, it's very simple. One head will bring about thirty dollars. Sometimes it's a little more, but when you consider the attrition rate during shipment, one thing and another, you can pretty well count on about thirty dollars a head. Turquoise Ranch is probably running around twenty thousand head, so there is more than half a million dollars in stock alone, let alone the value of the rangeland and its buildings."

"Are you sure about that, Dad? About the price of cattle, I mean."

Jake walked over to a rolltop desk and opened it. He picked up a small printed circular.

"Here is an offering from the Southern Pacific Railroad," he said. "They're paying thirty-one dollars at the railhead in

Flagstaff. If a fella wanted to shop around he might be able to beat that, but not by much."

"Would there ever be a reason for someone selling their cattle at twenty-five dollars a head?"

"Perhaps."

"Why would someone do that?"

"If they come by the cows dishonestly, they'll often discount them so that the buyer doesn't ask too many questions."

"Have you ever known anyone to do that?"

Jake frowned at his daughter. "You ask too many questions," he said. "One of these days you may get an answer you don't want to hear."

Suddenly Hilary had a most disquieting thought. Gil had told the cattle buyers that she would have her father's best interests at heart. Did that mean that Gil and her father were in partnership over some scheme to cheat the owners of Turquoise Ranch? What if the owners found out?

"Dad, why has the owner of this ranch never bothered to come look at it?" Hilary asked.

"Why do you ask that?" Jake asked.

Hilary didn't want to raise her father's suspicions, so she said, "It's just that Turquoise Ranch is so beautiful, surely anyone who owned such a bit of paradise would want to see it."

"I don't guess I can answer that question, darlin', 'cause I don't know who owns it," Jake said. "And the truth is, I don't think Gil Carson even knows."

"But how can that be? Surely he has to report to someone, doesn't he?"

"Yes, of course. Bit it's just to some lawyers who run things. It's a business, darlin', just like any other business, only in this business we raise and sell cows. So the ranch is owned by a cattle company."

"How cold," Hilary said. "How awful to reduce something like Turquoise Ranch to a bunch of numbers in a book."

"Perhaps so," Jake said. "But you fail to understand, darlin'. To you and me, and to those of us who live here, Turquoise Ranch is our home, and we love it. But to the businessman or businessmen who own it, it is simply another investment, like buying stock in a railroad or a shipping line. They know nothing about the ranch except its profit-and-loss picture."

"I am sure that if I ever meet the owner or owners, I shall not like them," Hilary said.

"It's not important that we like them, darlin'. The only important thing is that they like us."

"Why wouldn't they like us?"

Jake laughed. "Oh, there are a lot of reasons why they may not like us. They may decide that we're mismanaging the place, or they may decide to go out of business altogether. That's why we should save as much as we can, just in case we are ever thrown out."

"You mean a person should get all he can while he can?" Hilary asked.

"I wouldn't have put it in those words, but yes."

Hilary felt a great sadness. Now she knew what Stallings meant by the consequence of indiscretion. Gil and her father were involved in some scheme to cheat the owners. Her father and the man she was going to marry must be crooks.

After Hilary went to bed, Jake walked over to a liquor cabinet and took out a bottle of whiskey. He poured himself a drink, then sat down to enjoy it. Twenty-five dollars a head, huh? He had to hand it to Gil, he was getting a good price on the cattle he was stealing. Most rustlers had to discount their cattle by nearly half. And most rustlers took a greater risk all the way around than Gil was taking. Gil was taking no risk at all. He was merely cutting cattle out of the owner's herd, and selling them off.

It wasn't at all like it was in the old days, when cattle rustling could get a man killed.

Jake, Sam, and the others who had fought with him returned from the war to find their ranches in ruins, their herds gone and their reputations discredited.

Jake had inherited a small ranch from his father. The ranch itself wasn't small; there was land enough to run a herd many times larger than the herd Jake had, and Jake had grandiose plans for growth. He was going to marry the daughter of the man who owned the next ranch over, raise kids and cattle and make something of himself.

But during the war Jake's house was burned, his cattle run off, and his land confiscated for unpaid taxes. The girl Jake thought he was going to marry had married another, and Jake returned to find that he, and all the men who rode for him, were wanted men. The war had not ended for Quantrill's Raiders, nor for anyone who had ever ridden with him.

Jake had taken orders from General Fielding Nance. Fielding Nance had been one of the largest ranchers in the state of Texas before the war. Now he, too, was nearly destitute. His herds had been decimated, and much of his land confiscated. His house had not been burned, and he was not wanted for robbery and murder, as was Jake, but he, too, suffered from the defeat. When Jake went to see Nance, calling on him late one evening, he was struck with melancholy over what he saw. The once-proud rancher who had ruled over thirty thousand acres of land and a hundred thousand head of cattle, with the help of over a hundred cowboys, now sat in a rocking chair, a broken man. The house was in disrepair, the barns were tumbling down and the bunkhouses and fields were empty.

"General?" Jake said, tying his horse to a broken hitch rail in front of the General's house. "General, it's me, Jake St. John."

"Colonel St. John," General Nance said. He smiled and stood up. "Colonel St. John, how nice of you to come visit me. Come up here, have a seat, boy, have a seat."

Jake sat on an empty keg next to the General and looked at him. He sighed.

"We paid a terrible price, didn't we, General?"

"Yes," the General said. "But honor is dear, my boy. It is very dear."

"Honor? Is that what it was?"

"Of course."

"Some of us are still paying. My men, for example. And me. You know there are reward posters out on us, don't you? We can't even show ourselves in public. I had to sneak out here to see you when I was sure there was no one else around."

"Yes," General Nance said. "I know."

"I guess I could take it all right if it was just me. But my men were only following orders. My orders. And I was following your orders, General."

"Colonel, I must know," General Nance said. "The money. Did you keep any of the money you took?"

Jake glared at the General. "I would have hoped you would know better than to ask that question," he said. "Of course I didn't keep any of the money."

"Some of the raiders did. Quantrill, for example."

"Yes, but Quantrill stood condemned by the Confederate government, even before the war was over. Quantrill and all his men were nothing but a pack of murdering thieves, the lot of them. What are we to do with them?"

"You rode with them."

"Only for a short while, General, and only under your orders."

"I know," General Nance said. "Jake, I wish I could do something for you, I really do. I wish I could go to someone and have all the posters withdrawn." He held his hand out, taking in his ranch. "I wish I could put this ranch back the way it was, and your ranch, and the homes and ranches and farms of all the men from the South who gave so much in a losing cause, but I can't."

"I know," Jake said. "I know." Jake stood up and held onto one of the porch posts while he looked out over the empty ranch. That was when he got his idea.

"Maybe we can. General, how many acres of land do you have left?"

" 'Bout ten thousand," the General said. "But all the land's good for is to hold the world together. I don't even have a milk cow left."

"What if I got a herd? Could we run them here on your grass and water until we could sell them? We could split the profit."

"Where would you get a herd?"

"I've heard of some pretty large carpetbag spreads near here," Jake said. "Most of their cattle came from our herds. I'll just take some of them back."

"Legally, that's cattle rustling," General Nance warned.

Jake smiled. "I'd as soon have the game as the name," he said.

A log snapped in the fireplace, and the sudden noise brought Jake back to the present. He looked at his glass and saw that it was empty, and he wondered how long he had been sitting there just thinking. His rustling days were past, and he had already paid for them. He hoped he didn't get caught up in Gil's scheme.

He would make sure that he didn't . . .

Chapter Fourteen

"Pardner, it beats me why you want to take a train ride down to Phoenix," Curly said when Tom announced his intentions. "The only thing Phoenix has that Flagstaff doesn't is just more of the same, that's all."

"I'm sure you're right," Tom said. "It's just that I would like to see it, and with three days off, it seems like a fine opportunity."

"Ha," Curly said. "You'll use up a good portion of the first day just gettin' there, and the third day just comin' back. Think of how we could put that time to good use in Flagstaff. I sure hope you ain't plannin' on me goin' with you."

"You are certainly welcome to come along if you wish," Tom said.

"No thankee. While you're still ridin' on the train, I'll already be havin' me a fine time in Flagstaff."

Tom was certain that Curley would turn down his invitation, and in fact, that was exactly what he wanted him to do. Tom did want to go to Phoenix, but he was not exactly honest with Curly in telling him why he wanted to go. Tom wanted to go to Phoenix so he could wire his lawyers in Boston without danger of someone finding out. He was afraid to send a wire from Flagstaff because Flagstaff was so small that it would be impossible for him to hide his business. Phoenix was larger, and farther away, thus assuring him of some privacy.

It was hot in Phoenix. Tom had grown used to the cooler clime of Flagstaff, and he wasn't quite prepared for the blistering heat. He took his jacket off and tossed it across his shoulder, then braced himself to walk from the shade of the car shed out into the bright Arizona sun.

An old Mexican woman was operating a taco stand right across the street from the station. She didn't have any teeth and she kept her mouth closed tightly so that her chin and nose nearly touched. A swarm of flies buzzed around the steaming kettles, drawn by the pungent aromas of meat and sauce. She worked with quick, deft fingers, rolling the spicy ingredients into tortillas, then wrapping them up in old newspaper as she handed them to her customers.

Tom walked on down the street, taking in the sights and sounds of Phoenix. The city was undergoing a transition from a sleepy cow town of the Old West to a bustling city of the future. Electric trolleys whirred down the dual set of tracks in the center of the street, clanging their bells impatiently at the horses and carriages that had the temerity to get in their way. Both sides of the street were lined with poles which stretched electric wires along the length of the street, carrying telegraph and telephone messages as well as electricity for lights and the trolley cars.

The streets were long and wide and crowded on both sides with bustling businesses and busy hotels. Tom walked into one of the latter, a large ornate hotel known as the Adams Hotel.

"Yes, sir," the clerk behind the desk said as Tom stepped up. "You'll be wantin' a room?"

"Yes," Tom said as he filled out the registration form.

"With a bath?"

Tom looked up in surprise. It was a long time since he had enjoyed the pleasure of a private bathroom. "You have rooms with baths?" he asked.

"Absolutely, sir," the clerk answered proudly. "We've had guests from the East tell us that New York, Boston, Philadelphia and other such cities have nothing on us."

"Very good," Tom said. "In that case, I will take a room with a bath. Oh, and I would like to have this telegram sent. Would you tell me where the nearest office is?"

The clerk smiled. "We have a telephone here, sir. If you wish, you may leave your message with me, and I will call it in to the telegraph office."

For a moment Tom hesitated, then he smiled. Why not? After all, he wouldn't be able to keep the message secret from the operator anyway. Besides, Phoenix was certainly far enough away that there was little danger of his message falling into the wrong hands. He took the message he had written while still on the train and handed it to the clerk.

"Very well, have it sent at once, please, and give this hotel as the address for my answer."

"Right away, sir," the clerk said. The clerk handed a key to Tom. "Your room is on the third floor, in front," he said. "You have French doors which open onto a lovely balcony from which you can look out over the city."

"Thank you," Tom said.

Tom climbed the wide, carpeted stairs to the third floor, then found his room with very little difficulty. His room was equipped with a large bed, quite a change from the narrow bunk he was accustomed to using in the bunkhouse. There were also a sofa, table and chair, and a large wardrobe chest. In addition there was a door that led to a small bathroom. But, miracle of all, his room was equipped with an overhead electric fan. He turned it on to see if it worked, and was rewarded by a cooling breeze from the spinning paddles. He was surprised by the modern conveniences of his room. He wasn't sure what he expected, but the thought of electric lights and fans out here seemed strange to him. Though Phoenix certainly did have all the marks of a bustling community, and as electricity was quite common in the East, he really saw no reason why a city the size of Phoenix would be denied.

The bathroom had a white and black checkerboard tile floor. The white porcelain bathtub stood upon claw feet, and the water spigots were silver and enamel. When Tom turned them he was rewarded with a steady stream of water. He let the water run until the tub was nearly full, then he took off his clothes and settled gratefully into the refreshingly cool bath.

Nearly half an hour later Tom was clean and freshly dressed, standing on the balcony outside his room, watching the people below. The sounds of the city reached his ears, and he contrasted the noise of the city with the quiet of his ranch.

Tom smiled. It was *his* ranch, though in truth he had to force himself to think of it that way. He was so much a part of the cowboy scene now that even he sometimes regarded the ranch as being the property of some distant owner, and himself as but one of the pawns.

He wasn't a pawn, of course. He was the owner, and as such, he was the one who was being hurt by the improper administration of the ranch. It was to put a halt to the improper management that he had come to Phoenix. The message he sent asked his lawyers in Boston to recommend a Phoenix lawyer to whom Tom could go with his problem.

Tom watched the street for a while longer, then he went back into his room and lay on the bed to let the cool breeze from the spinning fan wash over his body. He had been on the train for quite a while, having left early in the morning. Perhaps a small nap would be in order before dinner.

Tom was dreaming. In the dream he was holding a plank against the wall of the barn while Curly was driving nails. The sound of the hammer was deafening, overpowering everything in the dream until finally it woke Tom up. He could still hear the pounding. It was not until that moment that he realized the pounding he was hearing was not a dream, but was really a knock on the door.

"Just a minute," Tom called. Tom sat up and rubbed his head. He must have been more tired than he thought, for he had slept so soundly that for a moment he had a difficult time getting his bearings. Then the spinning fan made him remember where he was and why he was here.

There was another knock at the door.

"Mr. Eddington? Mr. Eddington, are you in there?" a voice called from the other side of the door.

Tom stood up and walked over to the door, then opened it. A tall, gray-haired man stood in the corridor. He was well-dressed, and he smiled pleasantly.

"Are you Tom Eddington?" the man asked.

"Yes," Tom answered. He was confused. Who knew that he was here?

The man handed Tom a card. "My name is Dan Heckemeyer," he said. "I am a lawyer."

"A lawyer?"

"Yes," the man said. "You did wire your firm in Boston

informing them that you were looking for a lawyer, did you not?"

"Uh, yes," Tom said. 'Yes, I did."

"As soon as your firm heard from you, they wired me," Dan said. "You see, we have done quite a bit of business together in the past. In fact, I have even conducted some railroad business for your grandfather. Your grandfather is Andrew Eddington, is he not?"

"Yes," Tom said, and stepped back. "Won't you come in?"

"Thank you," Dan said. "That is most hospitable."

The two men walked over to the sitting area, where Tom sat on the sofa and Dan settled in the chair.

"Now, Tom, what is it that I can do for you?"

"I think I am being systematically robbed," Tom said.

"Robbed? By who?"

"By Gil Carson."

"Gil Carson? I've heard of him," Dan said. "Yes, he is the owner of the Turquoise Ranch, I believe."

"He isn't the owner," Tom said. "He is the manager."

"Yes, that's right," Dan said. "I believe I did know that. Wait a minute. Are you the owner?"

"Yes," Tom said.

"I see. And you think he is robbing you, do you? Well, that's a common enough thing, I suppose. There are many ranches owned by absentee landlords, which are having a portion of the profit shaved off by unscrupulous managers. It's easy enough to cover, you know. They report excess losses, don't report herd growth, report sales of less than they actually make. Have you confronted Carson with your suspicion?"

"No," Tom said.

"Well, Mr. Eddington, don't you think you should? After

all, you should hear his side as well. You shouldn't just depend upon unsubstantiated rumor. From whom did you hear he was robbing you, anyway?"

"It's just little things I've picked up here and there," Tom said. "I've been working on the ranch."

"I beg your pardon?" Dan said with some surprise.

"I've been working on the ranch for nearly two months now," Tom said. "I, uh, am working there as a cowboy. No one knows my identity."

"What?" Dan asked. "Let me get this straight. You are employed by Turquoise Ranch as a cowhand, and no one there suspects you are actually the owner of the ranch?"

"That's right," Tom said. "At least, I don't think anyone knows."

"You'd better hope they don't find out," Dan said.

"Why? What do you mean by that?"

"Well, outside the fact that it would be dangerous if Carson found out, I doubt that anyone else would take it too kindly either. They aren't the ones you'll have to worry about. You may lose a few friends. But if Carson is guilty, and if he finds out you're spying on him, you could lose your life!"

"Listen, I want you to know that I didn't get started in this charade in order to spy on people," Tom protested.

"Oh? Then why did you start it?"

"I wanted to learn the business," Tom said.

"I'm sorry, friend, but that argument doesn't hold water. Being a cowboy is no way to learn how to run a ranch. There are men who have cowboyed for half a century, and they don't know the first thing about the business end of the deal."

"Maybe so," Tom said. He smiled. "The truth is, I guess I was just looking for a little adventure and I thought concealing my identity would be the way to do it."

"Yes. Well, you may be letting yourself in for a little more adventure than you had planned on," Dan said. "I guess we had better go about finding out if you're being cheated, and if you are, put the guilty in prison."

"No," Tom said quickly. "No, I don't want to put anyone in prison."

"Oh? And may I ask why not?"

"I'm not sure how many are involved," Tom said. "And there are some that I don't want to get hurt."

"Even if they're hurting you?"

"Even if they're hurting me."

"Anyone in particular that you are trying to protect?"

"No, I . . . that is, I'm not trying to protect him. I don't really think he is guilty. In fact, he's one of the first people I heard about the impropriety from."

"A common trick," Dan said.

"What?"

"It's a common enough trick," Dan said. "If this person, whoever he is, had the slightest suspicion that you might be more than just an ordinary cowboy, it would be smart to avert suspicion from himself by saying something to you. Who is it?"

"It's Jake St. John, the foreman of the ranch."

"Jake St. John? Not the one they call Big Jake?"

"Yes," Tom answered.

"What do you know of Big Jake?" Dan asked.

"Not much," Tom admitted. "I think he came from Texas originally. I know he fought in the war, but that's about all I know. Everyone is pretty close-mouthed about their past. That's what has helped me to keep my own secret."

"Yes, well, in the case of Big Jake St. John, he has every reason to keep quiet about his past. You know he's from

Texas. Did you also know he was wanted there for murder and cattle rustling?"

"No," Tom said. "I've never heard that."

"I don't wonder," Dan said. "It isn't the sort of a past one likes to speak about."

"Are you sure?" Tom asked. "He doesn't seem like the type of man who would commit murder."

Dan laughed. "How many men have you known who have committed murder?"

"Well, none," Tom answered sheepishly.

"You're right about his having been in the war. But he didn't fight in the regular army. He rode with Quantrill. He and Quantrill, and the others like him, were out to get what they could from the war. They turned bad during the war, and didn't stop when it was all over. St. John was on the run for a long time afterward. Then I hear he shot it out with three lawmen at the same time and killed all three of them. But they were Federal lawmen, and a Texas court turned him loose. After that, things were pretty uncomfortable for St. John in Texas, so he left the state and came to Arizona. Believe me, in this case, Texas' loss was not Arizona's gain. Do you think he's involved?"

"I hope not," Tom said. "For Hilary's sake, I sincerely hope not."

Dan rubbed his chin and looked at Tom for a moment. "Tell me, Mr. Eddington, would Hilary happen to be St. John's daughter?"

"Yes," Tom admitted.

"Is she pretty?"

"She is beautiful," Tom said with more feeling than he realized.

"I see. So it isn't really Jake St. John you are concerned about, it's his daughter. Are you courting her?"

"Mr. Heckemeyer, I scarcely see that that is any of your business," Tom said rather harshly.

"Perhaps not," Dan said. "But if I am to do my job adequately, I feel that I should have all the information available. I don't want to go out on a limb and then have that limb sawed off behind me because you happen to be in love with the guilty man's daughter."

"In the first place, I don't believe Big Jake is guilty, regardless of what you say about him," Tom said. "And in the second place, what I feel or don't feel about his daughter has no bearing on anything. As it so happens, Miss St. John is engaged to Gil Carson, so I don't think it should enter into this at all."

"But it has entered into it," Dan said. He sighed. "Very well, you're the boss. If you don't want to put anyone in prison, we won't try. But if you don't want to put anyone in prison, just what the Sam Hill *do* you want me to do?"

"I want to find out if rustling is going on, and stop it."

"All right, maybe we can do that," Dan said. "With you working on the inside and me on the outside, it should be easy enough to accomplish. Now, what I will need from you is advance word about any large cattle transaction. If there is a big cattle buy or sale in the near future, you must let me know."

"How should I contact you?"

"Send me a letter," Dan said. "Not to my office, that might arouse suspicion if anyone saw the address on the envelope. Here is my post office box number. Send it there." Dan wrote a number on a piece of paper and handed it to Tom.

"All right," Tom said, taking the paper.

"You know, Mr. Eddington, if you do find out and confront Carson with the evidence, even if you don't have any plans to send him to prison, he may not take it kindly.

You'll be killing the golden goose, if you get my meaning, and he may not like that. It could still be dangerous for you."

"Yes, I know."

"And despite the faith you have placed in Jake St. John, you may be in just as much danger from him."

"I don't really think I'm in danger from Big Jake St. John."

"It's when you least suspect it that you may be in the most danger."

"I'll be careful," Tom said.

"Good," Dan said. He smiled broadly and stuck out his hand. "Then I shall look forward to doing business with you, sir, as I've enjoyed doing business with your grandfather in the past.

"Why do you ask?"

Gil poured wine into Hilary's glass, then put the bottle back on the table. Hilary had eaten dinner with him earlier, and though the housekeeper had cleared away the table, they were still sitting over their wineglasses, talking.

"It just seems unusual that you would sell the cattle for such a little amount. I happen to know that the going price is thirty-one dollars a head."

Gil took a sip of his wine and looked at Hilary over the rim of his glass. He smiled.

"Maybe there are some things you would be better off not knowing," he suggested.

"Gil, are you selling stolen cattle to those people?"

Gil laughed out loud.

"Now where would I be apt to steal fifty-five hundred head of cattle? That's an entire herd, my dear, as if you didn't know."

"I don't know where you would steal them. It's just that,

well, when I mentioned it to Dad, he said anyone who would sell cattle that cheaply must be selling stolen cattle."

"Did you tell him I was?"

"No. I wanted to hear what you had to say first."

"That was smart of you. Hilary, there are things about this business that you don't understand. There are things that you are better off not understanding."

"Like what?"

Gil poured another glass of wine for himself.

"Well, if you are better off not knowing, then I certainly shouldn't be the one to tell you, should I?"

"Gil, I love Turquoise Ranch, and my father loves it as well. I hope you aren't doing anything that could hurt the ranch."

"You forget, Hilary, I am the ranch," Gil said. "What happens on this ranch reflects directly on me. I'm not going to give all that up by doing something stupid."

"Are you telling me the truth?"

"Of course I am," Gil said easily. "Now, my suggestion to you is that you quit worrying so much. Your father and I know what we're doing."

"My father? You mean my father is involved?"

Gil laughed, a short, easy laugh. "Involved in what? I told you, there is nothing to worry about. The only thing I want you to be thinking about now is our wedding. That will be soon, you know."

"Yes, I know. Just two more weeks."

"Oh, I meant to tell you, I would like to postpone it for an additional three weeks. I hope you don't mind."

"No," Hilary said. In fact, she wouldn't have minded postponing it forever, though she didn't say anything.

"Good, I thought you would go along with me on it. It's just that I know you will want your father at the wedding, and as he will be on the cattle drive, he wouldn't have a chance to be here unless it's postponed."

"Cattle drive? What cattle drive?"

"To Phoenix, my dear," Gil said, smiling broadly. "We are going to have an old-fashioned cattle drive to Phoenix."

Chapter Fifteen

"A cattle drive? You mean we're actually going to make an old-time cattle drive?" Curly replied to Jake's announcement.

"That's right," Jake said. "There are fifty-five hundred head of cattle we have to deliver to an Indian reservation down near Phoenix."

"But why drive 'em, boss? They's railroad track running down to Phoenix."

"'Cause Gil Carson wants 'em driven," Big Jake said. "And as long as he is the manager of this ranch, I don't reckon we got much choice."

"Well, say, you ain't gonna get no complaint from me," Curly said. "It's been a while since I was on a genuine cattle drive. And won't ole Tom like it, though? He's gonna get him some real cowboyin' now."

"I guess we all are," Big Jake said.

"Are you gonna ramrod the drive, boss?" Curly asked.

"Yes," Jake said. He smiled. "That is, if I can remember

what to do. It's been that long since I was on a drive, I'm likely to be as green as Tom."

"Ha," Sam, who was also present, put in. "You, the man what took a cattle herd right out from under Yankee eyes, 'n drove 'em for near nine hundred miles? You makin' out like you wouldn't know what to do? Who you tryin' to kid?"

Jake laughed. "I hope I'm not tryin' to kid myself," he said. "And I hope we can get enough drovers who are willing enough to follow me to make a drive."

"Don't you worry none about that, boss," Sam said. "You ain't gonna have no trouble gettin' men to follow you. I 'member how it was durin' the war. They was men would soak their britches in kerosene and follow you to hell, jus' to see you kick the devil in the ass."

"A lot of things have changed since the war," Jake said.

"Some things don't ever change," Sam said. "And bein' a man others would follow is one of those things. You're a leader, boss, natural born. Always was, and always will be."

Sam and Curly left to attend to various duties, while Jake thought of Sam's words. He had been a leader men would follow. But it hadn't always been good for his men. The ones who followed him during the war, and who survived, came home to find themselves wanted men. Those who followed him down the rustler's trail after the war found themselves riding down a one-way street to nowhere. Some of them found themselves dead.

After making arrangements with Fielding Nance to keep the cows he rustled, Jake put together a band of riders and set out to take back all that he had lost.

Jake had come from a ranching area, and there were several good ranches around when he left for the war. There were several ranches there when he returned, but they weren't the same ranches. The original owners, those who were still alive, were living as destitute men, eking out a living the best way they could, while the new owners, carpetbaggers who had come down from the North after the war, were getting rich off the misery of others.

Large well-fed herds roamed the range, and men who, before the war, had been clerks and lawyers up North, now resided in luxury in the homes and haciendas of their victims. Those were Jake's targets.

Jake began hitting the herds hard, sometimes cutting out as many as five hundred to a thousand head of cattle and driving them away, almost right under the noses of the carpetbaggers. Many times he had help from the very cowboys who were riding with the herd, for they were Southerners themselves who took the jobs with the carpetbaggers because they were the only jobs available.

Soon it was no secret that Jake was the one who was masterminding the rustling operations, and though the reward posters increased and the Federal marshals roamed the ranges looking for him, Jake managed to stay just ahead of them.

In the meantime, General Fielding Nance was quietly restoring his ranch to its original grandeur, and men who had worked for him in the past deserted their new bosses to return. Jake had lost the war against the Yankees, but he was winning the peace.

Then, one afternoon as he was coming into town, Jake and four of his most trusted men were ambushed by a dozen bounty hunters. He was shot from his horse, but from the dirt of the road and with three bullets in him, he exchanged fire with the ambushers. All around him, his friends were being killed. Finally only Sam was left alive, and Sam managed to get Jake on his horse and flee. Behind them three of Jake's comrades lay dead as well as three of the ambushing bounty hunters.

As the bounty hunters were acting on Federal posters, the military governor tried to say that Jake had murdered Federal marshals. The Texas court didn't buy that, however, and when a Texas Ranger, who happened to be an old friend of Jake's, asked Jake to give himself up and plead self-defense, Jake agreed. Jake was found innocent of the crime of murder. The charges of cattle rustling were dropped. The Texas Ranger strongly suggested to Jake, however, that he would be better off if he left Texas.

Jake took the ranger's advice and moved to Arizona with Sam in tow. The ranger was right. There was no one looking for him in Arizona, and the Federal charges against him were eventually dropped.

Word that the Turquoise outfit was going to drive fifty-five hundred head of cattle south in an old-time cattle drive spread quickly, and soon men began to show up looking for work. It was good that extra men showed up because a lot more men would be needed to drive the cattle a great distance than would be required merely to watch over them on the range. Some of the men who returned were men who had worked on Turquoise Ranch before and had left, cursing Gil Carson and swearing never to come back. But they, like the others, were attracted by the opportunity to participate in a genuine cattle drive, for this was now a thing of the past.

"It will be something we can tell our grandchildren," the cowboys said to each other as they discussed the upcoming drive in the saloons and cafés of Flagstaff.

There were many applicants for the drive, so many in fact, that Big Jake had to put out a special table and sit behind it while he took the applications. The cowboys were lined up all the way across the yard.

"What's so unique about a cattle drive?" Tom asked Curly as the two men stood on the porch of the bunkhouse and watched the excited activity. "Isn't that normally the way you get your cattle to market?"

Curly laughed. "That was the way of it till the railroads come along. After that, they's been very few of 'em, 'n they's likely to be even fewer of 'em in the future. This here is gonna be just like the ole times, though, 'n that's why so many is showin' up."

"It must be good work."

"It's hard work," Curly said. "Most of these galoots don't have no idee what they're lettin' themselves in for. They jus' heard about it, 'n they wantin' to get in on it. The others, the older ones that have been on a trail herd are just wantin' to . . . to . . ." He let his voice trail off.

"To what?" Tom asked.

"I don't know as I can say it so's you can understand it. I ain't a educated man, 'n I can't talk fancy like you can, but it's like they're all awantin' to reach out 'n take aholt o' somethin' they think they had when they was young."

"They want to recapture their youth," Tom suggested.

"Yeah, maybe you could put it that way," Curly said. "The plain truth is, though, what most of 'em remember ain't what it's like a'tall. They jus' remember the good times, the days when they was plenty of water 'n lots of grass 'n no weather or animals or rustlers to spook the cows. They remember the friendly jawin' aroun' the campfires 'n the drinkin' and celebratin' at the end of the trail. They don't remember the bad parts."

"What are the bad parts?" Tom asked.

Curly looked at Tom, then Curly laughed and looked down at the ground in embarrassment.

"I don't know," he said. "I don't remember either. I reckon the truth of it is, I'm just as big a fool as any of them are."

Hilary did not intend to let this opportunity pass. If there was going to be a cattle drive, she was going to go on it. She had heard her father and the other men talk about the cattle drives of old. They had told so many wonderful stories about them that they had taken on a magical quality, and now that there was to be one, she wasn't going to let the opportunity pass.

Hilary said nothing to Gil about her plan to go on the drive. She knew that he would definitely be opposed to it. Actually, she felt that he really had no right to tell her whether or not she could go, since they weren't married yet. But she didn't want to argue with him about it, so she said nothing. Gil Carson wasn't the only person Hilary kept in the dark. She didn't talk to her father either. She just went to Sam and told him that she would be going with the trail herd as his assistant. She implied, though she didn't actually come right out and say it, that her father knew of her plans.

"I won't join you until midway the first day," she said. "I have several things that need to be taken care of at home before I can leave."

"Whenever you join, it'll be fine," Sam said.

Hilary didn't really have a lot to do. She just felt that her chances of getting away with it would be much better if she pretended that she wasn't going to go.

On the day of the drive the cowboys who were going were up before dawn. Hilary could hear them from her bed as they called out and shouted excitedly and laughed and whistled at horses and each other. They banged around the barn and corral, loading wagons and preparing equipment for the drive. Sam was getting ready too because Hilary could smell coffee and bacon from the cookhouse, and she knew that the cook had been up for hours already in order to prepare a breakfast for the men.

"Tom, yo Tom, take a look in that wagon and see if we packed away the spare harness," a voice called loudly. Hilary strained to hear Tom's answer, not because she was concerned as to whether the spare harness had been packed, but because she just wanted to hear Tom's voice. It came to her, clear and strong, and she felt a little shiver run down her spine.

The shouting and noise continued for another hour so that sleep was impossible, even for those who had no intention of going. Hilary didn't mind it, though, because she was enjoying the excitement, even from her bed. She wished she could get up and be a part of it, but she was afraid that if she did so, it would jeopardize her plans to go. She wondered how Gil could be so insensitive to the excitement. Hilary knew that Gil wasn't going. He was over in the big house, still in bed. Probably, he wasn't asleep, as it would be nearly impossible to sleep through all the noise.

Finally, after a good hour of preparation, during which time the men ate breakfast in shifts, the wagons and the horses started to move out. Just as they started, Hilary heard a light tapping on her door.

"Hilary?" her father called. "Hilary, girl, are you awake?"

"Did you really think I could sleep through all this?" Hilary asked.

Jake laughed. "I guess not."

"Come on in, Dad," Hilary called back to him. She sat up in bed to watch him as he came into her room.

"I just wanted to tell you we were leavin' now," Jake said. "And I didn't want to leave without tellin' you goodbye."

"You are looking forward to this, aren't you, Dad?" Hilary asked. She laughed. "I've been watching you. You're enjoying it."

"I have to confess that the thought of doing another trail drive is appealin' to me," Jake said. "I only wish I could feel better about it."

"Better about it? What do you mean? Dad, you aren't expecting some sort of trouble, are you?" Hilary asked.

"No, darlin', nothing like that," Jake said.

"Then what is it?"

Jake looked at Hilary for a long moment, then he summoned up a smile. "Nothin', darlin'. At least, nothin' you've got to worry your pretty head about. Now, I've got some cows to move. You be a good girl and go on back to sleep."

Hilary smiled. "That's what you used to tell me when I was just a little girl."

"You're still just my little girl as far as I'm concerned," Jake said.

Hilary lay back down after her father left her room, but she didn't go back to sleep. She was far too excited for that.

It was late morning by the time Hilary left the house. She kept herself occupied with busywork, both to help pass the time until she could leave and, also, to fool Gil into thinking everything was going along normally. She did a small wash and hung a few things out on the line, carefully choosing items that would dry quickly so she could take them in before she left. She waved gaily at Gil when she saw him get in the buggy for a drive into town. She had known that he was going to town, and that was what she had developed her plan around. She would leave while he was gone. He was going to stay in town overnight so by the time he returned tomorrow, she would already be with the drive and it would be too late for him to do anything.

Although the drive had been under way for three or four hours by the time Hilary left, she was able to cover the same ground on horseback in about forty-five minutes.

As she rode in the direction of the drive, it wasn't long before she could see a huge cloud of dust hanging just over the horizon.

She could sense the excitement even before she was close enough to hear anything. She could hear the sounds of the drive, the bawling and crying of cattle and the shouts and whistles of the wranglers, before she could actually make anything out in the dust cloud. Finally, she could see the cows moving forward relentlessly, prodded on by the drovers. She rode around the edge of the herd, keeping out of everyone's sight, and headed for the chuck wagon. The chuck wagon, she knew, would be far ahead of the herd, perhaps nearly to the location of the first night's camp.

"Lunch is generally what a drover can carry with him," Sam had explained to Hilary when he was telling her about the drive. "Generally it's no more 'n a piece of jerky and a swallow of water. Ever' now 'n then a handful of dried fruit. The only two meals the cowboys really get are breakfast and supper. Since them is the only two regular meals, I always do my best to make certain they are good ones. You see, what I do is, I fix 'em up a good breakfast, generally biscuits 'n gravy, or hotcakes, 'n lots o' hot, strong coffee. Then, after I've cleaned up, I break camp 'n go on ahead till I've gone whatever distance the trail boss tells me he plans to make that day. Then I make camp 'n start supper. Beans, most likely, or chili, or a good stew. If I got enough time, 'n I have a good, large piece of beef, why sometimes I even whip up a barbecue. Whatever it is, I try 'n be prompt, 'cause come nighttime the herd is caught up to the chuck wagon, 'n the drovers is ready for their vittles. That means I got to have it ready 'n waitin' for 'em, 'cause they generally ain't in no mood to wait."

"I'll help all I can," Hilary said. "Whatever you want me to do, I'll do."

That conversation had taken place on the day Hilary told Sam she would be helping him. Now she was reviewing the conversation in her mind. If she was going to be successful in convincing her father to let her stay, she was first going to have to convince Sam that she was a help rather than a hindrance.

Hilary passed the herd, riding far enough around the edge of it that no one saw her. Seeing the roundup in progress was much more exciting than listening to it from her room that morning. She could see the dark shapes of cattle moving under a billowing cloud of dust. She could see individual plumes of dust behind running horsemen as cowboys dashed hither and yon to keep the animals in check. She wished she could take the time to stop and study the herd to see if she could pick out her father and Curly and Tom. But she knew that she would have to ride hard to catch the chuck wagon if she meant to join up with Sam in time to be of any assistance for supper. So she rode on ahead, spurring her animal into a long, ground-eating lope which she knew he could keep up for hours. Finally she saw the wagon ahead, and she let out a little shout, then urged her horse into a gallop to catch up.

"You're just in time," Sam said when Hilary reached the wagon and swung down from her horse. Sam pointed to a sack of potatoes. "I'm gonna have a stew for supper. I need those potatoes peeled."

Hilary smiled. It wasn't much of a greeting but she would rather be greeted with the prospect of some work to do than to be told that she wasn't welcome. Willingly, she took the potatoes which were to be peeled and started to work.

Chapter Sixteen

Tom couldn't recall when he had been so tired. It was a bone-aching, back-breaking tired, and yet there was an exhilaration too that transcended the tiredness. The exhilaration came from the excitement of the drive and from the feeling of accomplishing some good, hard work. Tom wasn't the only one affected by the excitement of the day. He could see it in the eyes and on the faces of all the other drovers as well. The excitement was infectious and self-feeding and it seemed to grow as the day progressed. It was all around them, like the smell of the air before a spring shower, or the smell of wood smoke on a crisp fall day.

But it wasn't fall or spring. It was summer, and throughout the long, hot day the sun beat relentlessly down on the men and animals below. Mercifully, the yellow glare of the early summer sky mellowed into the steel blue of late afternoon by the time the herd reached the place where it would be halted for the night, and the cowboys were refreshed with a breath of cool air. To the west, the sun dropped all the way to the foothills, while to the east evening purple, like bunches of violets, gathered in the notches and timbered draws. Behind the setting sun, great bands of color spread out along the horizon. Those few clouds that dared to intrude on this perfect day were underlit by the sun and they glowed orange in the darkening sky.

Tom was watching the sunset with appreciation for its beauty when he heard Curly call to him.

"I'm over here, Curly," Tom called back.

Curly rode over to Tom, and the two of them looked toward the colorful display for a few, quiet moments.

"I've heard tell that the sunsets at sea are near 'bout as pretty as the ones we have out here," Curly said quietly, almost reverently. "But iffen you ask me, God'd be hard-pressed to make any sunsets better'n this here'n we're alookin' at."

"I've seen them at sea," Tom said. "And I agree with you, I've seen none more glorious than this."

Curly smiled. "Iffen someone would've asked me, I would'a told 'em you'd been to sea. I bet you been to Europe too."

"Yes," Tom said.

"You're a queer one for a cowboy, Tom Eddington. But they can't no one say you ain't earnin' your keep. Speakin' o' which, you ain't through for the day."

"Oh? Why, did I fail to do something?"

"Naw, you didn't leave nothin' undone," Curly said. "But don't go thinkin' you can get all cozied up by the campfire 'n lissen to the singin'. The boss has other plans for us."

"What sort of plans?"

"I figured the boss would go easy on you, bein' as this is your first drive 'n all, but what do you think? He's gone 'n tapped you 'n me for nighthawk."

"What do you mean, because this is my first drive?" Tom

asked with a laugh. "It's just about everyone's first drive, isn't it?"

"Yeah," Curly replied. "Yeah, I guess it is at that. Well, come on. Bein' as we got to nighthawk, we at least get to go to the head of the grub line. And I'm that hungry tonight that I could eat mutton."

"Mutton? Oh, wouldn't a couple of lamb chops be good right now, though?" Tom asked. "Maybe with a little mint jelly and asparagus."

"What?" Curly said. "Are you serious? Are you really talkin' 'bout eatin' one o' them wooly bastards?"

"Of course I'm serious," Tom said. "I think lamb is delicious."

Curly made a spitting noise, then shook his head. "Don't ever let a cowman hear you talk like that," he said. "I've known cowmen who would shoot a fella for such talk. You know, they's been many a range war fought between sheepmen and cowmen. Leastwise, iffen you are gonna carry on 'bout how good lamb is, you could have the decency to do it when I'm not aroun'. I wouldn't want to be hit by no stray bullets."

Tom laughed. "Thanks for the warning," Tom said. "I wonder what we will have. I'm a little hungry myself."

"Beans or stew," Curly said. "But either one is fine with me tonight."

Tom and Curly took their horses to the remuda and unsaddled them. They would draw fresh mounts for their night duty. They dropped their saddles where they could retrieve them easily after supper, took their mess kits out of their saddlebags, and sauntered over to the chuck wagon to get their meal.

"Uhmm, stew, from the smell of it," Curly said. They saw Sam stirring something in a big, steaming cauldron, and then they saw Sam's helper, a small thin cowboy who was busy with something at the far end of the wagon. Because of the late evening shadows, neither Curly nor Tom could see the assistant very clearly.

"You want to know how to get a few extras during a drive?" Curly asked.

"Extras? What sort of extras?"

"I'm talking about things like an extra biscuit, or an extra piece of pie . . . things like that."

"Sure," Tom said, smiling. "I'm always willin' to learn a few tricks of the trade."

"You got to make up to the cook's boy," he said. "The cooks nearly always got 'im some young boy helpin' out who really wants to cowboy, but helpin' the cook is as close as he can get. What you do is, you make friends with the boy, you know, let 'im ride your horse, show 'im a few things with a rope, stuff like that. Then you get to bein' sort of a hero to the boy, 'n the next thing you know, why, little extras start turnin' up in your plate." Curly pointed to the back of Sam's assistant. "Go on over there and get started."

"Oh, Curly, I don't know," Tom hesitated. "I'd feel a little foolish."

"What for?" Curly asked. "You don't have to feel foolish just to be nice to a body, do you?"

"No, of course not."

"Then go on over there like I told you. Besides, I never met anyone who could eat more'n me afore I met you anyhow. You gonna need all the extras you can get or you're likely to starve to death durin' this drive."

"All right," Tom said begrudgingly. Tom walked over to the slim assistant. "It certainly smells good around here," Tom said. "You must be doing a good job."

The assistant didn't answer, nor turn around. Tom looked back toward the head of the wagon where Curly was standing, holding his mess kit. Tom made a shrug with his shoulders, as if asking what he should do next, and Curly urged him on.

"I know you may think your job is unimportant," Tom said. "But believe me, it is every bit as important as mine, or any of the others. Why, without the knowledge that you and Sam were here working away to make certain that we had good, hot meals at breakfast and supper, I don't know if we could go on."

There was still no answer, so Tom cleared his throat and started again.

"Of course, I know you may not feel that way sometimes. When a boy has his heart set on riding herd, I guess it might be a little disappointing to be stuck on chuck wagon detail. But look, I'll tell you what I'll do. Anytime you would like to ride my horse, why you just come look me up and I'll be glad to oblige."

"Thanks," the assistant said, without turning around.

Tom was confused by the lack of response of the boy, and he wondered if he should say more. Then, fortunately Curly called to him.

"Come on, Tom, iffen we're gonna get re-mounts and back to the herd, we gotta eat now."

"Right," Tom said. He shrugged his shoulders and walked back to join Curly at the steaming cauldron.

"How'd you make out?" Curly asked.

"That's a quiet young man," Tom said. "I could hardly get a word out of him."

"Who?" Sam asked as he spooned a generous portion of stew into Tom's kit.

"The boy you got belly-robbin' for you," Curly said. "Me 'n Tom figured to make friends with him, but he didn't seem none too friendly."

Sam smiled broadly. "Tryin' to get inside for a little extra grub, are you?"

"Now Sam, you know me," Curly said.

"You mighty damned right I know you," Sam said. "That's why I said what I said. You don't think I'm some calf just birthed yesterday, do you? I been aroun' awhile. I know all the tricks you might come up with."

"Yeah? Well, it didn't work anyway," Curly said. "You done picked yourself one unsociable boy as your assistant."

"Well, now that's funny," Sam said, smiling again. " 'Cause I think my assistant is just about as sociable as they come."

"Is that so? Well, why don't you call him over here so we can get better acquainted," Curly suggested.

Sam smiled again and shouted to his assistant, "Come on over here and meet these two galoots who think you're so unsociable."

Sam's assistant sauntered over, then, at the front of the wagon, removed a hat which let a cascade of long strawberry blonde hair tumble down. Hilary laughed.

"Miss Hilary!" Curly gasped. "It's you?"

"One and the same," Hilary said.

Now it was Curly's time to laugh. "Well, I gotta say, you put one over on us, didn't she, pardner?"

"Yeah," Tom said. "Miss Hilary seems quite adept at amusing herself with cowboys."

A cool night breeze swept over Tom. It was not a strong breeze at all, for the nearby trees did no more than whisper with its passing, but its breath was pleasant against Tom's skin. In the distance a coyote barked, and he was answered by the long, plaintive howl of another.

Above Tom the white stars blazed bright, big and close. Before him, a large shuffling shadow within shadows, the herd stood, content for the moment with resting for the night. Behind him, a distance of nearly a mile, campfires winked tiny orange lights as the cowboys gathered around for their supper and evening discourse. Tom and Curly had already had their supper, and any discourse they would have now would have to be in the quiet shadows of the herd as they rode on their lonely night vigil.

Tom had spoken out harshly over Hilary's little trick. He was surprised to see tears spring to her eyes, and even more surprised to feel a sense of shame for his intemperate remark. Curly had looked at him in hurt surprise, and he knew that Curly couldn't understand what had motivated him to utter such a statement. He knew also that Curly wouldn't ask, for Curly was a strong believer in the right of privacy for any man. And yet, as long as Curly didn't know the reason, he would hold Tom in somewhat less esteem for hurting Hilary, for Curly loved her and didn't care to see her hurt.

Tom thought of Curly's love for Hilary. Curly might not even realize it, or, if he did recognize it, he might not be able to put his feelings into words, but he did love her, perhaps as much as Tom himself did.

A disquieting thought passed through Tom's mind. Had Curly and Hilary ever . . . ? No . . . surely not. And yet, she was not entirely without experience. That he had discovered on that wonderful morning at the line shack.

Abruptly, Tom jerked his head around, ostensibly looking toward the source of a sound, though in reality clearing his mind of the unpleasant thought of Hilary with other men.

The sound Tom heard was from iron striking stone. It came from Curly's horse as he rode up toward him.

"I've circled the entire herd," Curly said. "They was a handful on the other side was gettin' a bit antsy, but I pushed 'em on back into the herd. I figger they'll stay with the others, but we might want to take a look ever' now 'n ag'in."

"All right," Tom said.

The two men rode on slowly. The cattle lowed softly and the crickets chirped noisily. By a quirk of the evening breeze a cowboy's laughter carried to them.

After a long silent ride, Curly spoke.

"Pard, you was out of line to pass that remark about Miss Hilary tonight. I didn't say nothin' then, 'cause you are my friend 'n I didn't want to have words with you in public. But Miss Hilary is as fine a girl as there is to be had in the Arizona Territory, 'n you had no call to hurt her like you done."

Tom was silent under the quiet admonition of his friend. Finally, he heard himself asking words that pained him, even as he spoke them. From the moment the words were born on the tip of his tongue, he wished he could call them back, but it was too late. They were out.

"Curly, have you ever . . . been . . . with Hilary?"

"What?" Curly answered in a voice which, though quiet, dripped with cold anger.

"I mean . . ." Tom started, but Curly cut him off.

"I know what you mean," he said quietly. Curly stopped his horse. "You know, mister, it could just be that I have made a mistake about you. You might not be the kind of man I want to call pardner."

"Curly, I'm sorry," Tom said quickly, but Curly had already turned his horse and started to ride away. Curly stopped just long enough to call over his shoulder,

"I want you to know, I'd'a kilt any other son of a bitch that would'a asked me that question. Now, it's best you check on them cows what wandered off while ago," he said. "Make sure they're still with the herd."

Tom watched as Curly rode away then. He wanted to call him back and apologize to him again, to explain to him that he was in love with Hilary and that love made him speak as he did. He drew in a breath to call to him, but he let the breath die in a long, silent sigh. What good would it do to explain? Curly still wouldn't understand. Tom couldn't understand himself; why should he expect anyone else to?

The pots and pans were clean and the "necessaries" drawer straightened out, so at last Hilary's long day was finished. She hadn't even rolled out her bedroll yet, and it was late at night, and many of the cowboys had already fallen asleep, exhausted from the day's work.

"Hilary?"

"Oh, Dad," Hilary said, turning toward the sound of the voice. "I didn't know you were here."

"That makes us even. I didn't know you were here, either. What are you doing here?"

"I wanted to come."

"You might have ask me if you *could* come."

"Would you have let me?"

"I don't know. No, I don't think so!"

"Well then, so much for asking you."

"I wish you hadn't come. A trail drive is no place for a woman."

"Dad, haven't you told me the story many times of Mom going on the drive up to Denver with you?"

"That was different. She had me to look after her."

"How is it different? I have you to look after me too."

"It's not the same thing."

"Oh? Would you feel more secure about me if Gil were on the drive, looking out for me?"

"No, it isn't that. It's just that . . . well, this isn't an ordinary drive, darlin'. There's somethin' strange about this drive, 'n I'm not sure I like the smell of it."

"I know. You suggested that once before. But when I asked you if you expected trouble, you said no."

"Well, I don't expect trouble. That is, not the kind of trouble you think of when you think of trouble on a trail drive. But there's trouble and then there's *trouble*. And if it comes, I'd just as soon you not be around."

"Dad, you aren't going to send me back now, are you? Sam is counting on me. He thought I was coming along, so he didn't bother to hire anyone to help him. It's either me or you'll have to pull someone off the drive. Have you got enough men to do that?"

"No, and you know I don't." Big Jake sighed and ran his hand through his hair. "Hilary, I don't like bein' put on a spot like this."

"I know you don't, Dad, and I hated to do it. But I wanted to go on this drive and I knew that if I asked you, you would probably say no."

"You're right. I would have. I can't understand Gil letting you come."

"Gil didn't let me come," Hilary said.

"What do you mean?"

"I just came. Gil doesn't know anything about it."

Jake laughed. "You mean Gil doesn't even know you left?"

"No, and I doubt if he'll find out before tomorrow. He went into Flagstaff, and I think he plans to spend the night there."

Jake laughed again. "In that case, darlin', stay with the drive. Stay with the drive and Gil be damned!"

It was with some confusion that Hilary lay out her sleeping roll that night. She was glad that her father had consented to her staying with the drive, but confused by his strange reaction to the knowledge that her presence was secret from Gil. Her father had never been openly hostile toward her association with, or engagement to, Gil Carson, but he had never been warm to it either. Tonight he had come the closest he had ever come to letting his true feelings be known. It was now obvious that her father did not like Gil.

The question was, why not?

After all, Gil was everything a girl could want in a man. He was handsome, almost to a fault. He was ambitious, and his ambitions had already borne fruit, for he was the manager of one of the largest and most productive ranches in the country. It would seem to Hilary that any father would be more than pleased to have a daughter in love with such a man.

In love with?

At that thought, Hilary's musings stopped. She was engaged to Gil, and she was going to marry him. But was she in love with him?

Of course she was in love with him. Why else would she have agreed to marry him? She was in love with him, and had been from the very beginning. Any doubts she might feel now were caused by her strange reactions to Tom Eddington. Surely, Tom Eddington had caused her some degree of confusion. After all, she was strangely attracted to him. More than attracted, she admitted, for she had willingly, even eagerly given herself to him, not once, but twice. Why?

Tom Eddington wasn't handsome.

Tom Eddington wasn't wealthy.

Tom Eddington wasn't even ambitious, or he would certainly not be working as a mere cowboy.

In fact, Tom Eddington might even be fleeing some social or civil indiscretion that had occurred back East. So what was there about him that held such a strange attraction for her?

Hilary could not answer that question. She knew only that, for whatever reason, she had to get Tom's presence out of her mind, for if she didn't, any chance of a happy marriage to Gil Carson would be forever destroyed.

Chapter Seventeen

Jake left Hilary and walked through the sleeping men, beyond the chuck wagon, even beyond the remuda, before he found a rock that was just about the right size for sitting. He sat on the rock, pulled the makings from his pocket and rolled a cigarette. He lit up, then, savoring the satisfying taste of a good smoke, he thought of Hilary's remark about her mother.

Hilary reminded Jake of Maggie. Hilary looked so much like her that sometimes, in the shadow of an afternoon or in a certain trick of light, a sharp pain would come to his heart, because he could almost believe that Hilary was Maggie come back to him.

They were more alike than mere lookalikes, though. They were alike in spirit and personality. Maggie had been the daughter of a ranch foreman, just as Hilary was. And Maggie had made many drives with him.

In fact, as Jake looked around, he realized that it was very near here that he first met Maggie.

It was late in the fall when Jake and Sam reached

Arizona, following their long trek from Texas. It could have been late October, November, or even early December. It had been a long time since either man had seen a calendar, so they could only guess at the date.

Jake had thought nothing could ever take the place of Texas. He had fought a war in defense of Texas. Yet, from the moment he first set foot in Arizona, he knew that he had found a new place, a wild place, to love.

From the time they entered Arizona, they were surrounded by majestic mountain ranges. Ahead of them rose the rugged Mazatzals, while to their left, the towering cones of Four Peaks. They had passed through Sierra Blanca, and to their right was the lofty, snow-capped Mogollon Mesa. The Mogollon Mesa stretched for three hundred miles, and among its jagged peaks and purple canyons, he was to eventually find Turquoise Ranch.

But not for a while. Jake's days of adventure didn't end when he left Texas.

Their horses were travel worn and tired, but Jake and Sam pushed on. They had heard of a small town ahead, and they hoped to find some employment nearby, because they were nearly out of food and money.

"We just about got us enough for a plate of beans, a couple of drinks and some grain for our horses," Sam said. "But after that, we better get us somethin' fast, or, boss, me 'n you's gonna starve."

Jake chuckled. "Sam, I don't hardly see how you can call me boss now. I don't have anything to boss."

"You got me," Sam said. " 'N I reckon we'll find somethin' pretty soon."

"I'll give you this, Sam. You got confidence, if you got nothing else."

They rode on down the trail toward the town that they

hoped was just over the next rise, or perhaps beyond the next hill.

It was four more hills before the town was encountered, if the place could be called a town. There were only two streets, and they formed an X, with the bulk of the buildings near the crossroad. The buildings were low and wood, though several of them had wooden fronts which rose higher than the buildings themselves. A raised, wooden sidewalk graced both sides of the street for the length of the nicer of the buildings, but after a short distance, the wooden sidewalk ended, and there was nothing but a small dirt path in front of the shabbier buildings of the town. The biggest and most prominent building was a saloon, identified by the sign painted on front as, "The Gilded Cage."

"Well, I reckon that's as good a place as any for a fella to get a plate full of beans and somethin' to cut this dust," Sam suggested.

Jake agreed, and the two men tied their horses off in front of the building and went inside.

There were more than a dozen men inside, and they looked up with unbridled curiosity as Jake and Sam went in. In a town this remote, no stranger passed unnoticed. The bartender came over and passed a damp rag across the bar in front of them.

"What'll it be?" he asked. That was the only question voiced, but his eyes asked volumes.

"Whiskey, 'n a little grub, if you serve vittles here," Jake said.

"Beans," the bartender said. "With a hot pepper for seasonin'."

"Sounds fine," Jake agreed.

There was a sudden fanfare of guitar music, and Jake and Sam turned to see a Mexican man sitting on a stool, holding a guitar. A moment later a very pretty young woman came out, and began a flamenco dance to the young man's accompaniment.

"Well now," Sam said, smiling. "I'd say this is a right friendly little town, to set up a welcome like this for us."

The girl proved to be even more friendly, for after her dance, she answered Sam's smile and came to sit with the two men. Her name was Rosita, and she was the sister of the guitar player. Before too long, Sam discovered just how friendly Rosita could be, and he went to a small room in the back with her, while Jake obligingly offered to take care of the horses.

It was then that Jake saw Maggie for the first time. It was also nearly the last time, for Maggie and an older man who was with her were standing near the wall of the livery stable with their hands raised. Two masked men were holding drawn guns on them, and one of the gunmen was relieving Maggie's companion of his wallet.

"Ha," the gunman who had just taken the wallet said. "What did I tell you? He just sold five hunnert head of B Bar T cattle. I knew he'd be carryin' a fat wallet."

"That's not my money," the robbery victim said. "That belongs to Mr. Turner."

"Wrong," the robber said with a laugh. "It belongs to us now."

"I know who you two men are," Maggie said. "You're Billy Bates, and you're Charley Penrod. Dad, you remember. They're the two who ran off last year. They stole a couple of horses too, if I recall."

"Charley, what the hell?" one of the gunmen said, and it was clear by the expression in his voice that her recognition had disturbed him. "She knows who we are!"

"Shut up, you damn fool!" Charley replied. His voice, like that of his companion, was muffled by the hood he wore over his head.

"I see you aren't much better at robbing than you were at punchin' cattle," the girl's father said.

"You know the trouble with you two? You got too good'a memory, and too big a mouth. We're gonna have to kill the both of you."

"No you don't," Jake called. He had waited until now to make his presence known, just to make certain that things were what they seemed to be.

"Charley, shoot 'im!" Billy yelled, and both robbers turned toward Jake with their guns blazing. Jake had already pulled his gun before he challenged them, and he stood there as the two men shot wildly, and returned fire with deadly accuracy. Both men went down under his bullets.

"Are you two all right?" Jake asked, holstering his pistol after the two men were down.

"Yes, thanks to you," the older man said. He smiled and extended his hand. "My name is Abel Cole, mister. This here is my daughter, Maggie. I don't know that I've ever seen better shooting."

"The name is Jake St. John, and I got lucky, that's all," Jake said.

"No, sir. We got lucky when you came along. Tell me, Mr. St. John. Is there anything I can do for you? I'm sure Mr. Turner would like to reward you for what you did here."

"Mr. Turner?"

"He's the owner of the B Bar T ranch. I'm his foreman."

Jake smiled. "Well sir, Mr. Cole, my partner and I could sure use a job. Do you think you could use a couple of good hands?"

"You know anything about cattle?"

"We're from Texas," Jake said.

Abel Cole laughed. "I reckon that's recommendation enough for me. Where is your pard now?"

"He's tied up for the moment," Jake said, smiling and looking at Maggie really closely for the first time. What a beautiful girl she was.

"Miss, you wouldn't be married or anything, would you?" he asked, tipping his hat politely to her.

"Married?" Maggie replied. She smiled. "No, Mr. St. John, I'm not married."

"Engaged, or spoken for?"

Maggie laughed. "No, I'm not spoken for either. I'm my own woman, Mr. St. John."

"That's good," Jake said. "That's real good."

Jake decided then and there that this was the woman he was going to marry.

"Jake? Jake, is that you?" Sam called. Sam's voice brought Jake back from his memories, and he looked around to see his friend walking toward him.

"Yeah," Jake said. "It's me."

"I thought I saw you walking over here. You got a smoke?"

Jake took the makings from his pocket and handed them to Sam.

"I hope you don't mind too much my lettin' the girl come along," Sam said. "But the truth is, I'd rather have her along with us than back there with Carson."

"It won't be long, Sam, till she's with Carson all the time. She's goin' to marry him, you know."

"I keep hopin' somethin' will come up to prevent that," Sam said. He put the rolled cigarette in his mouth and lit it. " 'Cause iffen it don't, I'm just likely to prevent it myself."

"Sam, all we can do is stand by and watch," Jake said. "Hilary is a full-grown woman now. She's got her own mind to make up 'n her own life to live. If she decides she wants to live it with Gil Carson, I don't really reckon there's much we can do about it."

"Carson's stealin' Turquoise blind, you know," Sam said.

Jake sighed. "Yeah, I know."

"He's real slick with it," Sam said. "But he's gonna get caught, 'n when he does, the owners are gonna come down on him like a duck on a June bug. There ain't no way you're gonna escape that either."

"I know that too," Jake said.

"Seems to me like the best thing to do would be just to take Carson outa the picture."

"You mean kill him?"

"Killin' ain't no stranger to either one of us, Jake."

"I know. But neither of us have ever killed except in a gun battle."

"Well, I figure to just prod the son of a bitch till he draws on me," Sam said. "Hell, I might even give the son of a bitch the first shot. Then I'll kill him."

"He's too slick for that," Jake said. "And I don't know that I want him dead. I'd rather let him live and let Hilary see him for what he is."

"Do you reckon she will?"

"She'll come to her senses, Sam. I just know she will."

Gil Carson, the subject of their conversation, was spending the night in Flagstaff just as Hilary had known he would. What Hilary did not know was that he was not spending it alone. He was in the company of Bonnie Tyre, a soiled dove whose company he had enjoyed before.

Bonnie led Gil up the back stairs of Cahill's, and down a long, narrow hallway to the room that was hers. She lit a lantern as soon as she was inside, and the room was bathed in a quivering bubble of golden light. She smiled at Gil and pointed to the table.

"You know where it is, love," she said. "You've been here often enough."

"Yeah," Gil said. "I know where it is."

Gil reached for the whiskey and two glasses. He pulled the cork with his teeth and splashed the liquor into the glasses. Bonnie reached for one of them.

"Unh-uh," Gil said, holding the glass away from her. "Get undressed first."

"My," Bonnie said, smiling seductively at him. "You are hungry tonight, aren't you?"

"Just do it," Gil said.

Bonnie undid the yellow ribbon which held her hair, and she shook her head to let it tumble down. It fell softly across her shoulder. Then she began removing her clothes, never losing the self-assured smile. She pushed her dress down her body until it fell to the floor in a pool of silk, shimmering in the soft light from the lantern.

Gil watched, fascinated by the sight, as he was treated to the expanse of smooth skin, firm, well-rounded breasts and tightly drawn nipples. His gaze shifted to the small triangle of hair at the junction of her legs.

"Do you like what you see?" Bonnie asked.

"Yeah," Gil said.

"Show me how you like it."

Gil slipped out of his own clothes as Bonnie picked her dress up from the floor and folded it neatly. When she turned toward him again, her body was subtly lighted by the lamp, and she licked her lips seductively as she raised her arms to invite him to her.

Gil walked over to her and, fully aroused, pulled her to him, pressing his manhood against her, kissing her open mouth with his own, feeling her tongue dart against his. He moved her toward the bed, then climbed in after her, and without preliminary, crawled on top of her and entered her.

Bonnie warmed as quickly as Gil, and she received him happily, wrapping her legs around him, meeting his lunges by pushing against him. She lost herself in the pleasure of the moment until a few minutes later she could feel him jerking and thrusting in savage splendor as he obtained the release he so ardently sought.

Several minutes later, after they had finished making love, Gil walked over to the window and pulled the shade to one side to look out onto the street below. Behind him the bed squeaked as Bonnie sat up.

"Gil?" she said softly.

"Yeah," Gil answered without looking around.

"Gil, is it true you're going to marry the daughter of your ranch foreman?"

"Where did you hear that?" Gil asked.

"I heard it," Bonnie said. "I heard it from the woman she bought material from to make a wedding dress. Is it true?"

"What if it is?" Gil asked.

"You . . . you promised to marry me," Bonnie said in a quiet, hurt voice.

Gil turned toward her and laughed, a laugh without mirth.

"You?" he said. "Did you honestly think I would marry you?"

"You told me you would," Bonnie said.

"You shouldn't have believed me."

"Why not?"

"Because they were lies, told in a whore's bed," Gil said cruelly. "You've been a whore long enough now, you should be able to recognize them."

"I . . . I thought you were different," Bonnie said. "I thought I meant something to you."

Gil grabbed himself obscenely. "This is all you meant to me," he said. "And this is all you'll ever mean." He smiled. "But don't be sad. I'll still come to see you, even after I'm married. Nothing need change between us."

"You mean . . . you want to see me even after you're married?"

"Sure, why not?"

Shutters seemed to descend in Bonnie's eyes, and the windows that had opened to her soul suddenly closed. For a few moments, she had been vulnerable. But no more. Now she moved behind those shutters and covered herself up so that she could never be hurt again.

"Sure," she repeated. "Why not? Only it will cost you more."

"It will cost me more? Why?"

"I charge more when I have to go to bed with someone who is a son of a bitch," Bonnie said flatly.

Chapter Eighteen

The cattle drive continued without incident except for long, tiring days in the saddle and nights that were too short and too hot to allow the weary cowboys much sleep.

Hilary worked just as hard as any of the cowboys, and Sam paid her the supreme compliment of telling her that he had never been blessed with an assistant who was as good a worker as she was. But Sam didn't just tell Hilary, he told her father as well, and that made Hilary very glad about having come, for she knew that she was carrying her own weight. She commented on it.

"Oh, I'd say you're more than carrying your own weight," Sam said. He chuckled. "Your pa knows it too, or he would have probably sent you back by now. He won't tolerate laziness, 'n I don't reckon he'd put up with it in his own daughter any more'n he would in anyone else."

"Sam, you've known Dad a long time, haven't you?"

"I reckon I've known him awhile. We was friends even before the war."

"Dad never talks about the war," Hilary said.

"It ain't a chapter in our history folks need to be proud of," Sam said. "Neighbor fought ag'in neighbor, brother ag'in brother. 'Twas little honor in that war, girl."

"Were you a cook during the war?"

Sam chuckled. "Girlie, I was a little bit of ever'thin', and so were we all. We was irregulars, 'n we was behind the enemy lines most o' the time."

"What did you do behind the enemy lines?"

Sam chuckled. "We did things that would o' got us put in prison for sure durin' peacetime. We robbed a few Yankee banks. Only, when we come home, we discovered that the Yankees had done the same to us, 'n they weren't ready to give it back. So we took it back. We rustled some of our cattle back from the Yankees."

"You . . . you rustled cattle?" Hilary asked.

"That we did, girl. But you gotta understand, it was rightfully ours, even if the law didn't see it like that."

"Is Dad still rustling cattle?" Hilary asked quietly.

Sam looked at Hilary with a sharp expression on his face.

"Where did you hear that?" he asked.

"I didn't hear it anywhere," Hilary said. "It's just something I want to know."

"Look here, girl, you'd best be askin' your dad some o' these questions," Sam said. "It ain't my place to be answerin' for him."

"I was just wondering, that's all," Hilary said.

"Well, quit your wonderin' 'n make yourself useful. Here, go get some water," Sam said to change the subject.

Hilary didn't ask any more after that, because she didn't want to upset Sam. And in truth, though she didn't admit it even to herself, she wasn't sure she wanted to hear the answers that Sam might decide to give.

In the meantime she was genuinely enjoying the drive

despite the hard work and the long hours. In fact, there was only one troublesome note, and that was Tom Eddington.

Hilary had to see Tom every day. She couldn't avoid him; he came through the grub line twice a day. She couldn't carry on a sustained fight with him either without arousing some questions, so she decided to try and get along with him. She changed her tactics. Instead of being cold to him as she had been at first, she started going out of her way to be pleasant.

When Hilary first changed her attitude toward him, Tom was a bit wary of her conduct. He didn't believe her. After all, she had been practically hostile to him ever since that morning in the line shack.

But Hilary's persistence paid off, and Tom was finally convinced that she was genuinely changing her attitude toward him. Once he was over the fear of being further hurt by her he was able, like any of the other cowboys, to banter about and tease her.

But the banter and teasing was bittersweet for both of them. Hilary was able to see Tom's great sense of humor and fair play, and that, added to all his other qualities, made him all the more desirable to her. Tom saw a new side of Hilary, a warm, tender side to go along with her beauty and vivaciousness, and it made him want her all the more, even though he knew that wasn't possible. Because of the bittersweetness suffered by both, it had almost been easier on them when she and Tom were hostile, for then they could fool themselves into thinking that they didn't like each other. Now they knew what a lie that was. Not like each other? The truth, pure and unrestrained, was that they loved each other.

Hilary loved Tom so much that if he came to her now and asked her to marry him as he had on that wonderful morning in the line shack, she believed she would gladly leave with him. If it meant leaving Turquoise Ranch forever, if it meant disgracing her name, no matter what it meant, she would leave with him if he would only ask.

For Tom's part, he loved Hilary so much that he was ready to go to her and tell her that he was the owner of Turquoise Ranch. He would lay it before her feet if only she would marry him. And yet, despite the mental anguish being suffered by each of them, they remained mute as to their actual feelings. They each suffered alone.

One night, several weeks into the drive, Hilary lay on her bedroll trying to go to sleep. A campfire burned cheerily in the center of the cowboy's circle, about thirty yards away. Most of the cowboys were already asleep because morning came early and the chance to rest was rarely squandered. A few cowboys were still awake, though, and Hilary could see them moving around as their shadows crossed back and forth in front of the flickering flames.

"Hey, Harley Mack, I thought you had nighthawk," one of the cowboys called to another.

"Naw," Harley Mack answered. "Tom's got it. I had it last night."

"Well, come on over here, Bob's telling us 'bout the girls he's gonna fix us up with in Phoenix."

"Ha, I can just see the girls he can fix us up with."

Harley Mack joined the others and then their conversation grew so quiet that Hilary couldn't hear it, though she could hear the occasional bursts of laughter which came from the men.

Hilary turned and positioned herself a dozen times, but no matter what she did, sleep refused to come to her on this night. Finally, she decided to get up and take a walk in hopes that the night air would soon make her sleepy. She found herself walking toward the remuda, and almost before she realized what she was doing, she saddled a horse. Moments later she was riding out toward the herd.

After a minute or two Hilary was completely away from the camp, swallowed up by the blue velvet of night. The night air caressed her skin like fine silk, and it carried on its breath the scent of pear cactus flowers. Overhead the stars glistened like diamonds and in the distance mountain peaks rose in great and mysterious dark slabs against the midnight sky. Hilary was aware of the quiet herd, with cows standing motionless in rest. An owl landed nearby and his wings made a soft *whirr* as he flew by. He looked at her with great round, glowing eyes, as if he had been made curious by her presence.

Hilary rode quietly for several moments until she came to a small grass-covered knoll. Here, she heard a splashing, bubbling sound, and she knew that she was hearing the swift flowing mountain stream which had caused them to choose this as the camping spot for the night. The stream provided water for men and cattle. Hilary had seen it when they first arrived, for she had gotten water for cooking from it. In fact, the chuck wagon was parked beside it. But that was at another location. Hilary had not seen the stream here.

Hilary got off her horse and walked to the top of the grassy knoll to look at the water. Here the stream was fairly wide and strewn with rocks. The water bubbled white as it tumbled over and rushed past the glistening rocks. The white feathers in the water glowed brightly in the moonlight while the water itself winked blackly, and the result was an exceptionally vivid contrast which made the stream even more beautiful at night than it was by day.

Hilary felt drawn to the water, and she walked all the way down the knoll until she found a soft wide spot in the grass. She sat down and pulled her knees up under her chin and looked at the water. The constant chatter of the brook soothed her, and she sat there in contemplative silence.

"I thought it was you I saw ride over this way. At least, I hoped it was."

Hilary was startled by the sudden intrusion, and she turned to see Tom standing at the top of the knoll behind her.

"Aren't you supposed to be watching the herd?" Hilary asked.

"They're quiet," Tom said. "What are you doing out here so late?"

"I couldn't sleep," Hilary said.

"As hard as you've been working and as early as you have to get up, I can't imagine you having trouble sleeping."

"I guess I just have too much on my mind."

"Are you thinking about your wedding?"

In fact, Hilary had been thinking about her father, and wondering whether or not he was involved in dishonest dealings with the owner of the ranch. But she didn't want to tell Tom that, so she let him think that he had guessed the truth.

"Yes," she said. "I was thinking about the wedding."

Tom walked down from the top of the knoll, then sat beside her, even though she hadn't invited him.

"I've been thinking about it too," he said.

"You've been thinking about my wedding?" Hilary asked with a little laugh. "Why?"

"Because it should be *our* wedding. You should be marrying me, Hilary."

Hilary gasped. Those were just the words she had wanted to hear Tom say, though she had become convinced that he would never utter them again after her rejection of his earlier proposal. And yet, hearing them again, she knew that she would have to reject them this time, just as she did before. Only now it wasn't just because of Gil. It was also because of her father. If her father was mixed up in something dishonest, if there was to be scandal and disgrace, then she would have to stick by him.

"Tom," she said quietly. "Oh, Tom, you know that can never be."

"It can be, Hilary. Believe me, it can."

"Tom, there are things you don't know, things you can't understand," Hilary started.

"Perhaps I know and understand more than you think," Tom replied. "Anyway, I understand the most important thing. I understand that I love you."

"Oh, Tom," Hilary said, and the words may have been a sob, but they died in her throat, for at that very moment Tom moved to her, pressing his lips against hers.

As before, a tidal wave of pleasure washed over Hilary, and all her resolve not to get involved with Tom again, all her carefully reasoned logic for staying clear of him, dissolved under the fire of his kisses.

Tom pushed her down gently until she could feel the soft mat of grass beneath her. His lips broke contact with her lips, then traced a fiery path down to her throat, in the process melting any resistance she may have tried to mount. As had happened in the line shack, Hilary discovered how helpless she was before such a determined onslaught. She was totally subservient to Tom's desires, molded to do his wishes, bent to his will. When his fingers moved to open her shirt and she felt the cool night breeze against her naked skin, she was aware of nothing save the pleasure of the moment. Tom's hands found Hilary's soft, warm breasts and he moved to them with the gentleness of a new love, but the confidence of one who had been there before. Tenderly, he stroked the swollen, straining nipples with skilled fingers, and Hilary's body melted into a hot, quivering thing of desire.

"Tom," Hilary finally managed to say, but whether it was a weak entreaty for him to stop, or an urgent plea for him to go on, she couldn't be sure.

Tom continued to press his kisses upon her body, and her skin tingled as if it were being caressed by the delicate wings of a thousand butterflies, until suddenly, and with some surprise, she realized that she was now totally nude. Hilary had not remembered the actual removal of her clothes; she had only been cognizant of the ecstasy of the moment, not of the actual events. Now she was naked, and she could feel the soft breeze on her breasts and thighs, and she thought dimly that nothing could be more right.

Tom raised up from her long enough to remove his own clothes, and though he wasn't touching her with his hands, his hold over her was just as powerful, for she watched him with wide, hungry eyes, and was held mesmerized by the ecstasy of the moment. When, a short time later, she could see his smooth skin and rippling muscles gleaming in the bright moonlight, her passion was raised to even greater heights.

Tom dropped back down beside her then, and put one hand lightly on her breast, then moved it across the silken skin of her body until it rested just inside her thigh. All the while the swift mountain stream continued to splash on, seeming not oblivious to the lovers but supportive, and proving it by producing beautiful music to accompany them.

Tom moved over her, poised for the final connection, yet denying it to her. Hilary positioned herself for him, then reached for him, to urge him on.

"Tell me you love me," Tom said, pulling himself away slightly.

"Oh, Tom, please, what are you doing?" Hilary asked. "Do you know how you are torturing me?"

"Tell me you love me," Tom said again.

"Yes," Hilary said. "Yes, I love you, Tom Eddington. I love you, I love you, I love you!"

With Hilary's admission of love, the connection was made, and with a happy cry, Hilary rose up to meet him.

She felt his weight and breathed the male scent of him, and was overwhelmed by the liquid fire which rushed through her body as he loved her. He thrust against her again and again, and Hilary abandoned all thought of Gil and the ranch and even of her father's possible trouble. She thought only of the moment and of the fact that she loved Tom Eddington more than she ever dreamed it would be possible to love any man.

Then, deep inside, she felt the beginnings of that eagerly sought goal. It started small, then began moving out like one of the whirlpools in the stream beside them, spinning faster and faster, ever faster, until finally it crashed over her in one mighty torrent of pleasure. She felt a million tiny pins pricking her skin and she nibbled at Tom's lips and whimpered in the joy of her rapture.

As she coasted down from that summit she opened her eyes and looked into the night sky above, only to see a falling star. The jolt of a second orgasm hit her then, and she was lifted up, out of her body, high into the night sky where her spirit soared on the golden flame of that streaking heavenly body, and in that moment she captured a piece of the rapture to hold in her heart forever.

Tom managed to join her while she was streaking through the stars, and Hilary knew that for the rest of her life she could only hope to equal this moment. It would never be surpassed.

* * *

Tom's horse and Hilary's were standing together when the two lovers walked back to the top of the knoll. Tom held Hilary's horse while she climbed on, then he swung onto his own horse.

"You must get back and get some sleep," Tom said. "Your mornings come awful early."

"Only if you ride back toward the camp with me," Hilary said.

Tom clucked at his horse and the two of them rode slowly, quietly, back along the path Hilary had taken when she rode out. The cattle were still standing quietly, patiently, waiting for the morning, when they would be urged on.

"Hilary?"

"Yes."

"I . . . I won't hold you to what I forced you to say a few moments ago. I took unfair advantage of you."

"Are you telling me that you want me to take it back, Tom Eddington?"

"What? No, of course not," Tom said, startled by her reply. "It's just that, well, as badly as I want to hear those words, I want to hear them spoken in a way that will tell me they are from the heart, and not from the heat of the moment."

"Very well," Hilary said. "If that's what you want, that's what you shall hear. I love you, Tom Eddington."

Tom stopped his horse and looked at Hilary with a shocked expression on his face.

"Do you . . . do you mean that?" he asked.

"Yes."

"Are you sure?"

Hilary laughed. "Do you want me to shout it out loud and start a stampede?"

"What? No! I mean yes! I mean, I don't care how you

say it, just as long as it's true. Oh, Hilary, do you mean it? Do you really mean it?"

"Yes."

"Will you marry me?"

"Yes," Hilary said.

"I'm asking you to give up a lot, you know," he said. "You are giving up the chance of being the wife of the manager of the ranch, just to marry a common cowboy."

"Tom Eddington, whatever you are," Hilary said, "you are no common cowboy."

"When will you marry me?" Tom asked. "Right away, I hope. How about Phoenix? Will you marry me in Phoenix?"

Hilary laughed. "My, you are anxious, aren't you?"

"Yes, I'm anxious. I've got you now and I don't want to lose you, ever."

Hilary reached over and put her hand on Tom's arm.

"You won't lose me, darling. But we can't get married in Phoenix. I owe it to Gil to at least tell him to his face that I'm marrying you. You understand that, don't you?"

"Yes," Tom admitted. "I suppose I do. Though I must confess that the wait is going to be even harder now."

"Maybe so," Hilary said. "But, if it's worth having, it's worth waiting for, they always say."

"I'll wait. Not gladly, but I'll wait."

"Oh. And Tom? Let's not tell anyone about this. At least not yet."

"Not even your dad?"

"Especially not Dad," Hilary said. She laughed. "Although I daresay he'll be a lot happier over the idea of my marrying you than he ever was over the prospect of my marrying Gil."

"All right, I won't tell him," Tom said. "But Hilary, you must let me tell Curly. He's misunderstood something recently, and it's put a strain on our friendship. I think telling him would clear a few things up, and I value our friendship. I value it a great deal."

"All right," Hilary said. "You can tell him if you will swear him to secrecy."

"You don't have to worry about that any," Tom said. "I've never known a man better able to keep secrets than Curly. He won't say a word."

"Tell him if you must," Hilary said. They reached the edge of the herd, and from here they could see the soft glow of the campfire, now burning low after the last of the cowboys were turned in for the night. "Here is where I'll be leaving you."

"Hilary, before you go . . ."

"Yes?"

"Let me hear it one more time."

"Hear what?" Hilary teased.

"Let me hear it. It'll warm me for the rest of the night."

Hilary looked at Tom and smiled.

"I love you."

Chapter Nineteen

Though Hilary didn't tell anyone of her change in wedding plans, it was difficult to keep her new spirit of happiness away from Sam. After all, they rode together day in and day out, sitting side by side on the seat of the chuck wagon. They worked together getting the meals prepared, and when Hilary broke into spontaneous song or made jokes or went on about the glory of the sunset or the beauty of the flowers or the majesty of the mountains, Sam knew that something had changed. Finally, Sam could take it no longer, and he asked Hilary what was going on.

"What do you mean?" Hilary answered. She was mixing dough for biscuits, and she had flour up to her elbow and a bit on the end of her nose. "What makes you think something is going on?"

"Because," Sam said, "if there is anybody in this world who knows you as well as your pa, it's me. I know you, and I know when something is going on, and I tell you now, something has happened. Girl, you have changed since this drive began."

"Oh, I've changed have I?" Hilary teased. "Well, tell me, Mr. Sam Potter, have I changed for the better or for the worse?"

"For the better, I'd say," Sam said. "You seem a mite chirpier. A lot happier."

"Sam, you are looking at a girl who is in love," Hilary said easily. "Any change you see is due to the most wonderful man in the world."

"Wonderful man, huh?"

"A marvelous man," Hilary said.

"I wish I could see some of what you see in him."

"Oh? You don't agree with me?"

"Girl, it ain't my place to say nothin'."

"Say it, Sam. You're part of the family."

"You're makin' a mistake marryin' up with that galoot."

"Why do you say that?" Hilary asked anxiously.

"Because Gil Carson is a low-down excuse for a man, and I wouldn't . . ."

"Oh," Hilary said with a laughing sigh of relief. "It's not Gil Carson I'm talking about," Hilary said, interrupting Sam in mid-tirade.

"What? Look here, girl, are you tellin' me you are not goin' to marry Gil Carson?"

"That's what I'm saying," Hilary said.

"Does your pa know this, girl?"

"No," Hilary laughed. "He doesn't know a thing about it. My true love is a secret from everyone."

"Who is it? Tell me."

"We promised each other we wouldn't tell," Hilary said.

"We who?" Sam asked in exasperation. "Girl, you can't keep me in suspense like this. It would've been best if you'd never said a word."

"Maybe you're right. He's going to tell one friend, so I see no reason why I can't tell you," Hilary went on.

"Girl, if you don't tell me soon, I'm gonna bust a gut," Sam said. "Who in tarnation are you in love with?"

"You have to promise you won't tell Dad."

"Why do I have to promise that? Don't you think your pa has a right to know?"

"Of course he should know. But I want to surprise him. I've always suspected he wasn't really happy about my engagement to Gil anyway."

"Ha!" Sam said. "You sure got that right. Fac' is, he's been miserable over your engagement to that no-'count, Now, *who* are you in love with?"

"You haven't promised."

"All right, all right, I promise!" Sam said, holding up his right hand in the approximation of an oath. "Now, who is it?"

"It's Tom Eddington," Hilary said.

Sam smiled broadly and slapped his hand against his thigh.

"Ha!" he said. "I know'd it. I know'd it all along, that it was Tom Eddington."

"Oh? And how did you know?"

"I could tell by the way that you was shootin' moon eyes at him."

"Moon eyes?"

"Yeah," Sam said. "Just like the ones your mama used to give to your pa."

"Did Mama look at Pa like that?"

"That she did, girl, that she did."

"Tell me about Mama."

"Tell you about your mama? Shucks, girl, what can I tell you about your mama? You remember her well enough."

"No, I don't mean the mama that I knew. I mean the one before. Before I was born. Before she and Dad were married. Tell me about her then. Was she as pretty then as she was when I knew her?"

Sam smiled and got a faraway look in his eyes.

"Girl, your mama was that pretty that she could pure take a man's breath away. She had eyes the color of a frosty morning sky and hair as golden as ripe wheat. Beautiful? I'll say she was beautiful."

"Did Dad really rescue her on the very first day he ever saw her?"

"I'll say he did. Two desperadoes waylaid your mama and your gran'pa. Your gran'pa, you see, was foreman for old Frank Turner, of the B Bar T ranch. Mr. Turner was near on to seventy by then, 'n 'bout feeble. That left your gran'pa to run the place, so he was more'n a foreman. He was like a general manager. Anyway, he had brought in some cattle to sell, and Bates and Penrod, two no-'counts who'd worked at the B Bar T for a bit before they run off, jumped him. They knew about the cattle sale, and they were aimin' to take all the money."

"And Dad stopped them?"

"That he did. Your pa always was that slick with a pistol that he could'a earned his keep as a gun for hire iffen he'd'a had a mind to. Anyway, your pa braced them two men, 'n they was dumb enough to go up ag'in him. He shot 'em through, dead center, 'n cut 'em both down slick as a whistle. What that done was, it saved your mama and your gran'pa's lives, to say nothin' of Mr. Turner's money. Your gran'pa was that pleased with your pa that he hired us both that very day."

"Tell me about Mama and Dad's courtship," Hilary said.

Sam smiled again. "Well, I reckon you could say that it started that very day."

"Really?"

"As far as your pa was concerned, it did," Sam said.

"What makes you say that?"

"That night, me 'n your pa slept in the bunkhouse. That was the first time we'd had a roof over our heads in over two months. Well sir, we lay there 'n talked about our good luck at landin' us a job so quick. And that was when your pa told me he was gonna marry your mama."

"You mean he'd already asked her?" Hilary asked in surprise.

"Asked her? No, not a word of it. But that didn't make no never mind to your pa. He had it in his mind he was gonna marry her, 'n that was that."

"Tell me about Mama."

"Well, like I said, she was as pretty as a new-foaled colt. That part you already know. But did you know that they wasn't a soul in the territory that could touch her on horseback, and that's man or woman. She could ride like the wind."

"You mean she could beat Dad?"

"Oh, girl, your pa couldn't even come close to her."

"That must have been embarrassing to Dad."

"No. Your ma was that good that it didn't embarrass anyone to be beat by her." Sam chuckled. "Besides, your gran'pa always used to say that he never doubted for a moment that your mama wanted to be caught by your pa, 'cause they couldn't nobody catch that girl, without she was wantin' to be caught."

"Did Grandpa approve of Pa? Was he pleased that they got together?"

"Yes, I'd say your gran'pa was pleased. He always set a great store by your pa, and he stuck by him, even when there was trouble."

"What trouble?"

"Shootin' trouble," Sam said.

"You mean Dad was in another gunfight, other than the one you told me about?"

"You got to remember that after the war there was quite a bit of paper out on your pa back in Texas. It was only natural with as many folks arriving in Arizona from Texas as there was durin' those days that someone was goin' to come who would remember us."

"And did they?"

"Worse. Some bounty hunters came out, bound to make a little money on takin' our scalps back to Texas. The fac' is that by then all the warrants had been erased, and the paper was supposed to be all called back. Me 'n your pa wasn't wanted men no more. But bounty hunters are men with cow plop for brains. They had them a piece of paper that had a dead-or-alive reward on it, and that was all they cared about. They came lookin' for us, aimin' to turn our killin' into a little money in their pockets."

"What happened?"

"It was just before your mama and your pa got married. About a week before, I think it was. Me, your pa 'n your gran'pa had gone into town. Your gran'pa was at the bank for Mr. Turner, your pa was runnin' errands for your mama 'n I went into the Gilded Cage."

Hilary laughed.

"The Gilded Cage, Sam? Really . . . The Gilded Cage?"

"It was a bar and . . ."

"Sporting house?" Hilary teased.

"Watch your tongue, girl. You aren't supposed to know about such things."

"It was a sporting house, wasn't it? It was a place where soiled doves live and work."

"Girl, iffen your pa knew me 'n you was talkin' about such a place, he'd have a fit!"

"Tell me about it. Did it have red lace curtains and lots of gilt-edged mirrors?"

"Now, do you want me to tell the story or don't you?" Sam asked.

"I'm sorry," Hilary laughed. "Yes, I want you to tell the story. Please, do go on."

"All right. There I was, in the . . ."

"Sporting house," Hilary injected with a giggle.

"Sporting house," Sam agreed. "I was upstairs with Rosita."

"Rosita? I've never heard of Rosita. Who is she?"

"She was the prettiest señorita you would ever hope to see. Anyway, I was upstairs with her when all of a sudden the door to the room was just kicked open. No warning, no how-do-you-do, no nothing. And there, standing in the doorway, were two of the ugliest galoots you'd ever hope to lay eyes on.

" 'Which are you?' they asked. 'Colonel St. John or Sam Potter?' Well sir, when they asked for us that way, I knew they had to be bounty hunters from Texas."

"What did you do?"

"I told them those warrants had been withdrawn. I told them we weren't wanted men anymore."

"Did they believe you?"

"No."

"What happened?"

"They had the drop on me, so there was nothin' I could do except go with them. I told them that Jake was dead, that he'd died soon after we got out here, but they didn't believe me. They pushed me out into the street in nothin' but my underhauls."

"Sam, how scandalous!" Hilary teased.

"It weren't none too proper, I'll give you that. Especial, what with Rosita runnin' alongside, not wearin' even as much as I had on. She was yellin' at 'em in English and Mexican, cussin' 'em out good 'n proper, tellin' 'em to let me go, but they weren't havin' none of it. They figured to take me out into the center of the street 'n kill me there. That way, see, they'd have all the witnesses they'd need that I was dead 'n that they was the ones what kilt me. They needed such proof, you see, in order to collect the reward. They also figured that Jake would hear about it 'n would try 'n rescue me. When he did, they would catch him too."

"What happened?" Hilary asked, excited.

"Like I said," Sam said. "That's when your gran'pa stepped in."

"What did Grandpa do?"

"He come out of the bank and seen that them two men had the drop on me. His horse was hitched up in front of the bank 'n your gran'pa pulled his rifle outa the saddle holster. He walked right out into the middle of the street, holdin' that rifle. 'Who are you two men?' he shouted. 'And what are you doin' with my hand?'

"'Stay outa this, mister, unless you wanna get yourself kilt,' one man shouted. The other one raised his pistol toward your gran'pa, but your gran'pa, just as cool as a cucumber, cocked that rifle.

"'Shoot him,' the one holdin' a gun to my head shouted. 'Shoot the old geezer afore he shoots us.'

"The man who was pointin' the gun toward your gran'pa pulled the trigger, and his bullet carried away your gran'pa's hat. Your gran'pa raised his rifle 'n—get this, girl—he *didn't shoot the one who was shooting at him.*"

"He didn't? What did he do?" Hilary asked in surprise.

Sam was silent for a moment, and Hilary saw that he was swallowing hard. She also saw with surprise that his eyes had misted over.

"He shot the one who was holdin' the gun on me," Sam

said. "You see, he risked his own life just to make sure the fella who had a pistol to my head couldn't shoot. Well sir, that gave the other galoot a second shot at him, and the second time he didn't miss. He put a bullet in your gran'pa's shoulder. The gunman was so mad at your gran'pa, 'n so full of hate, that he started toward him, aimin' to finish off the job point-blank. That was when he made his mistake."

"Why?"

"Well sir, the dang fool forgot all about me. There was his partner lyin' in the road beside me, dead, with a loaded gun in his hand. It was easy enough for me. I just picked the gun up and plugged the other fella."

"Good for you."

"Maybe so. But I wound up bein' tried for murder."

"Sam, why would they try you for murder? What you did was in self-defense?"

"Accordin' to the law, them two galoots was actin' within their rights to make a citizen's arrest of me 'n your pa. We should'a gone back to Texas with them 'n proved our innocence."

"But they weren't going to take you back. They were going to kill you."

"That was what we argued in court, and your gran'pa hired us a high-powered lawyer to come up from Tucson 'n make the case for us. He stuck by us through all of it, 'n after it was over, we was never troubled by those old warrants again."

"And then Mama and Dad were married?"

"Right after that."

"How did we come to the Turquoise Ranch?"

"Your gran'pa knew ol' Ian MacMurtry pretty well. When he heard Mr. Mac was lookin' for a foreman, he recommended your pa. Bein' foreman of the Turquoise paid a lot more money than what your pa was makin' at the B

Bar T, and with a new wife, why, your pa needed the job. I come over to the Turquoise with him. Fac' is, ole Mr. Turner died not too long after that, 'n his property was bought up by the Turquoise anyway, so your gran'pa spent his last days on the Turquoise as well."

"The old B Bar T ranch is on the other side of Turner Creek," Hilary said.

"Yep. The creek was named after ole man Turner, though it was your gran'pa that found the spring and dug a channel for it. Do you remember your gran'pa, girl?"

"Yes, I remember gran'pa," Hilary said. "He died when I was still young, but I remember him." She laughed. "He always carried rock candy in his shirt pocket. I thought it was because he liked candy so much. It was a long time before I realized he was just doing that for me."

"Your gran'pa was a wonderful man," Sam said. "And your mama was a wonderful woman. Put them with your pa and, girl, you gotta turn out good, 'cause there ain't nothin' but good in you."

"I wish Mama were still alive," Hilary said. "I wish she could meet Tom. I wish she could know how happy I am right now. Who knows? Maybe she does know how happy I am. Maybe she's up in heaven right now, looking down on us. Do you believe in heaven, Sam?"

"I'm a God-fearin' man, yes," Sam said. "But I gotta tell you that there's somethin's I've never been able to figure out. And why good people like your gran'pa and your mama have to die before their time is one of those things. Course, I seen that happen a lot durin' the war, so I guess it's been goin' on for all time."

Hilary looked at Sam as he finished the preparations for tonight's stew. He was already bald, and his face showed the signs of living a hard life. To the average cowboy making this drive, the ones who didn't know him, he was nothing but another belly-robber, an ordinary cook. But she knew there was absolutely nothing ordinary about him at all. She was proud to call him her friend. And she was glad to be able to share her wonderful secret with him.

"Sam, why have you never married?"

"I got me a wife. Leastwise, I think I do. I ain't seen nor heard from her in a long, long time."

Hilary's mouth opened in surprise, and she stared at Sam.

"What? You are married? To who? Why have I never seen her?"

"I ain't seen her myself, since long afore you was born. I left her back in Texas."

"Oh, Sam, I'm so sorry," she said.

"Nothin' to be sorry about," Sam said. "That was a long time ago."

"Why have you never talked about her? You must have been terribly hurt by her."

Sam took the dough Hilary had made and began kneading it. He worked it hard, pounding it with his fists, as if to underscore his story.

"I was hurt all right," he said. "The onliest thang is, I was also a fool. You get wiser when you get older, but generally, especially for an old fool like me, it comes too late."

"Tell me about her. Why did you leave her in Texas? Was she pretty? Did my dad know her?"

"You ask a lot of questions," Sam said.

"I'm sorry," Hilary said. "You're right, I don't have any business butting into your affairs."

"We was married just before I went off to the war," Sam said. "There was those who told us it would be smarter to wait, but we didn't want to wait. She was sixteen, prob'ly too young to get married 'n settle down, but neither one of us could see that. Oh, we had a big military weddin', don't you know, with flags and bands and pretty uniforms. Course, none of us knew then what we was lettin' ourselves in for. War was somethin' we read about in history books and what we heard the old soldiers talk about. It was flags and uniforms and swords and bands and pretty girls wavin'. Only it weren't. It was dyin' and screamin' and men with their arms or their legs blowed off. And it weren't all that good for the womenfolk that stayed home, either. Lots of 'em seen their menfolk die, or come back maimed. Lots of 'em was scared, and when the times got rough, they was hungry, and sometimes the war come right to the home front."

Sam pounded on the dough with his fist. Hilary didn't say anything for a while.

"And some of 'em was lonely," Sam said. There was another beat of silence. "Lettie Mae was lonely. When I come home, I found out just how lonely she was. It was the talk all over the county, how she had took up with a Yankee carpetbagger while I was gone."

"Oh, Sam, how awful," Hilary said.

"I left her soon as I heard. She begged my forgiveness, but I wouldn't have none of it."

"No one could blame you for that."

Sam looked at Hilary, and she saw more pain on his face than she had ever seen in the face of any man.

"I blame me for that," he said. "What I should'a done was just take her with me and leave that place and all the gossip mongers. I should'a just forgot about what happened and made my life with her."

"But surely you don't mean that?"

"Why not?"

"Because she was unfaithful. You had a right to . . ."

"What are rights, girl?" Sam asked. "I'm tellin' you true that when two people love each other, they gotta have some bigness about 'em. They gotta know that we are only human, 'n sometimes we make mistakes. And they gotta learn what it's like to forgive."

"If you feel that way, why have you never contacted Lettie Mae?"

"Because the sin I've done her is a lot more'n anythin' she's ever done me. I'm not the one to do the forgivin' now. I'm the one to ask for it. And I would, only I don't know where she is, or how to find her, or even if she is still alive. And if she is, I don't know that I got the nerve to ask her to forgive me."

Sam was quiet for a long moment afterward as he continued to work on the dough. Finally Hilary kissed him on the cheek.

"Thank you, Sam, for sharing with me," she said.

Sam was quiet as she walked away.

Chapter Twenty

When Tom told Curly the news that he and Hilary were in love and were going to get married, Curly broke into a big smile and stuck out his hand.

"Well, put 'er there, pard," he said. "This here is the best news I've heard since they run Geronimo outa Arizona. So, you 'n Miss Hilary are gonna get married, are you? That is wonderful. That is truly wonderful for a fac'."

"I thought you would approve," Tom said. "Oh, and I also hope this explains a few things. I mean about the way I've been behaving whenever I was around her, and about some of the things I said. It hasn't been easy, you know, loving her and thinking that she loved another."

"Shucks, don't give it a second thought," Curly said. "I know how folks acts when they tumble head over heels in love sometimes. Especially iffen they think that love ain't bein' returned. They go plumb loco, like they ain't got no sense a'tall. Maybe that's what they mean when they say crazy with love."

"Maybe so," Tom said. "Anyway, I sure hope it helps explain a few things to you."

"Ha!" Curly said. "It's good enough news that my pardner is gonna get a swell girl like Hilary. Why, that's nearly as good as me gettin' her myself. But you wanna know what is the best part? This means that Gil Carson ain't gonna get her."

"Yeah," Tom said, smiling broadly. "I have to admit that I like that part of it myself."

Curly chuckled. "He's gonna be one mad fella, you can believe."

"Let him get mad," Tom said. "What can he do about it?"

Suddenly Curly got serious. "There is one thing he can do about it," Curly said. "And he probably will do it. You know you are gonna have to find another job somewhere. Yes, you 'n Big Jake too, 'cause when Carson finds out what's happened, he'll fire the both of you. You for takin' his girl, 'n Big Jake for lettin' it happen."

"I guess he will at that," Tom said. "But I don't care, and my guess is Big Jake won't either."

Curly smiled. "You're right, Big Jake is too much a man to let a little somethin' like that bother him. Course, what Carson don't know is that when he fires you 'n Big Jake, why, that's the same as firin' me 'n Sam too, 'cause we'll leave just as sure as a gun is iron. And I bet we ain't the only ones that'll be leavin' Turquoise either."

"Now that's one part I don't enjoy," Tom said. "I hate to be the cause of you losing your jobs. And I know how much Hilary loves Turquoise Ranch."

"Don't you worry none about that," Curly said. "Why, Big Jake is that good a foreman that he'll get on somewhere else real pronto, 'n when he does, why, I reckon the rest of us'll have jobs too. He'll see to that. And as far as Hilary lovin' Turquoise Ranch, well, I reckon everyone who has ever lived there loves it. 'Ceptin' maybe Carson hisself, 'n I don't think he loves anythin' but money 'n power."

"Curly, can you think of anyplace besides the Turquoise where there would be a spread big enough to hire all these people who might lose their jobs?" Tom asked.

"Don't worry about it. Truth to tell, I don't know but what ole Big Jake ain't been saltin' back for a rainy day anyhow. And this is likely to be that rainy day. Who knows? He may start his own ranch 'n we could all work for him."

"Salting back? You mean stealing from the Turquoise?"

Curly looked at Tom with a funny expression on his face.

"I didn't say that," he said. "I don't know that Big Jake has been stealin' at all. I don't even know that Carson has been stealin'. I just said I figured Big Jake had been saltin' things back for a rainy day. Anyhow, what difference does it make to you? You surely ain't got no loyalty to Carson and the Turquoise now, do you?"

"I don't look upon Gil Carson and the Turquoise Ranch as one and the same," Tom said.

"They are as far as *we* are concerned."

"Curly, what if we didn't leave the Turquoise? What if Carson had to leave instead?"

"Why would Carson have to leave?"

"He would have to leave if the owner discovered that Carson was stealing from him."

"Yeah? Well, how is the owner gonna find out?"

"If we found proof and sent it to the owner, don't you think the owner would fire Carson? He'd fire Carson and keep us on."

" 'N move Big Jake up to manager 'n me to foreman, I guess," Curly said.

"Maybe."

"No, thank you," Curly said with a surprising amount of

emphasis. "That'd be about the low-downest, meanest, most ornery thing I could think of."

"What?"

"Pard, maybe you still got a bit too much Eastern blood in you," Curly suggested. "But they ain't no way you'd ever get me to turn in one of our own to some Eastern dude who don't care enough about his ranch to even come visit it."

"One of our own?"

"Yeah, one of our own," Curly said. "For all that I don't like him, he's still a Westerner, 'n that makes him a better man than the absentee son of a bitch who owns this ranch. Besides, it'd be a pretty low life kind of fella who'd turn another man in just to get a little better treatment for hisself."

"I don't agree with you," Tom said. "If Gil Carson is stealing, he deserves to be punished for it."

"Then let the owner catch him and punish him," Curly said. "I don't want no part o' that."

Up until this conversation, Tom had contemplated telling Curly the truth. He wanted to confess to being the owner of Turquoise Ranch, not only to have someone with whom he could share the news, but also because he hoped Curly would help him get the goods on Carson. Now he decided it would be best not to tell Curly anything. At least not at this juncture.

The drive continued on to the San Carlos Indian Reservation outside Phoenix. It took at least two more weeks, but those were the happiest two weeks of Tom's life. It was all he could do to keep from shouting his love for Hilary, but he did manage to keep it quiet, as she had asked. That was particularly hard on him, for he saw her every day at meals.

He may not have said anything aloud, but, in the looks he and Hilary exchanged, they spoke volumes.

"I see you got an extra pancake," Curly said as he sat down beside Tom for breakfast.

"You said I should get friendly with the cook's helper," Tom teased. "I'm just following your instructions."

"Speakin' of instructions," Curly said. "Big Jake says we gotta be especial careful for a few days aroun' the cattle. We're comin' into a stretch where we are gonna have a long way between water holes, 'n when the cows start gettin' thirsty, they're awful easy spooked. They could stampede over the least little thing."

"Stampede?"

"Yeah, you ain't never seen one, have you?" Curly asked.

"No, I haven't. Have you?"

"I can't rightly say as I have," Curly admitted. "That is, no full-blowed stampede of as many cows as we got here. I've seen smaller herds panic 'n run, 'n believe me I got out of the way even then. Iffen this herd was to go, we'd have our hands full, I can tell you that."

"Curly, what's the best thing to do if they start to stampede?"

"Get the hell out of their way," Curly said. "The next thing is just to follow 'em, 'n when they get to where you can turn 'em, head 'em back in the right direction. But the best thing to do is to keep 'em from stampedin' in the first place."

Despite Curly's warning and all the good intentions, the herd broke into a stampede that very afternoon. There was no way the cowboys could have prevented it from happening. It was an accidental act of nature which was beyond anyone's control.

There had been no water since early in the morning, and

the cowboys had pushed the herd hard to get them through the long, dry passage. The cows were hot, tired and thirsty. They began to get a little restless, and Tom and the others working around the perimeters were kept busy keeping them going.

Then, at about three o'clock in the afternoon, one of the cows stepped on a dry branch of mesquite. The mesquite popped as loud as a pistol shot, and the noise frightened the cows nearest to the branch. They jumped and started to run and that spread through the rest of the herd. Then, like a wild prairie fire before a wind, the herd ran out of control.

"Stampede! Stampede!"

The call was first issued by one of the cowboys at the front, and it was carried in relay until everyone knew about it.

"Stampede!"

There was terror in the cry, and yet, grim determination too, for every man who issued the cry moved quickly to do what he could do to stop it.

Tom was riding on the right flank when the herd started. Fortunately for him, the herd started toward the left, a living tidal wave of thundering hoofbeats, millions of pounds of muscle and bone, horn and hair, red eyes and running noses. Fifty-five hundred animals welded together as one, gigantic, raging beast.

A cloud of dust rose up from the herd and billowed high into the air. The air was so thick with the dust that within moments Tom could see nothing. It was as if he were caught in the thickest fog one could imagine, but this fog was brown, and it burned the eyes and clogged the nostrils and stung his face with its fury.

Tom managed to overtake the herd, then he rode to the left, which, before they started running, had been the rear, and he tried to get in front of them to turn them. Tom, like the other cowboys, was shouting and whistling and waving his hat at the herd, trying to get them to respond. That was when Tom got a glimpse, just out of the corner of his eye, of a cowboy falling from his horse. The stampeding cows altered their rush just enough to come toward the hapless cowboy, and he stood up and tried to outrun them, though it was clear that he was going to lose the race.

Tom acted without thinking. He headed for the cowboy, even though it meant riding right into the face of the herd. When he came even with the running man he reached down and picked him up with one hand, using his great strength to lift him as easily as if he were a child. Tom carried the cowboy under his arm and turned his horse to get away from the herd. As he reached the edge, the cows turned again, and Tom and the cowboy he had rescued were safe. Tom set him back down, then rode off to join the others until finally they managed to bring the herd to a halt. At last the cows slowed their mad dash to a brisk trot, and when they did that the cowboys were able to turn them back in the direction they were supposed to be going. The stampede had at last come to a halt, brought under control by the courage and will of a dozen determined men. An aggregate total of less than eighteen hundred pounds of men were once more in control of two million pounds of cattle.

Tom was a hero around the campfire that night, and the last vestige of "Eastern tenderfoot" died. Tom was accepted as one of them by even the most reticent of the old hands, for by his action he had won their respect and admiration.

"You've come a long way, pard," Curly said as the two men sipped coffee and stared into the fire after supper. "You know, when I seen you at the railroad station that day, I would'a bet anyone that they was no way you'd ever make a cowman. But the truth is, you are already as good as anyone I ever rode with."

"I had a good teacher," Tom said.

"Now that's a fac', pard," Curly said, beaming under Tom's remark. "That's truly a fac'." Curly stood up and poured the last dregs of his coffee out. "Well sir, me for bed. 'N if you are still listenin' to what your teacher has to say, you'll be doin' the same, I reckon."

"That sounds good to me," Tom agreed.

That night, as Tom lay in his bedroll looking up at the stars, he thought of the events of the day, and of his acceptance by the cowboys that night. He thought also of Curly's remark that he was already as good as anyone Curly had ever ridden with. If that was truly the case, then his time of training was over.

It was time he made his identity known.

The only question was, *how* was he going to do it?

"You wait till after we deliver them cows," one cowboy said to another as they carried on their conversation not far away from Tom's bedroll. "The first thing I'm gonna do is get me a nice cold bottle of beer. No, two bottles. No, three bottles. And someone soft 'n pretty to drink it with. Then I'm gonna get me a bath."

"Ha," the other cowboy said. "If you don't get yourself a bath first, I guarantee you you won't find nobody soft 'n pretty to drink it with."

"And then I'm gonna find me a party," the first one went on, unperturbed by his friend's rejoinder. "A big party with lots o' eats 'n dancin' and pretty women."

A party! Tom thought. Yes, that's what he would do. He would throw a party for all the drovers on this drive, and there at the party, he would announce his identity. Of course that probably meant that he would not be able to get proof positive that he was being robbed, but that didn't matter. Whatever he had lost thus far was worth it for the lessons he had learned. He would simply let the ones who stole from him keep their ill-gotten gains. He would be satisfied to claim what was rightfully his. And at this point, one of those rightful claims was Hilary St. John.

When they came down off the last mountain pass, they could see the main village of the reservation stretched out in front of them. The village consisted of several small houses and tents scattered on both sides of a small creek. The creek which meandered through the village was Cave Creek, a narrow stream that flowed down from the high country, then broke into white water as it bubbled across the tiers of rocks just above the village.

Smoke curled from the roofs of several of the cabins. There were a couple of community corrals for the horses, and there were several dogs. A few of the dogs came out to meet them.

When they reached the bottom of the pass and started into the village, everyone came out of the houses or away from the wells, which were community gathering places, and came to meet them. A group of children, nut brown from the sun, ran to the village edge and began laughing and running in circles as they formed the vanguard of the impromptu welcoming committee. Many of the adults fell in behind the children and as they walked to the center of the village, they formed a small procession. Then several Indians on horseback came to take charge of the herd, and the cows were taken by the Indians to the private pastureland of the reservation. At that moment responsibility for the cows passed from the drovers to the Indians. At first, the cowboys didn't realize that they were finished. Then it dawned on them, and the cowboys, relieved at long last of their duties, headed for the well, where several of the women and children were drawing water for them. Tom and

Curly were among them, and Tom gratefully took a long, cool drink of water and looked around the village.

"Are you looking for Hilary?" Curly asked from the other side of the well. Curly poured some water from the gourd over his head and several of the children, seeing this, laughed at him. Curly drank the second gourd.

"Yes," Tom said.

"Sam took the chuck wagon on into Phoenix," Curly said. "He's gonna ship it back up to Flagstaff on the train. Fac' is, he 'n Hilary 'n Big Jake will be goin' back by train too."

"Then I reckon that's how I'll go," Tom said.

"We're supposed to ride back," Curly said. "Lessen we want to pay our own way."

"I'll pay my way."

"Pard, you sure must have more money than sense," Curly said. "Now me, I've got better things to do with my money than spend it on train rides, when I got me a perfectly good horse that can get me back home in two days."

Big Jake joined the two men then, holding an envelope in his hand. "It seems funny, doesn't it, that all these cows and all this work boils down to what I have in my hand."

"Boss, you gotta be kiddin'," Curly said. "You mean all the money that was paid for these here cows is put into that one envelope?"

"Yes. Well, it isn't cash, it's a bank draft. But it's negotiable, so it's the same thing as carrying cash. I'm going into town now to deposit it in the bank."

"You mean Turquoise Ranch does its banking in Phoenix?" Tom asked.

"If you would have asked me that question a few weeks ago, I would have said no," Jake said. "But my instructions are not to bring the bank draft home, but to deposit it in the Valley National Bank."

"It would seem to me that if Carson wanted to be dishonest about that money, hiding it in a Phoenix bank would be a good way to do it," Tom suggested.

"The account is in the name of the Turquoise Ranch," Jake said. "It isn't under Carson's name."

"Yes, but Carson has the power of attorney to draw from any working Turquoise account, doesn't he? That would just be a good way to cover up."

"I don't know, maybe you're right," Jake said. "At any rate, it isn't your worry. Or mine either, for that matter. I've done my job. All I want to do now is deposit this draft and get a good night's sleep in a bed, even if it is a hotel bed in Phoenix."

"Boss, you ain't gonna waste time sleepin', are you?" Curly asked. "When there's so many things to do in town?"

"Like what?" Jake asked.

"Well, like . . . like . . . like what, Tom? Tell 'im."

"Like come to my party," Tom said.

"Yeah, like come to Tom's party," Curly said. He looked at Tom in surprise. "What party?"

"I'm giving a party," Tom said.

"What kind of a party?" Curly asked.

"A big party," Tom said. "With lots of food, drink and fun. And every drover on this drive is invited to it."

"Tom, you're a damn fool to waste all your money on a party like this," Jake said. "Hell, man, somethin' like this'll cost you damn near as much as you was paid for the drive."

"It'll be worth it, Jake," Tom said. "Believe me, it'll be worth it."

"There's no way I can talk you outa wastin' your money?" Jake asked.

"I'm afraid not. And I'll be hurt if you don't come."

"Oh, I'll come all right," Jake said with a smile. "If some damn fool is dead set on spendin' all his money in buyin' free food 'n drink for others, then I sure want to get my share. I'll be there, you can count on it."

"Good," Tom said.

Jake started toward his horse. "I guess I'd better go ahead and get on into town. Oh, I suppose Sam and Hilary are included in your invitation?"

"They are especially included," Tom said.

Jake chuckled. "I rather thought they would be. All right, boys, I'll see you two in town."

Tom and Curly watched Jake until he rode away, then Curly looked at Tom and smiled.

"Pard, could it be you are going to surprise a few people with an announcement tonight?"

"I'm going to surprise everyone," Tom said.

Curly chuckled. "No, you forget, I already know about you 'n Hilary. You won't be surprisin' me none."

This time it was Tom's turn to chuckle.

"Pard," he said, imitating Curly's slow, Western drawl, "I think you are going to be the most surprised of them all."

Chapter Twenty-one

"A party? Dad, are you sure Tom said he was going to give a party?"

"That's what he said, all right," Big Jake said. Jake had come to the railroad station to see if Hilary and Sam needed any assistance in shipping the chuck wagon back to Turquoise Ranch. By the time he got there he discovered that arrangements had already been made. Now he and Hilary were walking down the plank sidewalk of the bustling city, headed toward the hotel where they would be staying.

"What on earth would make Tom throw a party like that? Why, it would take all the money he's made on this drive," Hilary protested.

"I told him as much," Big Jake said. "But that didn't seem to worry him."

"Well, it might not worry him," Hilary said. "But it certainly does worry me."

Big Jake looked at his daughter with a puzzled expression on his face.

"Girl, what do you mean, it certainly does worry you?" he asked. "Why would you be worried about what Tom Eddington does with his money?"

"Uh, well, no reason really," Hilary said. "I mean, of course I'm not worried, it's just that . . ."

"Daughter, is there somethin' you aren't tellin' me?"

"Not really, it's just . . ." Hilary paused for a minute, and then she broke into a big smile. "I guess maybe there is at that. Dad, Tom and I are going to be married."

"Married?"

"Yes. Oh, Dad, isn't it wonderful? Tell me you're pleased."

"But what about Gil Carson? You haven't forgotten that you promised to marry him, have you?"

"No," Hilary sighed. "I haven't forgotten."

"I hope you're going to tell him that you've had a change of heart," Jake said. "It wouldn't be seemly just to marry Tom without at least letting Gil know."

"I know," Hilary said. "If it weren't for that, Tom and I would get married here in Phoenix, today. But I feel that I owe it to Gil to tell him to his face rather than send him a telegram."

"How does Tom feel about that?"

"He agrees with me," Hilary said.

"Tom is a good man all right," Jake replied.

"Oh, Dad, you are pleased for me, aren't you?"

"Darlin', I'm pleased if you are pleased," Jake said.

"I am pleased," Hilary said. "Oh, I am so pleased. I love him, Dad. I love him more than I ever thought I could love anyone."

"Well, it seems to me that's what it takes to make a marriage work." Jake had a far-off, bittersweet look in his eyes. "I know I loved your mama," he said. "And though our time together was short, it couldn't of been any sweeter."

"That's just what I want it to be like with Tom and me," Hilary said. "And I don't care if he doesn't have anything. A cowboy is good enough for me, if that cowboy is Tom Eddington."

"Yeah? Well, if he spends money like he's spendin' it for this party, a cowboy is all he's ever likely to be too," Jake said. He looked at Hilary and smiled. "But then, I reckon he has cause enough to celebrate. He's got the love of the finest girl in the world, and that's worth all the money a man could ever want."

"Oh, Dad, I'm so happy," Hilary said. She hugged her father spontaneously, and he hugged her back.

"I'll let you in on somethin'," he said secretively.

"What's that?"

"I'm a sight happier about you marryin' Tom than I was over your marryin' Gil."

Hilary laughed. "I never did think I had your enthusiastic support," she said.

"It's your life, darlin', 'n your decision to make. I didn't figure then, 'n I don't figure now, that I got any say-so in it whatever. But I will tell you that I am happier with your decision to marry Tom than I was when I thought you was gonna marry Gil. Even if Tom is a damn fool who is going to spend all his money throwin' a party."

When Hilary and her father walked into the Adams Hotel, they saw their names printed on a small blackboard above the message, "Please check with the concierge."

"What do you suppose that's about?" Hilary asked.

"I don't know," Jake said. "Come on, we may as well check with him before we pick up our keys."

"Maybe they don't have room for us," Hilary said.

"No, there's no problem with that," Jake said. "I have already confirmed reservations."

A bellboy walked by and Jake reached out and stopped him.

"Excuse me," Jake said. "Could you tell me where to find the concierge, please?"

"Yes, sir," the bellboy said. "That's him, right over there, standing by the mailboxes."

"Thank you," Jake said. He led Hilary over to the concierge, a beefy, bearded man, who was busily poking letters and messages into a wall of post-office boxes.

"Excuse me," Jake said. "You have our names on the board there, asking us to see you."

"Are you Mr. St. John?"

"Yes."

"I have a message for you," the clerk said. "And you must be Miss St. John?"

"Yes," Hilary said.

"I have a message for you as well."

"Aren't we the popular ones, though?" Hilary quipped as the manager handed each of them an envelope.

Hilary's was from Tom, and she opened it eagerly.

Dear Hilary,

I am certain that, by now, you have heard of the party that I intend to give tonight. I am going to be extremely busy during the day taking care of some pressing matters, so I will be unable to see you until the party. I am going to make an important announcement at the party . . . one that I hope will please you. Don't worry, it isn't what you are thinking. That announcement I will hold off until we can make it together, as I respect your wish to clear up a few other things beforehand.

In the meantime, I will take great comfort in knowing that, despite the fact we can't make it public as yet, I do have your love. And you have mine.

> Tom

The words thrilled Hilary, and she held the letter to her heart as she would have held him, had he been there.

Hilary looked over at her father. She was anxious to share her letter with him, but when she saw the expression on her father's face, her own joy was momentarily suspended. Her father was positively ashen faced!

"Dad? Dad, what is it?" Hilary asked. "Is something wrong?"

"What?"

"The expression on your face. Have you received some bad news?"

"No," Jake said absently. He folded the letter and slipped it in his pocket, then he smiled. "No, why do you ask?"

Her father asked the question so innocently, and the smile on his face at that moment seemed so genuine that Hilary began to wonder if she had mistaken the expression earlier. Perhaps it was merely a trick of the light.

"No reason," she said. She held up her letter. "This is from Tom."

"Oh? And what does he have to say?"

"Just that he is going to be taking care of some pressing matters today," she said. "And of course, the fact that he loves me."

"Where is he now?"

"I don't know," Hilary said. "All I know is he said he would see me tonight at the party. Oh, and he said he is going to make an important announcement tonight."

"I thought you were going to wait until after you had confronted Gil Carson."

"We are," Hilary said. "That isn't the announcement."

"It isn't? Then what is the announcement going to be?"

"That I can't tell you," Hilary said, "for I don't know myself. I guess we'll just have to wait until tonight and find out."

"Yeah, I guess so," Jake said.

"Oh, look," Hilary said, pointing to a restaurant which opened off the lobby of the hotel. "Dad, let's have lunch. It's been a long time since I ate anything without the taste of dust in it."

"You go ahead, darlin', 'n eat without me," Jake said. "I've got somethin' that needs tendin' to."

"Oh, you and Tom," Hilary said in an exasperated tone of voice. "You are just alike. Both of you have such mysterious tasks to perform on our first day in Phoenix. Well, you just go right ahead. I, for one, am going to enjoy my visit to the city."

Jake smiled and kissed his daughter. "You do that, darlin'," he said. "I'll see you tonight."

Hilary watched as her father walked back out of the hotel to take care of whatever mysterious business had come up for him. Then she walked over to the desk to register and get her key. She heard a sound of laughter from the dining room and she looked inside. At first she thought about going right to lunch, but then she decided that it would be best to take a long, hot bath first. In fact, that sounded even better to her than food.

"Here you are, Miss Proctor," the clerk was saying to another young woman who stood at the far end of the counter. "Your room is three-thirteen."

"Thank you," the woman answered in a cool and

extremely cultured tone. "Oh, and would you have a boy bring my things to my room, please?"

Hilary looked over at the woman. She was exceptionally pretty, if a bit overdressed for this time of day. But it wasn't just her looks that attracted Hilary's attention. It was the sound of her voice. There was an accent to her voice, a well-modulated accent, which attracted Hilary's attention right away. Her accent was exactly like Tom's. Because of that, Hilary smiled at her.

"Hello," Hilary said. "Are you just arriving in Phoenix?"

The woman looked around as if surprised that someone had spoken to her. She looked at Hilary, dressed as she was in her trail clothes, and she screwed her face up into an expression of disapproval.

"I'm sorry, dear," the woman said. "If you are looking for a position as my maid, I don't intend to remain in this wretched town long enough to require the services of one. At any rate, I would require someone of better grooming."

"Maid?" Hilary answered, puzzled by the woman's strange remark. "What are you talking about?"

"Weren't you about to ask me for a job?"

"No," Hilary said. "I'm not asking anybody for a job!"

"Good," the woman said. "That should spare you the embarrassment of being turned down." She turned away and walked quickly and haughtily over to the grand staircase.

"Well, I'll be . . ." Hilary began, and but for the fact that she was in a strange hotel in a strange city, she would have let go with some of the more colorful language she had learned from her years on the ranch.

"That woman is one beautiful lady, isn't she?" the desk clerk said, coming over to Hilary at that moment. "From high society too. She's from Boston."

"Boston?"

So that explained why she sounded just like Tom when she spoke. Tom was also from Boston.

"That's what the register says. I'd certainly like to go to Boston some day. I've read that it's a most beautiful old city, with lots of history. Not like this town, which is barely thirty years away from being a couple of mud huts in the middle of a desert. Now, what can I do for you, miss?"

"My name is Hilary St. John. I'm with the Turquoise Ranch. I believe you have a reservation?"

"Ah, yes, Miss St. John, you have room three-fifteen. Here is the key. I hope you have a nice stay with us."

"Oh, I intend to," Hilary said, smiling and taking the key.

Hilary walked up the carpeted stairs to the third floor, then down the hall toward Room 315. She reached her door just as she saw the pretty but haughty young woman from Boston going into her own room right next to hers. The woman glanced over at Hilary with one final look of disapproval, then she let herself in quickly, as if she was afraid Hilary might actually say something to her. Hilary could have set the woman's mind at ease. She certainly had no intention of saying anything to her ever again.

The room had a high ceiling and an overhead paddle fan. Hilary turned the fan on, then was rewarded with a brisk, cooling breeze. She left the fan running and went into the bathroom to draw her bath. A few minutes later, she lowered herself down into a tub full of warm, soapy water, and then and only then did it feel as if the long, tiring days of the drive were actually over.

The tub was heaven. She felt as if she could stay in it all afternoon, and she did sit there for way over an hour, until the water went from hot to tepid and finally to cool. Then, reluctantly she stepped out of the tub and walked over to stand at the foot of the bed while she dried herself.

As Hilary stood there, drying her nude body, she could feel the gentle breeze of the overhead fan. Never had she felt anything as delightfully sensual as that, and all thoughts of going down to the dining room for lunch were suspended as she lay her tired body down on the bed to enjoy the silken sensations which were passing across her body at that moment.

The fan made a tiny hum and *whoosh* sound, and that soothing sound, plus the gentle breath of air thus moved, soon combined to send Hilary off into a most restful sleep.

Big Jake sat on a leather-covered bench in the waiting room of the office of the Arizona Cattlemen's Association. The walls were decorated with polished steer horns, the horns also serving as hat racks. Huge photographs of past and present officers of the Cattlemen's Association also decorated the walls, while against one wall stood a large grandfather's clock. The pendulum steadily swung back and forth as the clock ticked away its measured moments.

"Mr. St. John," the secretary, a smallish, bald-headed man, said.

"Yes."

"Mr. Appleton will see you now."

"Thank you," Jake said, and walked through the rail gate and back toward the office indicated by Mr. Appleton's secretary.

Appleton stood up as Jake entered, and he smiled and stuck out his hand.

"Jake," he said, "it has been a long time."

"It has at that, Colonel; it has at that," Jake said.

Appleton chuckled. "I don't hear that very much,

anymore," he said. "It's been a long time since anyone called me Colonel."

"Are you uncomfortable with it?"

"No," Appleton said. "Ours may have been a lost cause, but it certainly wasn't a shameful one. I'm proud that I did what I considered to be my duty, and whenever I meet someone who shared that duty with me, I feel good about it. Now, sit down, let's talk."

"I got your note," Jake said. "The one where you said the Colorado Cattle Company was crooked."

"No one has been able to prove them guilty of any wrong-doing," Appleton said as he settled behind his own desk. "But nearly everyone has their suspicions."

"And what are those suspicions?"

"The Colorado Cattle Company deals only in stolen cattle," Appleton said.

"I was afraid of something like that," Jake said. He sighed. "I just delivered fifty-five hundred head of cattle to the Indian reservation. It was a deal worked out with the Colorado Cattle Company."

"Your own cows?"

"From Turquoise Ranch," Jake said.

Appleton rubbed his chin. "Jake, I'd be willin' to bet that the owner never sees that money."

"Yes, he will," Jake said.

"Don't count on it."

"He'll see it," Jake said, "because I'm going to send it to him. Or them. Whoever it is."

"You mean you don't even know who owns the ranch?"

"No. All our dealings have been with some lawyers' corporation back in Boston," Jake said.

"Then how are you going to get the money to the owner?"

"I'll send it directly to the lawyers in Boston."

"Uh-huh. And how do you know these lawyers aren't in cahoots with Gil Carson? It wouldn't be the first time a crooked ranch manager teamed up with a bunch of lawyers to cheat the rightful owner."

"I don't know," Jake said. He sighed. "Maybe you're right. Maybe there is nothing I can do about it."

"You could leave the money with us," Appleton said.

"With you?"

"Sure. Sometimes we manage funds for our members. You could just leave the money you get for these cattle with us. That way we could look around, find out who the real owner is and get the money in the right place. Of course, it would mean your job, in the meantime."

"I got a feelin' my daughter has already taken care of that," Jake said.

"What do you mean?"

"My daughter was engaged to marry Gil Carson," Jake said.

"You say she *was*? You mean she isn't anymore?"

"No. She met a cowboy on the drive, and now she's engaged to him. Well, actually she didn't meet him on the drive; she knew him even before. But somethin' must have happened, 'cause it's all changed around. And knowin' Gil Carson as I do, I'm pretty sure he's gonna be a sore loser about it. That probably means I'll be fired as soon as we get back. Tom too, I'm sure."

"Tom?"

"Tom Eddington," Jake said. "A finer man than Gil Carson, by far. It's worth losin' my job to be knowin' that I won't have Gil Carson as a son-in-law."

"Well, after this money reaches the real owner, you may find that you haven't lost your job after all. It may be Gil Carson who is out in the cold."

"I figure Gil Carson will be turned out in the cold," Jake

said. "And that's the way it should be, him bein' a crook 'n all. But I won't be makin' no profit by it."

"Why not? You would deserve it for getting the goods on Carson."

" 'Cause I won't be doin' this for a reward," Jake said. "I'm not one to profit by another man's problems."

"That's silly, Jake. Even if the other man's problems are of his own doing? I mean, after all, he is a thief, isn't he?"

"Yes, I reckon he is."

"Then what's so wrong in seeing that both of you get justice?"

"I lived for a while with paper out on my head," Jake said. "When you got a reward out for you ever'one you see can make a profit from you if they want. All they have to do is turn you in. It makes you feel like an animal."

"Yeah," Appleton said. "I guess I can remember those days. Some of you got a pretty bad deal when we came back from the war."

"I'm not complainin' or apologizin' for anythin' that ever happened to me," Jake said. "I reckon I cut my own trail, 'n whatever cards life dealt me I had to deal with myself. For the last twenty years or so I've had a real good life. But the memory of dodging bounty hunters has stayed with me. That's why I don't figure to be a bounty hunter for anyone."

"But this isn't bounty hunting," Appleton protested.

"It's the same thing," Jake said. "I turn Gil Carson in . . . he loses and I profit! No, sir. I'm willin' to see Gil Carson get what's comin' to him, 'n I'm willin' to see that the owner gets the money that's rightly his. But I'm not willin' to make any gain on the deal. So, whether the owner offers me a job or not, I'll be movin' on."

"Well, a man has to do whatever he considers right, I guess," Appleton said.

"That's always been my motto," Jake said. Jake took an envelope from his jacket pocket. "Here is a bank draft for one hundred thirty-five thousand dollars. I'd like you to keep it."

"I'll be glad to," Appleton said. "Listen, would you like to have dinner with my wife and me tonight?"

"No thank you, Colonel, but Tom Eddington is throwing a big party at the Adams Hotel tonight."

"Is that the cowboy you said your daughter was going to marry?"

"The same."

"Isn't the ballroom of the Adams a little expensive for an ordinary cowboy?"

"Tom Eddington isn't your ordinary cowboy," Jake said.

"No, it doesn't sound as if he is," Appleton said. He wrote out a receipt for the bank draft and handed it to Jake. "I'd like to meet him sometime."

"I'm sure you will," Jake said, taking the receipt and putting it in his billfold. "And I want to thank you for holding this draft for me."

"I think you're doing the right thing, Jake. If there is any chicanery going on, then you're protected. If there isn't, why then there's no harm done."

Jake left the Cattlemen's Association office a short time later, feeling much better than he had when he went in. Not only was he rid of the burden of carrying around a draft for so much money, he was also glad that he had covered himself against any possible repercussions from Gil Carson's cheating.

He felt as if a great weight had been lifted from his shoulders.

"I don't understand," Gil said. "Are you certain they said the funds had not been deposited?"

Gil was sitting at the desk of the vice-president of the Cattlemen's Bank and Trust in Flagstaff. He had come to town earlier in the day in order to have a wire transfer made of the money that was being deposited by Jake in the Valley National Bank of Phoenix.

"Here is the return telegram, Mr. Carson," the vice-president said. "You can see for yourself."

Gil took the telegram and read it.

> IN RESPONSE TO YOUR REQUEST THAT ALL FUNDS DEPOSITED TO TURQUOISE ACCOUNT BE TRANSFERRED YOUR BANK BE ADVISED THAT TOTAL FUNDS AVAILABLE ARE EIGHTY-TWO DOLLARS AND FIFTY-ONE CENTS.

"But that has to be a mistake," Gil said. "I gave St. John specific instructions to deposit all that money in the Turquoise account."

"Perhaps he misunderstood, Mr. Carson. Perhaps he's bringing the money back with him."

"He had better be," Gil said. "If he doesn't have that draft on him when he gets off the train, I will have him arrested."

"I am certain it will all work out for you," the vice-president said.

"Yes, I'm sure it's all right," Gil said. He stood, shook hands with the teller, then left the bank.

Damn! He should have taken a train to Phoenix and been there to personally take receipt of that money. He had managed to take a little money off the top of the ranch operations before, but never had he taken this much money. This was over one hundred thousand dollars!

One hundred thousand dollars! The very term had a magnificent sound to it, as if it were set to music. One hundred thousand dollars, all in one lump sum, and all for his own, personal use. He had managed to cover up the shipment beautifully. The lawyers back in Boston would have absolutely no idea the magnitude of his victory in this little deal.

He just hoped the whole deal wasn't queered now by Jake St. John's inexplicable neglect to deposit the money in the special account he had set up in Phoenix. He needed that money right now if he was going to make the Trailback deal go through.

Gil looked up at the large clock over the bank. It was fifteen minutes after two. He had an appointment at four, after which he would be the sole owner of Trailback.

But until four, there was time for Bonnie.

Chapter Twenty-two

A door slammed at the far end of the hall, and the noise awakened Hilary. It was good that happened, for Hilary had fallen asleep from pure exhaustion, and had she not been awakened she might have slept through the entire night.

Hilary sat up in bed. She had a moment of confusion. She didn't know where she was, or why she was nude. Then she remembered that she had lain down right after taking her bath, just for a moment, she had thought. That moment had stretched into hours, and now her room was filled with the shadows of early evening.

Hilary feared that she might have slept through the party, so she walked over to the window and peered through it at the large clock on the front of the bank across the street. The clock said 6:45. She gave a sigh of relief.

Hilary turned away from the window and looked at a package which lay on the dresser. She had gone shopping this morning, even before the arrangements had been made for shipping the chuck wagon back to Turquoise, and she bought a new dress. Maybe it was a bit extravagant on her part, but she had not brought anything with her on the drive except trail clothes, and she intended to dress up at least one night while she was in Phoenix. When she bought it, she knew nothing about the party; that just turned out to be a happy coincidence.

The basic dress was beige colored, and it was designed to fit Hilary's slender figure with a sheathlike closeness. From a distance, the beige color took on a fleshlike appearance, and so molded to her body was the dress that, except for the maroon design overlay on the dress, one might have thought from first glance that Hilary was nude. It was not a dress that could be worn by many, but Hilary's slender figure was perfect for it.

Hilary dressed quickly, then she left her room and walked through the carpeted hallway and down the stairs.

Hilary could hear the sounds of the party even before she got there. Bright lights, conversation and laughter spilled out of the ballroom, welcoming all who might wish to come.

Hilary stopped at the door that led into the room and looked around. As she was late, the party was already in full swing, and the excitement was all it promised to be. There were more than a dozen young women there, though where they came from Hilary had no idea. They did add life to the party, though, because their bright dresses and flashing earbobs formed collection points around which all the cowboys were gathered.

It wasn't just cowboys, though. There were all sorts of men present, from the denim- and leather-clad drovers, to the clerks and merchants of the city, fashionably dressed in three-piece suits and gold watch fobs.

A band was playing, but as yet no one was dancing.

Hilary looked for Tom, but she didn't see him. She did see her father, though, so she walked over to talk to him.

Jake gave a low whistle. "Darlin', you're gonna break every cowboy's heart in this room lookin' like that."

"Do you like the dress?" Hilary asked. "I bought it this morning."

"It's quite a dress," Jake said. "What do you think of the party?"

"There are so many people here," Hilary said, looking around. "I thought it was going to be a private party."

"I think it was supposed to be," Jake said. "But these things have a way of growing."

"Is Tom here? I haven't seen him," Hilary said.

"I haven't seen him either. I thought perhaps the two of you were together."

"I took a nap," Hilary said. "What about you? What have you done with yourself all afternoon?"

"Oh, I took care of some business," Jake said. "Hilary, in case something goes wrong, there's something I think you should know."

"What?" Hilary asked. "What do you mean in case something goes wrong? Wrong with what?"

"Well, it's something I did with the money."

"What money?"

"The money I was paid for the delivery of the cows."

"Dad, you're frightening me," Hilary said. "What are you talking about?"

"I didn't deposit the money where I was supposed to."

"Why not? Dad, you aren't in any trouble, are you?"

"I hope not," Jake said. He smiled. "But don't you worry about it," he said. "Just know that I did it for you."

"I don't like it when you make a secret out of things. I just hope you aren't in any trouble."

"I hope not too."

"Oh, where is Tom?" Hilary said in exasperation.

"Ah, don't worry about him," Jake said. "He'll show up soon enough."

"Excuse me, Miss Hilary," Curly said, coming up to them at that moment. "Tom asked me to look after you and to tell you that he's gonna be detained for a couple of minutes."

"Where is he?"

"He's talkin' to the sheriff about somethin'," Curly said.

"The sheriff? What about? Curly, is Tom in some sort of trouble?"

"He don't appear to be," Curly said. "He just asked me to look after you."

Hilary laughed. "I don't really need to be looked after, you know. I'm not some child who is likely to wander away."

Curly laughed too. "I know," he said. "I think the lookin' after part was just 'cause he's bein' nice to me. How 'bout a sarsaparilla? They got 'em here, good 'n cold."

"A cold sarsaparilla? Yes, that would be nice," Hilary said. She turned to her father. "Excuse me, Dad, I'm about to drink a sarsaparilla."

Jake smiled. "You haven't outgrown your taste for them, I see. You go ahead. I'm going to see if I can't find something a little stronger, for my taste."

"Miss Hilary, Tom told me about you two plannin' on gettin' married," Curly said.

"He said he was going to tell you."

Curly smiled broadly. "Well, I want you to know how pleased I am about it."

"You mean you're more pleased now than you were when you drove me in to Flagstaff after you heard I was engaged to Gil?"

"Yeah," Curly said, laughing. "Yeah, you might say that."

Curly and Hilary weaved through the crowd of people until they reached a bar, at which Curly ordered a beer for himself and a sarsaparilla for Hilary. Both drinks were served cold, and Curly lifted his beer and tapped it against Hilary's glass.

"The best to you," he said. "The best to both of you. I've never met two people I liked more, 'n that's a fac'."

Hilary drank the toast, then she looked across the room and saw her father leaving the party in the company of two men.

"I wonder where Dad is going?" Hilary asked, her voice expressing a small degree of worry.

Curly looked in the direction Hilary had indicated, then he shrugged.

"I don't know," he said. "Maybe Tom asked for him. That's the sheriff and the other fella I saw with Tom a few minutes ago."

"Oh," Hilary said. "Well, then whatever it is, I'm sure it's all right."

"Hey, it's Tom!" someone suddenly shouted. "Look at Tom, will you?"

Hilary looked toward Tom and gasped in surprise. He wasn't dressed in the denim and leather he ordinarily wore. He was wearing a suit, and, despite his great size, he looked quite at home in such garb.

"Look at what he has on," Hilary said.

"Yeah, ain't it somethin'?" Curly replied. "I seen that he was all dressed up, but I didn't want to say nothin' to spoil the surprise."

"Tom, why are you so dressed up?" someone shouted.

"He's just wantin' to show the rest of us galoots up, that's all," someone else said, and they all laughed.

Tom laughed with the others, then he held his hands up to get the attention of everyone there.

"Maybe I am being just a bit of a showoff," he said. "But I have a reason for it, believe me."

"It must be some reason," one of the drovers said. "I can't think of nothin' that would make me get dressed up in a monkey suit like that."

There was more laughter, and again Tom held his hands up, calling for quiet.

"Friends, I have an announcement to make."

"An announcement? What sort of announcement?" someone called.

"Well, maybe if you'll just shut up, he'll tell us," another said.

"Go ahead, Tom."

"What is his announcement?" Curly asked quietly. "He's not gonna tell 'bout you 'n him being engaged, is he?"

"No," Hilary said. "At least, I don't think so. He wrote me a note and told me he was going to make an announcement, but he said it wouldn't be what I thought. I haven't talked to him all afternoon, so I don't have any idea what this is about. I guess I'll just have to listen like everyone else."

The crowd grew quiet then, not only out of respect for Tom's wishes, but also because they were curious as to what the announcement was going to be.

"As you know," Tom started. "I've spent the last several weeks working on the Turquoise Ranch. It isn't by accident that I came to work here. I came to Turquoise Ranch by design, because I wanted to gain some valuable first-hand experience and knowledge of the business."

Tom looked over at Curly and Hilary.

"I've learned a great deal from my friend Curly, as well as from the rest of you. I don't believe I am the same man who arrived here, fresh from Boston, last spring."

"I'll have to confess that your feet aren't quite as tender," Curly called out, and the others laughed.

"No," Tom agreed. "My feet aren't quite as tender, nor am I quite the babe in the woods I once was. That's why I feel I am ready to quit being a cowboy . . ."

"Quit being a cowboy? Tom, no, you aren't giving it up, are you? Are you leaving us?" someone called.

Hilary gasped when he announced he was going to quit being a cowboy. Did this mean he was going to return to Boston? If so, she would go with him, because she loved him and she wanted to marry him. But she also loved ranching, and the West, and she had thought that he shared some of that love.

Tom smiled and held out his hands, again asking for quiet.

"Now wait a minute," he said. "I didn't say anything about leaving. I just said I was going to quit cowboying."

"What are you gonna do?"

"I'm going to run my ranch," Tom said.

"*Your* ranch? What are you talking about? Do you own a ranch?"

"Yes," Tom said. He looked over at Hilary, and Hilary knew he could read the shock which was mirrored on her face.

"What ranch do you own?" Curly asked, still puzzled by the announcement.

"I'll tell you what ranch he owns!" Sam Potter suddenly shouted from the door of the ballroom. Everyone looked toward Sam in surprise, because his voice sounded loud and strangely angry in this room of fun-seekers.

"He owns Turquoise Ranch," Sam said.

Hilary quickly looked back toward Tom. Her face registered complete shock from the revelation.

"Is . . . is that right, Tom?" Hilary asked. "Do you own Turquoise Ranch?"

"Yes," Tom said. "I own Turquoise Ranch."

"But why didn't you say anything? Why have you kept it a secret?" Hilary asked.

"Tell her," Sam said, coming on into the room. "Tell her how you kept it secret so you could trump up some phony charge to have Big Jake arrested."

"What?" Hilary screamed. The others in the room shouted out in quick, angry surprise at Sam's announcement, and the room instantly erupted into the excited babble of dozens of voices.

"Where is my father?" Hilary asked, starting toward Tom.

"He just got took off to jail," Sam said angrily. Sam pointed an accusing finger at Tom. "Eddington had him arrested."

"No!" Hilary screamed.

"What . . . what does this mean?" one of the cowboys shouted.

"I'll tell you what it means," Curly said angrily. "It means Big Jake, Sam, Miss Hilary, me 'n all of you have been taken in by Mr. Eddington." Curly slurred the words "Mr. Eddington" so that they sounded like a sneer. "The son of a bitch has been spyin' on us!"

"No, Curly, Sam, wait!" Tom said. "No! That isn't true! You can't believe that!"

"What else do you call it?" Curly said. "A rich man like you doesn't go slummin' with the cowboys lessen you got a reason."

"What have you done with my father?" Hilary asked.

"Nothing," Tom said. "And he is not under arrest. We're just going to ask him some questions, that's all."

"Why'd you have to take him to jail just to ask a few questions?" Sam spat. "Seems to me like you should'a got all you needed from your spyin'."

"I wasn't spying," Tom insisted.

"Then what was you doin'?"

"I was trying to learn about ranching," Tom said. "I thought you would be the men to teach me."

"You might'a learned a little about pokin' cows," Curly said disgustedly. "But you sure didn't learn nothin' 'bout ranchin'. It takes a man to be a rancher."

"Fellas, I don't know 'bout you, but I've kind'a lost my taste for this here party," Sam said.

"Yeah," someone else said. "Most any place would be better'n this."

There was a mass exodus then, and in less than a minute the only people left, other than Tom and Hilary, were the bandsmen busily putting up their instruments.

Tom stood on one side of the room, and Hilary stood on the other. The floor of the room was already strewn with residue from the party, and the tables were covered with glasses and bottles in varying degrees of emptiness. The two stared at each other across the empty room for a long, silent moment.

"Hilary, it isn't like they said," Tom started.

"Where is my father?" Hilary asked.

"We just want to ask him a few questions," Tom said. "We . . . that is, I don't intend to press any charges. That's the God's truth!"

"You don't intend to press any charges? What makes you think there is anything to press charges on?" Hilary asked.

"I don't know," Tom replied. He sighed. "I just mean that . . . if there is, I won't press charges."

"Tom, how could you do this?" Hilary said. "Let alone what we had . . . what we thought we had . . . between us. You worked for my father. Isn't there such a thing as loyalty?"

"Loyalty? What about me?" Tom replied. "I own the ranch. Isn't there some degree of loyalty due me?"

"But no one knew you owned the ranch," Hilary said. "You just came among us, like a wolf in sheep's clothing. Whatever my father may have done, it isn't as underhanded as what you just did."

Tom walked over to Hilary and stood in front of her.

"Hilary, please," he said. "Try to understand. I was just doing what I thought was right. I didn't want to get your father into any trouble. I still don't. I just want what is right, that's all."

"And Gil? Are you going to have him arrested too?"

"I don't know. I hope I don't have to. Oh, Hilary, don't you see? I'm as trapped by all this as Gil and your father now. I didn't set out to do this. I just came to learn the business before I took over the ranch. I didn't plan on all this. It just happened."

Tom reached for Hilary, but as soon as he touched her she spun away from him. Oddly, she wasn't as angry as she was hurt.

"No," she said. "Please, don't touch me. Don't talk to me anymore. Just tell me where my father is, so I can go to him."

Tom raised his arms again, but this time he didn't quite touch her. Instead, he let them fall back to his side with a sigh.

"He's at the sheriff's office."

"I'm going to him," Hilary said.

Hilary pushed through the doors of the sheriff's office a few minutes later, and saw one of the sheriff's deputies sitting behind a desk, reading a newspaper. He looked up when Hilary walked in, and his eyes reflected his surprise at seeing such a beautiful girl before him. The fact that she was still dressed for the party made her appearance all the more striking.

"Yes, miss, something I can do for you?" he asked.

"My father," Hilary said. "I want to see my father."

"And who might your father be?" the deputy asked.

"Jake St. John."

"Oh. Yes, he's here," the deputy said.

"Where?" Hilary asked anxiously. "Take me to him at once. I want to see him."

"Now hold on, miss," the deputy said. "I got no authority to take you to him. That's up to the sheriff."

"Where is the sheriff? Let me talk to him."

"Why, the sheriff is with him now," the deputy said. "Why don't you just have a . . ."

The deputy was interrupted in his statement when a door opened and three men came through it. One of the three was Jake St. John.

"Dad!" Hilary shouted, and she ran to him, throwing her arms around his neck.

"Hilary! What are you doing here? Why aren't you at the party?"

"I came as soon as I found out where you were," she said. "What's happening? What are they doing to you?"

"Nothing," Jake said.

"Nothing?"

"Your father is not guilty of anything," the sheriff explained. "We only wanted to ask him a few questions, that's all. He's answered them all to our satisfaction, and therefore we have no reason to hold him any longer."

"Dad, please tell me what is going on!"

"It would appear that there has been some misunderstanding," Jake said. "But it's all cleared up now. I guess you know that Tom Eddington is the owner of Turquoise Ranch."

"Yes, I know that now," Hilary said.

"Evidently," the sheriff explained, "Mr. Eddington believed that he was going to be cheated out of the money due him for the sale of the cattle to the Indian Reservation. But Mr. Appleton, of the Cattlemen's Association, has confirmed that your father deposited the money with his organization, on behalf of the owner of Turquoise Ranch. Therefore, everything seems to be cleared up."

"You mean he can go?" Hilary asked. "He can leave with me?"

"Of course," the sheriff said. "As far as the territory of Arizona is concerned, we have no evidence to show that either your father or Mr. Carson is guilty of anything. Mr. St. John, I thank you for your cooperation."

Jake and Hilary left the sheriff's office and returned to the hotel. Hilary told her father what had happened at the hotel, and of the reaction of all the cowboys.

"They just walked out and left him," she said. "It was awful! But he deserved it, doing something as low-down and sneaky as all this."

"Darlin', don't be too hard on Tom," Jake said. "After all, he was just lookin' out for his interest. In fact, the sheriff informed me as soon as he started talkin' to me that Tom Eddington had already told him he wasn't goin' to press charges, no matter what."

"That . . . that's what he told me too," Hilary said. "But I didn't believe him."

"It's true."

"Dad, is this what you were talking about earlier tonight when you said you didn't deposit the money where you were supposed to?"

"Yes," Jake said. "I did it just in case something like this happened."

"Dad, is Gil cheating Tom?"

"I don't know," Jake said. "Maybe now we'll never know. As it turns out, what I did was the best thing for the both of us, because now we are both in the clear, whether he had any intention to cheat or not."

"I'm glad you did what you did," Hilary said. "Not only because it kept you from getting into trouble tonight, but also because it set my own mind at ease."

"Your own mind? You mean you suspected me too?"

"No, of course not, it's just . . . well, there were a few things I didn't understand, like why you sold the cattle so cheaply, for example."

Jake chuckled. "So you're not really angry with Tom for suspecting me, are you? You're angry with yourself."

"Maybe," Hilary admitted.

"Tom had a pretty rough time of it tonight, didn't he?"

"Yes, I guess he did."

"Why don't you go to him?" Jake asked.

"Dad, I don't think I can. Not now."

"Why not?"

"Because I . . ."

"Hilary, I told you, he wasn't going to press charges against me, even if I had been guilty. How can you blame him for suspecting me? Unless, of course, you're blaming yourself and taking it out on Tom. After all, even you suspected me."

"But he had no right."

"Of course he had a right," Jake insisted. "He owns the ranch. If there is some chicanery going on, I as foreman would certainly be the number one suspect. Now, you can't blame him, can you?"

"No, I guess I can't."

"Then go to him," Jake said. "That is, if you really do love him. You do love him, don't you?"

"Yes, but—"

"There are no buts to it. Go to him. In the meantime, I'll find Curly and the others and straighten things out with them." Jake smiled broadly. "Look on the bright side of things, darlin'. You aren't gonna marry the ranch manager, you're gonna marry the ranch owner. There'll be no question of you havin' to leave the Turquoise now."

"No," Hilary said. "No, I guess not."

"And you do love him, don't you?"

"Yes," Hilary admitted. "I love him."

"Then go to him, darlin'. Tell him you understand."

"Do you think he'll take me back after that awful scene?"

"Of course he will," Jake said. "Go to him."

Hilary smiled. "All right," she finally agreed. "I'll go to him. But where will I find him?"

"You might try his room," Jake suggested.

"Yes," Hilary said. "Yes, I'll try his room."

Chapter Twenty-three

Tom stood at the window of his room and looked out over Central Avenue. Across the street he could see Melczer Brothers liquor store, and next to that a gun store, and then a plumbing and electrical supply store. How typical of this brash, Western city, he thought, that a gun store would share prominence with a modern electrical supply store. It was as if Phoenix had one foot in the Wild West of old, and another ready to step into the twentieth century.

A carriage moved down the street, driven by a liveried driver. The horses' hooves clopped hollowly on the smooth road, and the well-dressed passenger in the carriage was sitting in the back seat, unconcernedly reading the *Arizona Republican*.

As Tom saw the suit the carriage passenger was wearing, he thought of his own fine clothes, and unconsciously he put his finger to his collar and pulled it away as if it were too tight for his neck.

After what had happened down in the ballroom, not only

the collar felt too tight, but the entire suit felt oppressive. He wished he had not worn it, for its very presence seemed to exacerbate the separation he felt from the others.

In fact, Tom had bought the suit for just that reason. He planned to tell everyone that he was the owner of Turquoise Ranch. He had worked and ridden with these men for over three months now, and he needed something to underscore his statement, something to enable the others to take him seriously. He thought the suit would do it, and that was why he bought it.

Across the street from the hotel, upstairs above the liquor store was the law office of Norton and Heckemeyer. Tom had gone to see Dan Heckemeyer earlier in the day.

"Tom, you've hired me to represent you, so I'm going to give you some advice right now," Dan had said after learning that the cattle had been sold and the money already collected. "Don't let that money reach his hands. You know, out here possession is nine-tenths of the law, and if Carson gets his hands on that money, it may be his for good."

"That's just what I was thinking," Tom said. "That's why I came by to see you. I happen to know that Jake St. John is going to deposit that money in the Valley National Bank today."

"In whose name?"

"He told me it would be deposited in the name of Turquoise Ranch. But, of course, as Carson has access to that account, it really doesn't mean anything. He could get it out anytime he wanted."

Dan smiled. "Not if we change the account."

"You think we can do that without any problem?"

"Absolutely. I know Ed Mason, the president of the bank, very well. I will verify your identity to Ed, and he'll fix the account so that once the money is deposited, only you can withdraw it."

"That sounds good to me," Tom said.

The Valley National Bank was a two-story building constructed of adobe brick. It was situated on the corner of Central and Washington, and the bank entrance was under a red and white striped awning, right on the squared-off corner of the building. Tom entered the bank with Dan, and a few moments later they were with Ed Mason in his office. When Tom was introduced, the bank president, a small man with a round face and rimless glasses, lit up in a big smile, and he reached out to shake Tom's hand.

"You have quite a successful enterprise," he announced.

"I'm afraid I can't really take any of the credit for it," Tom said. "It has been administered in a trust for some time now. I've just recently arrived to take charge."

"Well, in that case let me say that we are glad to have you with us. And, I also want to tell you how glad we are that you have done so much business with us in the past. I do hope it will continue."

"Yes, I'm sure it will," Tom said. "Tell me, how much business have we done in the past?"

Ed looked at Tom and then at Dan with a puzzled expression on his face.

"I don't understand. Doesn't he know?"

"No," Dan said. "The truth is, Ed, we fear that the manager of Turquoise Ranch may have been using blind accounts with your bank to hide funds he has stolen from Mr. Eddington."

"Oh," Ed said. "Oh, dear me, I certainly hope not. That would be just awful. Uh, I can get the records and look that information up if you would like."

"Yes, if you would, please," Tom said. "That would be most helpful."

"You gentlemen just wait right here. I'll be right back."

Tom and Jake waited in the president's office for a moment while he hurried to secure the bank record books. Tom looked at the wall, at a calendar which had the date, July 18, 1893, featured prominently below a large drawing of a "bird's-eye view of Phoenix." Tom studied the drawing with interest until the bank president returned with a large ledger book.

"Uh, in the past year, you have done forty-seven thousand, three hundred and nine dollars' worth of business with us."

"I see," Tom said. "Is the account still active?"

"Oh, yes sir, it is."

"How much money is in the account now?"

"At the moment, less than one hundred dollars. Large amounts are never left in for too long."

"He obviously uses this as a place to hide the money," Dan said.

"Mr. Mason, I would like to put a freeze on the Turquoise account, so that Gil Carson cannot withdraw any more money."

"I'm afraid we can't do that," Mason answered.

"What? Why not?"

"Well, you see, this account was opened by Gil Carson. His name is on the signature card. He is the only one who can withdraw from the account, and he is the only one who can give us instructions as to its disposition."

Tom looked at Dan in confusion. "I thought you said we could take care of it."

Dan smiled. "It depends on how you go about it," he said. "Ed, what if we open another Turquoise account? If any money is placed into the bank in the Turquoise account, could you make certain it goes into the new account?"

"Certainly," Mason said, smiling. "That wouldn't be a problem."

"All right," Tom said. "Let's open a new account."

Tom opened the new account, convinced that the money earned from the cattle drive could not be stolen.

Tom turned away from the window and went back into his room. He lay on his bed with his hands clasped behind his head, and looked up at the spinning fan. One hour ago, he thought. One hour ago, he had stepped into the ballroom of the hotel on what he thought was going to be one of the happiest nights of his life.

"I hired a band, Mr. Eddington, just as you requested," the concierge had said that evening as Tom stepped into the lobby. "However, I would like to apologize for the bar girls. I'm afraid they took it upon themselves to show up."

"Good, good, the more the merrier," Tom said happily. "All the drovers have had to look at for the last several weeks have been each other. It will do them good to see a few new faces, and if some of those faces happen to be pretty, why, that's all the better."

A burst of laughter exploded from the ballroom.

"It sounds like the party is going to be successful," Tom said, smiling.

"Yes, sir," the concierge said. "It is certainly the most successful party we have had around here in quite some time."

Tom started to go in to join the party when he saw Dan coming in through the front door.

"Dan, it's good to see you," Tom greeted his lawyer happily. "Did you come for the party?"

"No," Dan said. "Tom, I have some disturbing news."

"Disturbing news? What sort of news?"

"There wasn't any deposit made today."

"What? But surely there was. Jake already had the money. I saw the draft! And he said he was going to put the money in the bank today."

"He may have said he was going to, but he didn't do it," Dan said. "If you ask me, you've got two men to worry about. Gil Carson and Jake St. John. Don't forget, Jake St. John has done some rustling in his own past."

"Perhaps so," Tom said. "But if so, I would be willing to bet that it wasn't this type of sneaky operation. I just don't believe Jake is mixed up in this!" Tom said.

"Believe it. We had the bank watched all day, and there was no deposit made."

"We?"

"Yeah, I notified the sheriff. In fact, he and his deputy are out front. Why don't you come talk to them?"

"All right," Tom said. "I'll talk to them. But I don't believe Jake stole that money."

Tom followed Dan through the front door of the hotel. The sheriff and his deputy were standing out on the porch, and they greeted Tom when he was introduced to them.

"Tom, what are you doin' out here? Why aren't you at the party?" Curly asked, stepping up onto the porch at that moment.

"I'll be right in," Tom said. "I just have a little business to discuss with the sheriff."

"The sheriff?" Curly asked, looking at the two men who were wearing badges. "Look here, Tom, is there anything wrong?"

"No, nothing is wrong," Tom said. "Really, nothing is wrong."

Curly looked at the sheriff suspiciously, and Tom,

seeking to mollify him, smiled and joked with his former partner.

"Well, look at you. Can this be the Curly I know? You are actually wearing a clean shirt and clean trousers."

"Yeah, but they sure ain't nothin' like them duds you got on. Is them the kind of clothes you wear back East?"

"Sometimes," Tom admitted.

"Well, I reckon you got reason enough to want to look good now," Curly said. "Miss Hilary is enough to make any man want to slick up for. And speakin' o' slickin' up, it ain't just my clothes that's clean."

"It isn't?"

"No," Curly said. "I took me a bath over to the barbershop, and put on some o' that witch hazel. Wanna smell?"

"Curly, I swear, none of your friends are going to know you," Tom teased.

"Well, you been learnin' all about cowboyin' from me," Curly said. "But I learned a bit from you too." Curly looked again at the sheriff and the other two men. They had said nothing since his arrival.

"Look here, Tom, are you sure ever'thin' is all right?"

"Yes, I'm positive," Tom said. "Why don't you go on inside and look after Hilary for me? I'll be along in a few minutes."

"Look after Hilary, you say?" Curly smiled. "Why, that'll be pure pleasure."

Tom waited until Curly was inside, then he turned back to the sheriff and the others.

"Look, I really don't think I'm going to need you," Tom said. "I'm sure Jake hasn't done anything wrong."

"Well, we know he didn't deposit the money," Dan said. "That means he's kept it. If so, we need to get it from him before he gives it to Carson. At least let's do that."

Tom ran his hand through his hair.

"All right," he said. "Go ahead and do that. Ask him for the money."

"And if he has deposited it to his own account?" the sheriff asked.

"I won't press charges," Tom said. "No matter what, I won't press charges. Just remember that! And don't go into the ballroom with me!"

"All right, if that's the way you want it."

"That's the way I want it."

Tom went on into the party, leaving Dan, the sheriff and his deputy standing on the front porch. There was one other man standing on the front porch as well, but Tom didn't see him. That was because the man didn't want Tom to see him. When he saw Tom talking to the sheriff, he stepped back into the shadows. He couldn't hear clearly enough to know all that was going on. But he did hear enough of the conversation to realize that Tom was the real owner of Turquoise Ranch. And he thought he heard Tom say something about pressing charges against Jake St. John. That was important to him, because Jake St. John was his oldest and best friend.

The man who had overheard parts of the conversation was Sam Potter.

Tom sighed and sat up on his bed. Not only Hilary had turned against him, but the two men whose respect he had most wanted had turned against him as well.

Tom wished he had never left Boston. If he could go back to a time in his life when he could start over, he would go back to the voyage he had made with his grandfather to the Bahamas. It was during that cruise that he made the final decision to come West. He wished he had known the hurt and pain such a decision was to cost him.

There was a knock on Tom's door.

"Tom?" a woman's voice called. It was muffled by the door, and Tom heard what he wanted to hear, so he stood up quickly.

"Hilary!" he said. "You've come back!"

Tom rushed to the door and opened it with a happy smile on his face. He was shocked when he saw, not Hilary but Evelyn Proctor. His mouth fell open in surprise.

"Are you surprised to see me?" Evelyn asked coyly.

"Evelyn! Evelyn, is it really you?"

"Yes," Evelyn said, smiling prettily. "It's really me. Are you glad to see me?"

"I'm flabbergasted!" Tom said. "What are you doing here?"

"Well, if you would invite me in, perhaps I could tell you," Evelyn said.

"Come in!" Tom said. "Of course, come in!" Tom stepped back to invite her in.

Evelyn came into the room. She kissed Tom coolly and chastely on the lips.

"That was from your grandmother," she said. She kissed him again in the same fashion. "And that is from your grandfather. I'll save my own kiss until later." Evelyn looked around the room. "Well, at least I'm glad I found a hotel with some of the modern conveniences, rather than in some Indian tepee somewhere. I must say, I'm surprised that they even know what electricity is out here. Perhaps they are not as savage as I thought."

"Evelyn, I can't believe my eyes! What are you doing out here?"

"I just got tired of waiting for you to return," she said. "In fact, I was beginning to think you might not come back at all. So, if the mountain won't come to Muhammad, Muhammad will go to the mountain. Here I am."

"Evelyn, what did you hope to accomplish by coming out here?"

"I hoped to talk some sense into you," Evelyn said. "I hoped I could convince you to come back home."

Tom sighed.

"Evelyn, at this very minute, I . . ."

"Yes?"

Tom was about to tell her that he was hopelessly in love with Hilary and couldn't think of coming home. Then the word "hopeless" came back to him, and he recalled his wish of a few moments before, when, if he could, he would have gone back to Boston.

"At this very minute, I must confess to you that the idea of coming back home does not sound all that unattractive to me," he heard himself say.

"Tom! You mean you will come back?"

"No," Tom said. "I didn't say that exactly. But I have had some unpleasant moments."

Evelyn smiled. "Maybe I can make you forget whatever unpleasantness you experienced," she said. She put her arms around him and moved against him, raising her lips to his. "I told you I was going to save my kiss until later, didn't I? Well, here it is."

Evelyn kissed Tom, and he found himself kissing back. Her mouth was soft and resilient, and it opened to draw his tongue inside.

The intensity of the kiss surprised Tom, for never in his entire relationship with Evelyn had she been anything except very, very proper. Chaste kisses under very controlled situations and the cool touch of a hand was the limit of all previous intimacy between them.

"Evelyn," Tom said when at last the kiss ended. "What are you doing?"

"Are you surprised?" Evelyn asked, leaning against him so that he could feel the heavy warmth of her breasts and the inviting press of her thighs.

"Yes," Tom said. "You've never been so . . ."

"Wanton?" Evelyn asked, raising her eyebrow and smiling.

"I wouldn't put it that way."

"I would," Evelyn said. "But if you think that's wanton, you haven't seen anything yet." Evelyn began to unbutton her dress. "I want you, Tom Eddington, and I'll do anything I have to do to get you. Anything," she added huskily as she began to slip out of her dress.

Tom knew that he should stop her now. She was obviously doing this to persuade him to come back to her, and if he wasn't careful, she just might succeed.

"Evelyn, no," he said. "No, you don't know what you're doing."

"Oh, yes I do," Evelyn said, and now the dress was off, and she began slipping out of her undergarments. She stood before him totally nude and completely unashamed. The nipples of her breasts were tightly drawn and protruding like tiny rosebuds. "Don't you want me?" Evelyn asked.

Tom started to protest again, but though he opened his mouth, no words of protest came forth. And why should they? After all, hadn't Hilary just left him without even giving him the opportunity to explain himself? It was over with Hilary. It was over before it ever had the opportunity to begin.

"Yes," he heard himself say. "Yes, I want you."

Gently, Tom put his hand under Evelyn's chin and turned her face up toward his. He kissed her again and pulled her against him, feeling her nude body against the buttons of his suit. A tide of feeling swept over him, and though he knew the pleasure he was feeling now was, at best, a surrogate pleasure, he nevertheless decided to take whatever it offered. A few minutes ago he had been a broken and dispirited man. In his heart he was still broken and dispirited, and it was that very thing which caused him to reach for whatever comfort, whatever love there might be available. If Evelyn was here to provide that comfort and love instead of Hilary, then he would take it from her. He would take it wherever he could get it.

Tom stepped out of his own clothes, then pulled her to him again, this time naked body against naked body. He kissed her with slow, hot lips, and gently moved her toward the bed where they lay down, side by side.

Tom's hand cupped one of her breasts, warm and vibrant, and the nipple, which was already swollen, strained to be touched. A soft cry of ecstasy emerged from Evelyn's throat as he moved his hand from her nipple down across her incredibly smooth skin to dip into the soft mound at the junction of her legs.

Tom moved his body over hers then, and he could feel her downy soft legs beneath his own. He looked down at her face. Her eyes were closed in the ecstasy of the moment. The face was that of Evelyn Proctor, but that wasn't the face he saw in his mind. The face he saw in his mind was Hilary St. John.

Evelyn thrust against him, and soon Tom felt himself slipping away, melting into a white flash of heat and sliding down through the connection that was between them. Then, at the supreme moment, he didn't want to see Evelyn's face, felt it would be blasphemous to do so, and he looked away from the girl beneath him.

He heard, or sensed, a presence, and he looked toward the door.

Hilary was standing there! Her face was screwed up in shocked horror, and she was biting on the edge of her hand to keep from calling out.

"Hilary!" Tom shouted out in an agonizing scream just as Evelyn called out her own rapture beneath him.

Chapter Twenty-four

Tom jumped up, leaving Evelyn gasping beneath him.
"Tom! What is it?" she asked.
"It's Hilary!" Tom said in an anguished cry. "I have to go after her. I have to get her back!"

Tom pulled on his clothes and ran after her, but she made it to her room before he could catch her. Tom stood outside her door for nearly an hour, telling her how much he loved her and begging her to forgive him. Despite all his pleading, Hilary would have nothing to do with him.

Broken and dispirited, Tom returned to his room. Evelyn was still there, sitting on the edge of his bed in the dark. She had not yet dressed, but so upset was Tom by what had just happened that he scarcely noticed.

"Who was that woman?" Evelyn asked quietly.
"What?" Tom replied, his heart so heavy with sorrow that he didn't hear the question.
"That woman. Who was she?"
"Her name is Hilary," Tom said. "Hilary St. John."
"I see."

Evelyn got up then, and padded naked over to her clothes. Slowly, she began to get dressed. Tom sat in a chair, then he saw her and realized how she must feel.

"Evelyn," he said. "Evelyn, I'm sorry, I . . ."

"No," Evelyn said, holding up her hand to hush him. She brushed a tear from her eye. "No, don't say anything!"

Tom went to her to try and comfort her, but, gently, she pulled away from him. "You are in love with her?" she asked.

"Yes," Tom said. "I'm sorry."

"Why should you be sorry? I think she's a lovely girl."

"But the way I acted, leaving you like this to . . ."

"Tom," Evelyn said quietly. "I have a confession to make."

"A confession?"

"I haven't come out here flying true colors." Evelyn was silent for a moment, then she choked back a sob. "I'm pregnant, Tom."

"Pregnant? But how? I mean, I didn't . . ."

"No," Evelyn interrupted quickly. "No, I was doubly foolish. I played the chaste virgin with you, and the wanton whore with another. Had you been responsible for my condition, I know that you would do the right thing. In fact, I came here for the sole purpose of trapping you. After tonight, I hoped to be able to convince you that the baby was yours. That was before I knew that you had found someone else."

"Found her and lost her," Tom said.

"No," Evelyn said. "You haven't lost her."

"What do you mean? After tonight, I've no doubt but that she will never see me again."

"You will win her back," Evelyn said. "If you really want to."

"Of course I want to. More than anything in the world, I want to," Tom said.

"Then do it! Go back to your ranch and tend to cows, or whatever it is you do in that godforsaken place, and win her back." Evelyn smiled sadly. "I'm not sure I would have made a very good cowgirl anyway."

"Evelyn," Tom said, looking at her. "I'm sorry things didn't work out for us."

"You aren't the only one," she said.

In her shock, hurt and anger, Hilary had recognized the woman. It was the same woman she had watched check into the hotel, and who, Hilary discovered later, had a room right next to hers. She was the one who had mistaken Hilary for a maid.

Hilary refused to see Tom that night, and she refused again the next morning. She took a separate train the next day so as not to have to see him on the way back to Flagstaff.

Tom returned to Turquoise, but even there, Hilary managed to avoid him. After the first few days Tom gave up trying to see her. In reluctant deference to her wishes Tom kept his distance from her, so that avoiding him was easier physically, if not emotionally. The enforced and painful separation went on for the next several days.

It was early in the morning, and Hilary was standing on the place that had been her private retreat for so many years. She was at the grassy precipice which overlooked the ranch. She was here, she realized, for what was probably the last time.

When Hilary returned to Turquoise Ranch, she didn't break off her engagement with Gil—she confirmed it. Her experience with Tom made her more determined than ever to marry Gil Carson and get away from Tom Eddington, once and for all.

It was the impending marriage to Gil Carson which had drawn her to the precipice this morning. She needed the solitude, and she wanted to take one last, lingering look at Turquoise. She was saying good-bye to the mountains, trees, streams and valley that she loved so much, because marrying Gil meant that she was leaving Turquoise.

Hilary's father was remaining. Jake's job as ranch foreman was not only secure, it was made even more significant by being upgraded to a position that was almost equal to the one formerly held by Gil Carson. Gil Carson's position, of course, had been taken over by Tom himself, and Tom had moved into the big house once occupied by Gil.

Gil left Turquoise Ranch, but he didn't go far. He moved to a large neighboring spread named Trailback Ranch. Trailback was nearly as large as Turquoise. At first, many were surprised that Gil was able to raise the money needed to buy Trailback, then they learned to their surprise that he only had to buy half of it. He had been an active, though secret partner in the operation of Trailback Ranch for as many years as he had been managing Turquoise. Many swore that Gil would soon make Trailback into a spread that would rival Turquoise for supremacy in the area.

A few others were less kind in their assessment of Gil Carson's frugality. They pointed out that the similarity in the brands, *TR* for Turquoise and *TR* with an arrow slash for Trailback, was more than a coincidence. Some commented on how unusual it was that the *TR* part of Gil's brand always managed to heal into an older looking wound than the arrow which was overlayed on the top, as if the *TR* brand had merely been altered by the addition of an arrow slash. Those same people also thought it significant that, whereas the

Turquoise herd had lost several cows during the harsh winters in the previous years, Trailback had gained animals. From a ranch that few people even knew of until Gil moved to it, there suddenly sprang a herd nearly as large as that which was on Turquoise.

That could only mean one thing. Gil Carson had been planning something like this for quite a while, and he had prepared for it by quietly stealing stock from Turquoise Ranch.

Despite the obviousness of Gil's cheating him, Tom had made no effort to press charges against Gil. In public, Tom let it be known that he was content to have his ranch and all that rightfully belonged to him. Privately, he indicated that he would do nothing that might bring further embarrassment to Hilary. Prosecuting Gil would do so, especially if she married him.

In his own way, Tom was able to exact a payment of sort from Gil Carson. In a business where a man's reputation and integrity were of vital importance, Gil had been discredited. By not pressing charges, Tom had shown himself to be the superior man of the two.

Curly was one of those who was quick to point out this fact to Hilary. Sam Potter was another. After their initial anger with Tom, which they had expressed at the party, they learned the whole truth from Jake. They were won over to Tom's side from that moment on and they, as well as most of the other drovers from the Turquoise, went to Tom to apologize and beg his forgiveness. Tom accepted them warmly. Now they were committed to helping Tom make certain that Turquoise Ranch survived the damage Gil had inflicted upon it. They also mounted a concerted effort to show Hilary the error of her ways. Despite their attempts to win Hilary over, however, she remained obdurate. When they even so much as mentioned his name, Hilary would threaten to walk away from them.

"Darlin'," Jake said quietly.

Hilary turned around, startled by the sudden and unexpected intrusion into her domain.

"Dad? What are you doing up here?"

"I figured this would be as good a place as any to talk to you," Jake said.

Hilary turned away from him and looked back down over the ranch.

"It won't do any good," she said. "I'm leaving the ranch today, and I'm going to marry Gil."

"You're makin' a mistake, girl. You're makin' the biggest mistake of your life."

"Dad, you don't know. You can't understand what it was like, how it made me feel to . . ."

"Maybe I don't," Jake said. "And maybe I'm speakin' outa turn now. But I do know that you should hear Tom's side of things."

"Dad, please. Curly and Sam have tried to talk to me, but I won't talk to them."

"I know," Jake said. "They are good men, doing what they think is right. But you haven't given them a chance. Just like you haven't given Tom a chance. If you would just listen to his side of the story . . ."

"As I have no intention of ever speaking to him again, I should think that will be rather difficult," Hilary interrupted.

"Then you are going to listen to it from me," Jake said. "I'm not Curly and Sam that you can send away. I'm your father, and you are going to listen!"

Hilary didn't answer for a long moment. Finally she

sighed. "All right. Go ahead. Explain Tom's side of it to me if you can."

"Consider the circumstances, daughter," Jake said. "At the moment of Tom's greatest happiness, he suddenly saw his whole world come crashin' down on him. Curly and Sam turned on him—and so did you! You were the one woman he loved, and *you* turned against him!"

"I thought he had betrayed you," Hilary said quietly.

"But he didn't."

"I didn't know that."

"You owed him the opportunity to explain," Jake said.

"I was willing to forgive him when I found out."

"You were willing to forgive him? Darlin', there was nothin' for you to forgive! He had done nothin' wrong. The wrong that was done was done by you 'n Curly 'n Sam when the three of you accused him. At least, Curly 'n Sam have made up for it. You haven't."

"Curly and Sam didn't see him in bed with that woman," Hilary said quietly. "I did."

"At least, daughter, she wasn't just some floozy Tom went out and picked up. It was a girl named Evelyn Proctor. He was once engaged to her when he lived back East."

Hilary turned to her father with an agonized expression on her face.

"But that's even worse! Don't you understand? I would have felt better if it had been some floozy. If it had been a floozy Tom went out and picked up, then I could accept that he was looking for some sort of consolation from the hurt I did him. That, I could understand. But to turn so quickly to a girl he had known before . . . I would never be sure that the old relationship wasn't dead."

"It is dead," Jake said. "You can believe me."

"Because Tom told you it is dead?"

"Yes," Jake said.

"And you believe him?"

"Yes," Jake said. "It turns out that the girl was pregnant."

"Pregnant? My God, you mean Tom?"

"No," Jake said quickly. "It wasn't Tom. It was someone else. But of course Tom knew that it wasn't his."

"How could he be so certain?"

"Very easily," Jake said. "He had never been with her."

"He can't make such a high and mighty claim now, can he?" Hilary said.

"No, I don't suppose he can. But then, darlin', can he make that claim about you?" Jake asked pointedly.

"What?" Hilary replied, feeling the breath leave her body. Her face flamed pink. "You . . . you know?"

"I didn't until this moment," Jake said.

Tears sprang to Hilary's eyes, and she looked away.

"Darlin', I don't judge you for anything you done, if you did it out of love. 'N though I'm not in the preachin' business, my bet would be that God wouldn't judge you either. But I tell you this. It would be a greater sin for you to marry Gil Carson and live with him without lovin' him, than what you and Tom may have done. You think about that! Oh, one other thing. Sam asked me to tell you."

"What's that?"

"He asked me to tell you not to make the same mistake with Tom that he made with Lettie Mae."

"Sam said that?"

"Yes," Jake said. "Think about it, girl. Just think about it."

Jake turned and walked away from his daughter, and Hilary watched him leave with vision which was now blurred by tears . . .

* * *

Gil Carson went to great extremes to make Trailback a festive place on the day of the wedding. There were several Mexican workers on his ranch, because very few of the local cowboys would work for him. The Mexican workers knew nothing of the heartache and deceit behind the upcoming marriage. They knew only that it was going to be a festive occasion. For that, they were happy, and they all wore their most colorful costumes and they laughed and sang and danced to the music of guitars and maracas. Their children played games, then blindfolded each other so they could swing long sticks at the gaily decorated piñatas which hung from the trees. Whenever one of the children hit one there would be a whoop of joy as they ran to discover what prizes had spilled from the smashed vessel.

The house was festooned with flowers and greenery and inside, a band furnished music for the entertainment of the visiting ranchers and their wives. The dining room furniture had been pushed to one side and a large punch bowl containing an alcoholic fruit punch was put in the center of the table. The cowboys stood grouped together near the punch bowl, drinking and exchanging self-conscious jokes about their unaccustomed clean shirts and trousers.

In a back room of the house, Hilary was standing in front of the mirror. Mrs. Ivery, who not only had made her reception dress for her, but had also altered her mother's wedding dress so that it would fit, stood behind her. The noise of the celebration from outside floated in and a child's squeal of delight told them that another piñata had been broken.

Hilary moved over to the window and looked through it.

"Now Hilary, if you don't stand back over here where I can see what I'm doing, I never will get that hem straight," Mrs. Ivery complained.

"I'm sorry," Hilary said quietly. She returned to stand in front of the mirror.

Mrs. Ivery got on her knees and folded the hem up. She pinned it in place.

"Now, turn around and let me look," she said.

Hilary turned as ordered, and Mrs. Ivery looked up at her. Then she gasped, because she saw that Hilary was crying.

"Hilary? Oh, dear, what is it?"

"I . . . nothing," Hilary said, wiping her eyes. "It's nothing."

Mrs. Ivery stood up and put her arms around the younger girl.

"Maybe it's just nervousness," she said. "Nearly everyone gets nervous at their wedding. I know I did."

"I'm sure it is," Hilary said.

Hilary moved through the rest of the preliminaries as if in a dream. She responded to Mrs. Ivery's questions and comments automatically, but she couldn't have told anyone what she was actually saying, or what was really going on.

Her father had come to the wedding, of course. And so had Sam, Curly and most of the men who worked on the Turquoise. They did it for her, and not for Gil, and Hilary knew and appreciated it.

Tom Eddington was conspicuously absent.

The actual marriage ceremony was to be conducted on the front lawn, and all too soon everyone moved outside to get into position.

"This is it, darlin'," Jake said, coming over to stand beside her. "It's not too late to change your mind."

"I . . . I'm going through with it," Hilary said resolutely.

Jake sighed.

"You're a full-grown woman," he said. "I can't make

your decisions for you. But believe me, girl, if I could stop it, this is one weddin' that would never take place."

The ceremony was to be performed by Father Dan Perkins, an Episcopal priest from Flagstaff. Father Perkins had set up an altar on the lawn, and now he, in his vestments, and Gil, wearing a cutaway and tails, stood just before the altar, waiting for Hilary and her father to make the walk from the house across the lawn toward them.

The band began playing, and everyone turned toward the front of the house where Hilary and her father waited at the top of the steps on the front porch.

In the distance, behind the altar, Hilary saw a lone horseman slowly riding toward them. At first, she was struck only by the incongruity of a single horseman dressed in denim trousers and a cotton shirt, amidst so many people who were so finely dressed.

The music began playing the familiar processional, and Hilary and her father walked slowly and stately toward the altar.

The horseman drew closer to the altar from the opposite side, though as yet no one besides Hilary saw him.

Hilary looked into Gil's face. He was smiling at her, but his smile wasn't one of love. It was a smile of victory. He was regarding Hilary as some sort of prize he had won. She was a symbol of his besting Tom Eddington. He was not thinking of her as a woman with whom he would be sharing his life. He was thinking of her as his rightful spoils of victory.

The rider continued to come toward them, moving in a slow but steady gait.

Oh, God, Hilary thought, fighting hard to hold back the tears. Please, God, I have made a mistake! I don't want to marry this man. I can't marry this man! Please, don't let this happen!

"Dad," she suddenly said quietly, squeezing her father's arm. "Dad, that's Tom!"

"Yes!" Jake said, for now the rider was close enough that he could see him clearly. "What's he doing here?"

No one other than Hilary and her father had noticed Tom yet. Instead, all eyes were turned toward Hilary and her father as they proceeded toward the altar.

"He's come for me," Hilary said with a sudden knowledge. "Dad, he's come for me!"

"Go with him, girl," Jake suddenly urged.

Hilary turned to look at her father. "Oh, Dad, would you be terribly shocked? Would you be too embarrassed to ever show yourself again?"

"Do you love Tom?"

"Yes! Oh, yes!"

"Then do it," Jake said. "Go with him."

Hilary smiled broadly, and many in the congregation smiled with her, because they thought she was a young woman bursting over with happiness on her wedding day.

Father Perkins and Gil positioned themselves to let Hilary join them at the altar.

Hilary kept walking, right past the altar. Tom arrived on the other side, then, as if planned, stretched his arm to Hilary. She swung up into the saddle behind him.

The congregation gasped in shock, and Gil shouted out, "Hilary! Hilary, what are you doing? Tom Eddington! Eddington, come back here!"

Tom turned away and started riding back as slowly and as deliberately as he had ridden up.

"Yahoo!" Curly suddenly shouted. He stood up and threw his hat into the air. "Hurrah for Tom!"

Curly's unabashed cheer broke the ice, and the others who had come to the wedding out of a sense of obligation to Hilary cheered with him.

"I'm going for my gun!" Gil said, starting toward the house.

Jake reached out and grabbed him.

"No," he said. "No, you aren't."

"You can stop me now, but you can't stop me forever," Gil said angrily. "Tom Eddington is going to die, if it's the last thing I do."

Jake looked at Gil with eyes that were cool and dangerous.

"Carson, you better pray for Tom's health. If he so much as gets a scratch on his little finger, for any reason, I'm going to kill you."

"But he has no right," Gil sputtered, pointing at them. Tom and Hilary were now growing small in the distance.

"That's where you are wrong," Jake said. "He has every right."

"What right do they have to do that?"

Jake looked at Tom and Hilary and saw that they were now locked in an embrace.

"They have the right of two people in love," he said. Then he added pointedly, "And they have a father's blessing."

Paula Fairman

Romantic intrigue at its finest—
over four million copies in print!

- ☐ 41-795-0 **FORBIDDEN DESTINY** $2.95
  A helpless stowaway aboard the whaling ship *Gray Ghost*, Kate McCrae was in no position to refuse the lecherous advances of Captain Steele.

- ☐ 41-798-5 **THE FURY AND THE PASSION** $2.95
  From the glitter of Denver society to the lawlessness of the wild West, Stacey Pendarrow stalks the trail of her elusive lover for one reason: to kill him.

- ☐ 41-783-7 **JASMINE PASSION** $2.95
  Raised in a temple and trained in the art of love, the beautiful Eurasian Le' Sing searches California's Barbary Coast for the father she has never met and for a man who can win her heart.

- ☐ 40-697-5 **PORTS OF PASSION** $2.50
  Abducted aboard the *Morning Star*, heiress Kristen Chalmers must come to terms not only with immediate danger, but the desperate awakening of her own carnal desires.

- ☐ 41-800-0 **SOUTHERN ROSE** $2.95
  Amidst the raging furor of the Civil War, the beautiful actress Jaylene Cooper is torn between her passion for a dashing Southern rebel and the devoted love of a handsome Yankee officer.

- ☐ 41-797-5 **STORM OF DESIRE** $2.95
  The only woman in a rough and brutal railroad camp in the wild Southwest, young Reesa Flowers becomes enmeshed in a web of greed, sabotage, and lust.

- ☐ 41-006-9 **THE TENDER AND THE SAVAGE** $2.75
  In the wild and ravaged plains of the Dakota Territory, beautiful young Crimson Royale is torn between her savage lust for a Sioux Indian and her tender desires for his worst enemy—a captain in Custer's Army.

- ☐ 41-749-7 **VALLEY OF THE PASSIONS** $3.25
  Forging her destiny in the harsh Oregon wilderness, Sara Landers must choose between the love of two men—a powerful rancher and the muscle-bound foreman who murdered her father.

- ☐ 42-034-X **WILDEST PASSION** $3.25
  Wrenched from the wealthy embrace of New York society, beautiful Courtney O'Neil sells herself as a mail-order bride in the untamed Northwest—never forsaking her dream of triumphant love.

Buy them at your local bookstore or use this handy coupon
Clip and mail this page with your order

PINNACLE BOOKS, INC.
Post Office Box 690
Rockville Centre, NY 11571

Please send me the book(s) I have checked above. I am enclosing $_____ (please add $1 to cover postage and handling). Send check or money order only—no cash or C.O.D.'s.

Mr./Mrs./Miss _____

Address _____

City _____ State/Zip _____

Please allow six weeks for delivery. Prices subject to change without notice.